The Wine Broker

by

Ian Rodney Lazarus

For the ones who read between the lines

Cherish those who seek the truth,
but beware of those who find it.

Voltaire

1

Gregory Zukov was already dead. He just didn't realize it.

"Am I enjoying myself? Seriously?"

He snapped back at the waiter who initiated the conversation as he approached the table, the young man who could not have been more than seventeen years old.

"Am I enjoying myself?" Gregory repeated, a bit louder this time, as if any more drama were necessary in the moment.

He then unpacked his grievances. "The guest elevator doesn't work, I have cockroaches in my bathroom, the internet is down most of the time, and my toilet doesn't flush properly," he said, raising his left nostril just enough to signal his disgust.

The young man straightened his back and shifted his weight onto his back heels as he took in the criticism of the hotel, then said something that put it all in perspective for Gregory.

"Señor, your first time in Cuba?" he asked.

Any other covert agent would probably have been delighted to be assigned to Cuba, but Gregory, now in his fourteenth year of service to the agency, wasn't convinced he was trading up from his prior assignment in Shanghai. There was no caviar nor Coca-Cola, for starters, and much of Havana looked like a war zone. At the Hotel Nacional de Cuba, he could at least momentarily forget these shortcomings—until he was asked about the condition of the hotel, which, prior to the revolution, accommodated dignitaries from Winston Churchill to Walt Disney. It was well past its prime by the time Gregory signed the guest register.

Indeed, quality is relative, he thought to himself, and the waiter who asked him if he had ever visited Cuba recognized this fact before Gregory did.

He looked to his left, across the Calle Malecón, to the American Embassy. As an operative, he would not be able to visit the Embassy, but he took some comfort in knowing it was there. Instead, he cradled his whiskey on the back porch of the hotel, watching the palm trees sway in the wind.

In the distance, ocean waves crashed against the breakwater that ran around the perimeter of the island, spraying seawater as high as eight feet. The warm breeze was intense, as evidenced by the number of cocktail napkins that leapt from the tables of other guests. Occasionally, the sky blinked in bright blue-white hues as a result of a lightning storm sitting off the west coast of Florida.

A series of lamps shone down on the grounds from the roof of the hotel, revealing the coordinated ballet of runaway paper products. It was about 10:30 p.m., and guests who had just finished dining were walking about.

A musical trio entertained small groups lounging on the outdoor wicker furniture, whether they liked it or not, playing a few Latin tunes before collecting gratuities and moving on to the next victims. Gregory stared at them as he inventoried his fortunes—or misfortunes, depending on his point of view at the time. He was staring down at his drink when the waiter stopped by his side, giving rise to his ill-advised eruption. Above all else, agents were trained to never bring attention to themselves.

Gregory Zukov was brought to the United States by his parents when he was seven years old. Russian was the predominant language spoken at home, and his ability to speak it, combined with a degree in political science from the University of Michigan, is what originally generated the CIA's interest in him. During previous assignments in New York, Moscow, and Shanghai, Gregory felt he was in the center of the party universe, participating in a range of activities from official ceremonies to wild, erotic raves that ran into the morning hours. Now he was as isolated as he could be on an island nation that time forgot.

"You've earned this, Gregory," his supervisor and handler told him when he was summoned back to the U.S. from Shanghai for a new appointment. "Lean into it," he said.

Gregory's assignment was to mix with the significant Russian tourist population and to investigate the origin of "Havana Syndrome." The condition had affected two dozen American and Canadian diplomats on the island by the time of his arrival, but reports of symptoms similar to Havana Syndrome outside Cuba had ballooned to 1,500. When the news program *60 Minutes* reported in 2024 on its five-year investigation into the issue, the agency was under intense pressure to step up resources.

He was also expected to gather intelligence on the Chinese and Russian convoy of ships arriving for the purpose of conducting "joint military exercises" in the Caribbean. Russia began deploying warships and nuclear submarines to Cuba in 2024, purportedly in response to the U.S. permitting Ukraine to use weapons they supplied to hit targets within Russia's sovereign territory. Cubans were permitted to tour the Russian frigate *Gorshkov* for a few hours on one random day during the week. Military analysts believed the *Gorshkov* was capable of anti-submarine warfare and carrying surface-to-surface and surface-to-air missiles. Gregory was to use his forged credentials to verify as many details as possible.

The high level of humidity outside the hotel wrapped Gregory in a warm, virtual blanket. That, combined with the effect of several drinks, made him numb to the prick on the shoulder as an apparently drunk guest stumbled

4

into him when he rose from his table. He took no special interest either when the guest whispered "ma-af," the Indonesian equivalent of "excuse me."

As Gregory reached the elevators, he was reminded that they weren't functional and that he would have to take the stairs back to his room. When he finally entered his room on the fourth floor, he dropped face down on the bed, fully clothed. The following morning, he was discovered there by the housekeeping staff, in the same outfit. He had died from an apparent cardiac arrest, and not so apparent blood poisoning.

2

Jose Lopez slowed the 24-foot Wellcraft he called the *Maravilla* to a crawl as it approached the GPS markings for the USS *Hogan*, about a forty-minute ride from the boat launch on Shelter Island in San Diego Bay. The *Hogan* was a WWII Navy destroyer sunk on November 8, 1945, when it was decommissioned and used by the Navy as a target ship for bombing tests. Today it sits 120 feet below the surface and is a popular site for advanced divers to explore. Little of it remains, but it is as popular with wolf eels as it is with divers, and the two often get the opportunity to stare at each other on the remains of the wreck.

Lopez was alone on the boat. There were intentionally no dives scheduled for that particular day. Still, he raised his dive flag after tying off the Wellcraft to a buoy attached to the bow of the *Hogan*. After doing so, he lay down to take a nap.

It was a warm Monday afternoon, the skies were clear, and there was a slight current trying to push the boat toward the south. An occasional seagull would land on the transom to see if any fish scraps could be scooped up. It would have been unusual for another dive boat to visit the wreck during the week, as most commercial dive charters accommodated customers on the weekends. However, the U.S. Coast Guard and Mexican Navy were potentially patrolling the area, as the *Hogan* sat just north of the international border. So long as the boat remained on the buoy designating the site of the wreck, there was no reason for any enforcement agency to bother him. In fact, most patrol boats were quite familiar with the sight of the *Maravilla*.

Lopez would remain there until just before sunset. Then, he would release the boat from the buoy and head toward Los Coronados Islands, about seven miles into Mexican waters. He would proceed slowly to avoid creating a wake that might attract the attention of the Navy and not use any lights. His visa and passport were in order, but the Navy had a reputation for harassing American boaters, and traveling after dark would invite soldiers to board his vessel in search of drugs or migrants. Lopez was as experienced as anyone in this operation, having grown up in Tijuana and operating charter boats on both sides of the border.

Once he reached the small island chain, he motored quietly to the opposite side of the North Island, in a spot where islands on both sides would conceal his presence, about fifty yards off the dive site known as "Keyhole." It was there that he lifted the wooden crate, which was about the size of a large ottoman, and lowered it gently via a line off the side of the boat. He dropped the line once he was sure the crate landed in the shallow water. Then, he motored back to the marina in San Diego. The cargo he dropped into the ocean had a market value of nine million dollars.

***

The intruder was aware that the home had state-of-the-art security, as he was well informed by the owner. The house on Hobart Boulevard was one of the more impressive properties on a street consisting exclusively of impressive properties, bordering the Griffith Park area of Los Angeles. He sat in his vehicle around the corner of the home until the owner and his wife, Mr. and Mrs. Alexander Sisky, left for the evening at 9:30 p.m., as promised. The couple would be attending a dinner party in the Russian neighborhood of West Hollywood that was guaranteed to run into the early morning hours. There would be no need to hurry, apart from the fact that the security system, once penetrated, would alert the neighbors and local law enforcement.

At 9:30 p.m., he stepped out of his car and walked to the corner, pausing to light a cigarette, a black backpack slung over his right shoulder. The evening air was crisp and cool, and a light, misty fog hovered beneath the street lamps along the boulevard. A series of automobiles filed past him; they were all heading down from the park and into the megalopolis of L.A. As he leveled his head, he could see a mixture of breath and smoke shoot into the evening air, and just as quickly disappear. He watched as the Siskys' car pulled out of the driveway and drove in his direction. He continued on to the house with the casual demeanor of someone out on an evening stroll.

Although he had seen pictures of the house, he walked past it to observe more of the neighborhood. Then, he abruptly turned around, headed back, and stopped when he reached the home he would be entering. He took his phone from his back pocket and set a timer for five minutes, allowing for one minute to enter the house and four minutes before the police would likely arrive once the alarm went off. When it did, it triggered in him a rush of adrenaline.

The man moved quickly, knocking over chairs, pushing an ashtray off the coffee table, and breaking the glass in a china cabinet. He next pulled a bottle from his backpack and placed it in one of the empty cells of the wine rack.

The bogus burglary stunt was a necessary condition of the espionage operation. Sisky demanded "plausible deniability" of his involvement because he was aware that he was under near-constant surveillance by the CIA, and he could not be seen with a person who, for all he knew, was also being monitored.

Once the intruder accomplished what he came to do, he left through the back door and lurched himself over the back fence. He fell clumsily on the other side and twisted his ankle, causing him to curse and limp. He would pick up his car on the next block and drive back into the city. He didn't have an abundance of time, as he was scheduled to appear at the comedy club for an 11:00 p.m. performance.

***

Jack Tanaka paced backstage as he waited his turn. There was one comedian ahead of him delivering a monologue, and by the sound of the audience, he knew it would be a tough act to follow. While other comedians would prefer to hang out in the "green room," Tanaka believed he could amp up his own enthusiasm and delivery by observing the performance ahead of his own. When the "one minute warning" light was illuminated to alert the performer ahead of him, he had sixty seconds before being introduced. At that point, he ignored everything in his orbit apart from the lines he had rehearsed countless times.

"And now, ladies and gentlemen," announced the emcee, "our very own Jack Tobacco!"

Tanaka took to the stage, galloping as best he could after his injury earlier that evening.

"Hello, hello! Hello, everybody!" said Tanaka as he approached the microphone, doing his best to conceal his injury. "Hey, do you know how Asian spices say hello?"

Tanaka waited a few seconds.

"Wassabi!"

A few beads of sweat immediately emerged on his forehead as the spotlight beat down on him.

"I know you guys weren't expecting a fat Asian guy tonight," he continued, "but I wanted to tell you that I am, actually, on a seafood diet. Now, when I see food, I eat it."

"Heard that one," yelled a customer from a table in back of the club. The comeback echoed through the cavernous club and generated more laughter than the joke itself. Tanaka ignored it.

"Oh, hey, do you know how to *really* insult an Asian?" he said, determined to maintain a certain tempo. "Say, your mama got more chins than a Chinese phone book!" A few members of the audience chuckled, but most were speaking to each other and ignoring the stand-up comic.

"But I do feel sorry also for my father; he had a stroke and lost feeling in his left side. He's all 'right' now." He held up a pair of air quotes as he delivered the line.

"I also feel bad for my brother," he continued, "he has a stuttering problem and went to prison for a botched robbery. I worry he'll never finish his sentence."

Tanaka's decision to take up improv and stand-up comedy was not dissimilar to how he ended up a member of the yakuza, the centuries-old Japanese criminal syndicate. His therapist, who was Jewish, likened it to the condition that created "self-hating Jews," a disdain for how his culture was viewed by the rest of the world that compelled him to join with negative opinions toward it.

The unfortunate reality for Tanaka was that he was impulsive and often careless, and the yakuza felt they had to settle by bringing him into the organization in order to strengthen their presence on American soil. He consistently felt he didn't fit into either American or Japanese culture, but at least within the yakuza, he had an identity. Things may have turned out differently for him if his family hadn't experienced so much discrimination in the U.S.

Tanaka would have loved to pursue a career in law enforcement, but he believed, correctly, that his excess weight, combined with racist attitudes, would have made it near impossible to be accepted. When he realized he could not lose weight, he allowed the hairs under his lower lip to grow long in an attempt to conceal the double chin underneath. Unfortunately, it merely drew attention to it.

Tanaka was a third-generation U.S. citizen. His grandparents were incarcerated in 1942 among 120,000 other Japanese and U.S. citizens of Japanese descent. Despite the significant challenges that followed families eventually released from internment, his parents both worked hard and lived frugally in order that they could send Jack to UC Berkeley, where he eventually received a degree in chemistry.

During his adolescence, Jack was often reminded that his family suffered the stigma of being second-class citizens. Lieutenant General John L. DeWitt, who administered the relocation and internment program, often told newspapers, "A Jap is still a Jap," an insult that many Japanese Americans could never forget. Tanaka's parents were proud to be American citizens, but the experience in camps forever scarred them and their family. Tanaka was not spared the humiliation; he was often bullied in school as a "half-breed."

And so, to cope with a near absence of self-confidence, as well as to create a cover for his role in a criminal syndicate, he would sign up for improv and stand-up gigs in and around the L.A. area. He intentionally spoke in broken English as part of his on-stage persona, even though he spoke perfect English with no accent at all other times. Occasionally he would fall *into* character when engaging with others in the community and start speaking in broken English again. It was a useful tool when he might want people to believe he was naïve, persuading them to let down their guard.

The stage spotlight on Tanaka was intense, and it didn't help that he wore a long-sleeve shirt buttoned up to his neck to conceal the many tattoos he collected as a member of the yakuza. Due to his large frame, he could have been mistaken for a football player. He wiped his brow with a handkerchief as he wrapped up his performance following a series of one-liners and self-deprecating stories.

"Thank you, you've been a great audience, and just to come clean, I wrote many of these jokes with the help of JAP-GPT."

Tanaka stood, hoping for some validation from an audience full of strangers. Appreciation would only come when it was clear, according to the emcee's announcement, that he would be leaving the stage.

"Let's give it up for Jack Tobacco, everybody!"

3

The sun began to make its presence known in the sleepy coastal town of La Bufadora, Mexico, in Baja California. Even in October, the temperatures could reach 80 degrees by the time most people would be waking up, although most fishermen would have left the village before sunrise. Gabriel Rios, however, was preparing his dive boat for customers who were still sleeping in the home he converted to a B&B. His customers arrived from Orange County the night before, and he would be taking them out later in the morning after his wife served them a traditional Mexican breakfast of chorizo, potatoes, and eggs.

La Bufadora is one of the largest blowholes in the world, where wave action forces seawater through a natural spout, resulting in a thunderous sound and shooting water up to 100 feet. It is a popular tourist destination and attracts scuba divers for its accessibility to underwater pinnacles, natural caves, and abundant wildlife. Crucially, it is about a 2.5-hour boat ride from Los Coronados Islands.

As he loaded the fifth scuba tank on the dock and stood it next to the four others, Gabriel's cell phone rang. He recognized the number from the U.S. and knew what the call would be about.

"Hola," he said, looking up at the rising sun and squinting at the cloudless sky.

"Buenos días, mi amigo," came the voice from the other end of the line. It was Jack Tanaka, doing his best to finesse a Mexican accent as he spoke.

"Hola, señor, ¿cómo estás?" replied Gabriel, who, although he did not consider Tanaka anything more than a business associate, was mindful of the need to be considerate at all times with his American customer.

"¿Tienes las botellas, amigo?" said Tanaka, asking the question that Gabriel knew was coming.

"Sí, señor, todo está aquí."

"Any problema yesterday?" Tanaka asked, demonstrating his lack of proficiency in the local language.

"No, señor, no problema."

In a continuation of Spanglish, Tanaka explained that the bottles would be collected that evening by a young courier who had been meticulously vetted for his honesty and reliability. The courier was a day laborer with dependable transportation. He was not one to ask questions apart from the payment he would receive to pick up and drop off what was very likely contraband: guns, drugs, or stolen goods. He would draw the line at transporting people, as that situation carried with it special risks and obligations.

For his trouble, which included the collection of the bottles from the shallow waters around Los Coronados, "Gabe" would earn enough in American currency to help keep his tiny dive business afloat. He also was not inclined to ask any questions about the bottles and why such a clandestine operation was necessary to transport them over the border.

From La Bufadora, the bottles would travel over Mexican roads to Port Pajaritos in Veracruz, a journey taking nearly two days. The courier was advanced a certain amount of funds to pay off any police who might stop him along the way, asking questions where the only purpose was to expedite the offering of a bribe. Ultimately, the cargo would be loaded on the Cuba-flagged tanker *Vilma*, which was in Mexico principally to collect and transport desperately needed oil to the island nation.

From Cuba, the bottles would be collected, separated, and sold to a variety of nation-states, the mafia, and other criminal organizations, with each bottle fetching anywhere from $100,000 USD to just over $1 million.

"Yo, Richard, wait up!"

Special Agent Richard Anthony O'Brien was walking with a cup of coffee in one hand and a muffin in the other. He had arrived for a morning meeting at FBI headquarters in Los Angeles, stopping first at the coffee cart just outside the lobby doors. Running behind him to catch up was his old partner, Jeff McAuley.

"Oh, hey Jeff, how are you doing?" asked Richard.

"Doing good, man, doing good. I caught some early waves this morning. Nothing can ruin this day now!" McAuley replied.

The FBI in Los Angeles operated out of the 17-story Federal Building on Wilshire Boulevard, a building that also housed the Department of Veterans Affairs and the U.S. Passport Agency. It was common to have a large crowd outside in the morning. Civilians would be screened upon entering the east lobby, while FBI agents and other government officials entered from double doors on the west side. Elevators in the east lobby provided access only to the first 10 floors. FBI personnel could access floors from 10 to 17. But in order to get to the FBI entrance, Richard first had to navigate past a crowd of people waiting for their appointment to obtain a passport.

McAuley jumped ahead of Richard and grabbed the door for him to enter the building, relieving him of having to negotiate the challenge with both hands occupied.

"Appreciate it," he said politely. Richard and McAuley had grown apart since their days at the Academy and a short stint as roommates in the beach community of Hermosa Beach. McAuley was always there for Richard, particularly during the dark days when Richard lost his connection to his girlfriend, Sarah Goodman. But Richard couldn't embrace the bohemian lifestyle that defined McAuley, and he worried that too close an association might threaten his fledgling career in the FBI. He also couldn't be 100% certain that McAuley had given up his recreational drug habits.

If there was any distance between the two men, McAuley wouldn't have noticed. His nearly unflappable demeanor resulted in him treating every man as his brother.

"Dude, it's good to see you," McAuley said as the two stood outside the elevator. As the door opened, however, it was clear that the two would not be having much of a conversation. About a half dozen men and women in white shirts and dark suits were there. They gravitated to the sides of the elevator to accommodate the two new passengers.

"How often are you surfing these days?" Richard whispered, not that he was entirely interested in the answer.

"Nearly every day, man, nearly every day," McAuley replied, loud and proud. "It's what keeps me from killing somebody." McAuley winked at Richard as he spoke.

Richard knew immediately the game McAuley was playing. Announcing intent to commit murder in an elevator packed with FBI agents was a stunt that only McAuley could conceive. Richard felt the urge to announce, "he's kidding," but decided that McAuley didn't need an alibi and didn't deserve the additional attention.

The doors to the elevator soon parted at the 12th floor of the building. All occupants filed out and walked into the conference room immediately opposite them. The room was similar to all other conference rooms in the agency: a number of banquet tables organized in a huge rectangle, with office chairs lining the perimeter. Opposite the entrance, a series of windows provided a view of the expansive, lush lawn from a former golf course. At the far end of the room, a screen hung from the ceiling. Behind it, the same clock found in elementary schools everywhere indicated the time. It was eight in the morning, or what agents would call "oh eight hundred."

The last agent to walk in, after most others were seated, was John Swanson. Swanson transferred from the FBI office in Manhattan to replace Paul Michaelson, the previous Assistant Director in Charge of the LA headquarters, who retired several months prior. The job was a promotion for Swanson, who was viewed as an often tactless and hard-headed leader—a man who led by intimidation. Apparently, this didn't prevent him from rising through the ranks.

Richard had worked with Swanson briefly in New York, and matters got ugly when Richard began dating Sarah Goodman, another FBI agent who had a brief romance with Swanson. Swanson was not the type of person to forget O'Brien moving in on a woman he felt was his exclusive property.

"Morning, everyone," Swanson barked to the audience.

"I don't have too much for you this morning," he continued. "But there was a burglary last night near West Hollywood, and LAPD has asked us to assist in the investigation."

"Sir?" came a response from an agent. It was well understood in the agency that the FBI did not interfere with local law enforcement; however, there were rare exceptions. Such exceptions were generally not very rewarding opportunities for agents seeking a path to career advancement.

"The victim is a former member of the Russian consulate out of DC," Swanson said. "Although he's technically retired, the Russian embassy asked that we not investigate, which means, of course, that we will. The State Department asked us to join the investigation largely for appearances."

When local law enforcement requests FBI assistance, it's generally due to a lack of resources or technology to meet the demands of the investigation, in which case they are grateful for the help. However, when assistance is "forced" on them, agents can feel unwelcome. This appeared to be a case of the latter. *Politics are everywhere,*

Richard thought as he sat through the briefing. His train of thought was interrupted by Swanson.

"O'Brien," he barked aloud. "You will meet LAPD Officer Gary Schaeffer at the residence. The two of you will interview the owner."

Richard knew that Swanson was picking him simply to emphasize his seniority over him. If it was true that Swanson was punishing O'Brien with such a trivial assignment, no one else in the room was wise to it.

Swanson continued. "The Russian Embassy asked that we give them 48 hours before we enter the home. We are giving them 24 hours," he said. "Remember, O'Brien, diplomatic immunity means their citizens are protected from arrest, not those that engage in crimes against them."

All Richard could think of, while aware of the answer, was, "why me?"

***

There was only one thing that concerned Richard more than driving north through LA traffic to Griffith Park—and that was meeting up with a likely uncooperative LAPD officer. As he exited Highway 101, the disintegrating concrete jungle of downtown Los Angeles gave way to clusters of oak trees, tall residential hedges, and gorgeous homes. The surroundings seemed to become more impressive with each passing block.

Richard had done some preliminary research on the homeowner: Alexander Sisky was a career diplomat, sent to Washington, D.C., in 2019 as a cultural attaché to the Russian Embassy. Had his career not been cut short by Moscow, it would have been natural to assume Sisky was a spy, not unlike the various undercover agents dispatched to Eastern Europe as cultural attachés by the U.S. during the Cold War. However, Sisky's employment was apparently terminated in 2021, whereupon he relocated his family to a popular Russian neighborhood in West Hollywood. Two years later, he bought a 4,500-square-foot home in the prestigious neighborhood near Griffith Park.

Sisky's purchase of the spacious home raised a few eyebrows when he first arrived in the neighborhood. How, after all, could a mere civil servant in the Russian administration afford a home that would be out of the reach of many Hollywood actors and film industry executives? Sisky never integrated enough with his neighbors to provide many answers.

Richard slid his car behind the patrol car on Hobart Boulevard, a street that cuts through most of Los Angeles's suburbs, terminating in the north after finally twisting slightly to hug the perimeter of Griffith Park. Homes sat on one side of the street, their backyards facing the road that visitors to Griffith Observatory would take to exit the park after visiting the historic site. These were massive homes, many with security gates, including the Sisky residence. Given that homes only sat on one side of the street, it was an ideal location to stage a break-in; there were no neighbors across the street to observe it.

Richard parked and walked toward the patrol car. Two uniformed policemen were leaning against it. One of them looked at Richard, then the massive Casio G-Shock watch on his wrist. Richard took a deep breath. He was already spent from the stop-and-go traffic he had to tolerate to reach the home. He wasn't in the mood for a confrontation. Fortunately, neither were the two officers.

"Agent O'Brien, I presume?" said Sergeant Schaeffer, smiling. Schaeffer turned toward Richard and extended his hand.

"Yeah," Richard replied, still a bit high-strung from the drive and showing it. "Hey, sorry I'm a bit late."

"No worries," Schaeffer replied, still smiling. "It's a shitshow this time of day. I'm Sergeant Schaeffer, and this is my partner, Jay Parker." Parker, the one who was checking his watch when Richard arrived, half-smiled at Richard without offering his hand.

"Hey," the two signaled to each other nearly simultaneously.

"Have you met the owner yet?" Richard asked.

"No," Schaeffer replied, "not yet. Our orders were to wait for you."

Richard recognized the awkwardness of the situation. These officers probably handled cases like this every day and were far better trained in how to investigate a break-in.

"Yeah," Richard started, "about that…"

"No, look, it's no big deal," Schaeffer interrupted. "The more the merrier. And it's always good to have a different set of eyes in some of these situations. This one doesn't pass the smell test from three districts away."

"How do you mean?" Richard asked.

"The owner would not have reported the burglary at all if not for the neighbors next door." This time it was Parker speaking. "Seems these Russians either don't like the cops or don't like Americans in general."

The three men stood outside the patrol car for a moment in a tight circle, looking down at the pavement, when Schaeffer broke the silence, saying, "Well, shall we?" They proceeded to walk past the open gates up the winding path to the front door of the house. Richard hung back to allow Sergeant Schaeffer the opportunity to speak for the team. The door to the residence opened moments after Schaeffer rang the doorbell.

"Mr. Sisky, good morning. I'm Sergeant Schaeffer, LAPD; this is my partner Jay Parker, and this here is Special Agent Richard O'Brien with the FBI. We are here to inspect the premises following the report of a break-in last night."

Sisky was a short and frail man with a scowl so finely honed that it appeared permanent. He looked in the general direction of the officers without making direct eye contact with any of them. He had long ago lost most of his hair, save for a few strands that lay aimlessly on the top of his scalp. Sisky may have been taller in the past, but by now suffered from a hunched-over frame that reduced his stature by at least four inches. He hesitantly backed up and opened the door wide enough to let the men pass, revealing a team of blue-gloved agents already on the scene, taking photos and dusting areas that the intruder may have touched.

"I don't know why you are all here; this is completely unnecessary," he said in a thick Russian accent as the three new visitors walked past him. "My wife and I have already looked through our things, and nothing of importance is missing."

"I understand, Sir," Schaeffer replied, "but we have to take every unlawful break-in seriously. It helps us catch criminals that may have harmed other members of the community."

The four men were now standing in the foyer of the house, facing each other.

"Mr. Sisky," Schaeffer said, "we'd like to take a look around the house. Can you show us where the perpetrator gained access?"

Sisky pointed to a window at the far end of the living room. "As I told these men already, over there," he said.

The living room was richly furnished and a bit gaudy, with a large bookcase on one side and a huge picture window facing the front lawn on the other. The bookcase had an integrated wine rack that was nearly full. A lamp on a nearby end table was lying sideways on the floor next to a couch, and behind this, the broken window. The three officers spread out in the general direction of the large room.

Schaeffer went to the window first. The glass was shattered, and the screen was cut down the middle.

"The alarm company confirmed that zone was breached," Parker said as he looked out the picture window, admiring the view.

Schaeffer stuck his head through the screen and out the window. He tried to imagine the perpetrator slicing the screen, smashing the glass, and unlocking the window from the outside. As he looked down, shards of broken glass on the ground reflected the sunlight back to his face. He pulled his head back inside.

"Do you mind if we look upstairs?" Schaeffer said to Sisky.

Sisky rolled his eyes and walked away from Schaeffer. "You'll find some jewelry on the floor," he said as he walked toward the kitchen just off the living room. "We went through it all last night. Everything is there."

Richard was staring at the wine rack and noticed that in a lattice structure that held probably thirty bottles, three cells in the center were vacant. It seemed odd to Richard that a person with such an immaculate home, and likely wine collection to match, would not have filled all the cells.

"Was any of the wine taken?" he asked, addressing Sisky for the first time, who was now in the kitchen and out of view. Sisky didn't reply.

Richard pulled one of the bottles out and took a picture of the label. Then he proceeded to take bottles out of other cells and to take pictures of them as well. It would be odd that Sisky would not admit to the wine being stolen, but then everything about this break-in was odd.

"Mr. Sisky," Richard repeated, now standing outside the entrance to the kitchen and in view of Sisky, "were any bottles of wine stolen from your collection?"

Sisky, whose back was turned to Richard, said firmly, "No."

Richard was about to walk away from the wine rack when he noticed a card standing up above it. He took the card to look inside. It was from a local seller of fine wines. The message inside was handwritten:

> *Mr. Sisky, we hope you enjoy this complimentary bottle of Lost Mountain Bordeaux-style wine, and we look forward to seeing you soon at our weekly wine tasting at Art Du Vin.*

Richard remembered seeing this bottle inside the wine rack and already had a picture of it on his phone. He took a picture of the card. He couldn't imagine Sisky socializing with others in the community.

By now, Schaeffer was walking back down the stairs, and Parker, who was looking for anything out of place, had moved to the foyer. Sisky came from the kitchen, and the men were once again in a loose circle.

"Mr. Sisky," Schaeffer said, "thank you for your cooperation. I'd like to give you my card if you find out anything that might help us to find the perpetrators. Do I understand then that you haven't found anything missing?"

"That's right," Sisky replied.

"All right then, we will be on our way."

The men did not bother to offer a handshake to Sisky. It was obvious he wouldn't value the best manners he was offered.

The officers remained silent until all three were standing by their vehicles.

"Well, that was weird. This is a fucking setup," Schaeffer said.

"How do you mean?" asked Richard.

"Well, first of all," Schaeffer continued, "who breaks into a home like this, heavily secured, and leaves without taking so much as a piece of jewelry? But it's more than that. The window was broken to make it look like the intruder entered there. Glass shards on the outside of the house indicate the blow came from someone already on the inside."

"You mean…" Richard started.

"He probably came in through the front door," Schaeffer said. "I am thinking this is some kind of scuffle between Russians in the mafia or something like that. Something was probably taken from the property, but Sisky doesn't want to report it because it's something that doesn't even belong to him, he has no right to own, or he doesn't want to go on record as having acquired it. The perpetrator wanted us to come here to hassle Sisky, and they've now accomplished that goal."

Richard wasn't sure that Schaeffer had it exactly right, but he probably wasn't too far from wrong. The CIA had naturally followed Sisky's departure from the consulate and concluded he did not have access to intelligence of any value now that he had settled in L.A., and that he did not pose a threat to national security. Still, they never stopped watching him.

But what nobody suspected was that, rather than something being taken from Sisky's residence, instead, something was placed there.

4

Jack Tanaka guided up the heavy orange garage door that served as the entrance to his 10x15 storage unit on the fourth floor until it snapped in place at the top. The building, which sat at the corner of Pico and Crenshaw in West LA, was built in 1928. It could easily be mistaken for a hotel, or even a fortress from some fantasy novel. For Tanaka, it represented his opportunity to escape the reality of his circumstances in real life. He entered the dark, damp space and then reached up to pull a cord that ignited the fluorescent lights running across the ceiling.

The spacious room was well organized. On one side, a series of grey metal shelves ran from floor to ceiling. On some shelves were various manuals and books that he had collected on the subject of spy craft. On other shelves were electronic devices that he might use from time to time: night vision goggles, burner phones, and a handgun he had for protection but had never used. Another shelf contained various combustible chemicals and a zip-lock bag containing dried mushrooms. And on the bottom shelf were twenty-two bottles of wine with no labels.

On the other side of the room was a sofa bed for those occasional nights when Tanaka didn't feel safe being at his apartment, and a coffee table. On the table was a bottle of Perrier, a fifth of scotch, and a single rocks glass. In the far back of the room was a long banquet table that served as his desk. Underneath that was a small two-drawer file cabinet, and next to this was a paper shredder. A mini-fridge was off to the other side. On the far left of the table was an HP printer, and several cables ran from there until they hung off the front, available for a connection to his laptop. Tanaka pulled the backpack he was carrying around his shoulder and laid it gently onto the desk. As he did, several bottles inside banged against each other.

Tanaka fell into the office chair with a thud. He was exhausted. He had put on extra weight in the past year that he didn't need. He reached into his pocket to retrieve a handkerchief, which he used to wipe the sweat off his forehead and face. He put his wireframe glasses on the table and buried his face in the cloth.

He got to bed late the night before after his stand-up routine at the comedy club, and, in addition to the sprained ankle, he also had a bruise on his knee from where he climbed the fence in the back of Sisky's yard and landed hard on the concrete on the other side. He was rubbing the injured area as he looked ahead to the world map taped up behind his desk.

Tanaka had a new set of problems. Since the fermentation of wine in U.S. coastal areas was declared illegal by the Food and Drug Administration, he needed to establish an entirely new approach to the distribution of his product. In August 2023, the U.S. Coast Guard removed and later destroyed 2,000 bottles of wine that had been submerged in 70 feet of water about 3.7 miles off the coast of Santa Barbara, put there by a company called Ocean Fathoms. It seems the company violated a series of environmental laws in submerging the bottles, including the destruction of wildlife that grew on the bottles and did not survive after the bottles were removed. Then there was the concern that the bottles may have been contaminated during the many months they remained underwater.

The business concept behind ocean-aged wines was irresistible to investors: the young wine enjoys a pure anaerobic environment, stable temperatures, low light, and gentle agitation, with near-zero overhead expense apart from dropping and collecting the product. What these startups didn't anticipate was U.S. government interference—after all, the industry trend was already taking root in many European countries, including Spain, Italy, and even France.

For Tanaka, it was not so much starting a business that he needed to do, as it was to establish the right network through payments and bribes following the FDA ruling. He had originally dismissed the case of Ocean Fathoms as a one-off and established an agreement with the Chinese Ministry of State Security to drop a crate of wine in the shallow waters off Big Diomede Island in the Bering Strait, which was possible during the summer before ice flows made navigation a challenge. The crate would be connected to a surface buoy for easy retrieval when the U.S. Coast Guard was not patrolling the area.

The Diomede Islands sit on the international date line between Chukotka, an autonomous region of Russia, and the State of Alaska. The Big Island belongs to Russia, while the smaller island belongs to the United States. At their closest point, the islands are only 2.4 miles apart, so it made the perfect spot for the illegal transfer of goods to Chinese intelligence.

The Chinese Coast Guard had begun patrolling the area with the tacit approval of the Russian Navy, and the Chinese research vessel *Xue Long 2* was also known to pass through the region, so Tanaka had a couple of solutions for getting the product to his customer. However, when the USCG Cutter *Storis* detected a suspicious-looking fishing vessel about to cross into Russian waters, they dispatched a rigid inflatable to board the vessel and confiscated the crate containing the wine. Tanaka was fortunate the captain of the vessel didn't expose him, but as a result, the wine was sent to a USCG warehouse in Anchorage.

Tanaka also recognized the arrangements he made with Jose Perez and Gabriel Rios were unacceptable to the yakuza. They created too much exposure to "outsiders," with the risk of being blackmailed if even the wine was able to make it as far as Mexico without being confiscated by the Coast Guard or Mexican Navy. They were also chronically unresponsive or unavailable and could disappear at any time as the business was ramping up. It was unsustainable as a current approach, and he would eventually need to establish another distribution channel to replace it.

What Tanaka really wanted to do was to start an operation out of Florida that would drop the wine off the coast of Cuba. With regular flights out of Havana to Moscow and Beijing, this made the most sense of all. He mused that this would be worth pursuing as soon as he delivered the various orders that were now delayed by the recently confiscated wine.

Tanaka leaned back in his office chair, staring at the wall again. One thing he knew for sure: he could not continue to deliver bottles one at a time, as he had done for Alexander Sisky. This was not a scalable approach; it was exhausting and expensive. But moreover, it exponentially increased the odds that he would get caught. And this was certainly the reason why he was being called back to Tokyo for a meeting with the Oyabun, the head of a yakuza clan, the most feared organized crime syndicate in Japan.

***

"One of the first things you want to do," said the instructor, "is hold the glass at a 45-degree angle into the light."

Richard looked quizzically at the pretty woman seated next to him, then raised the glass of cabernet in front of his eyes.

"If you really want to impress people that you have a handle on the fundamentals," the instructor continued with a delicate British accent, "hold a white napkin behind the glass for better contrast with the color of the wine." The instructor stood in front of the group and demonstrated the technique, holding the glass with her right hand and a white napkin behind it with her left. "The depth of color will give you clues to the age of the product," she added.

Now fully acclimated to the Southern California lifestyle, Richard O'Brien was renewing his commitment to continuing education, and taking a class in wine tasting at Art Du Vin in Long Beach seemed to be as good a place to start as any. The investigation into the Sisky burglary was one timely form of inspiration, and the wine-tasting event described on the card he photographed provided all the details. He was also aware that this was an excellent venue to meet well-educated, attractive, and available women.

"The color looks a bit purple to me," he said, leaning his body in the woman's direction. "I'm calling this a relatively young wine, probably a troublemaker," he continued. Richard could think of a few other comments, like "she's barely legal," but such comments would have definitely been a higher risk. The woman smiled back as she laid her glass back on the table, revealing a wedding band on her left hand.

"Are you a troublemaker?" she whispered. Before Richard could answer, the instructor continued with the program. Married women were off-limits as far as he was concerned. But now that he had concluded she was unavailable, he noticed the instructor was more likely just his type. She was slender and petite, with long, straight black hair and a nice smile. She had a bronze complexion and appeared to be of Indian heritage. And she was staring right at him.

"So now you are going to take your first smell of the product," she said, smiling at her audience. "This is to prepare your olfactory senses for the real test." The instructor pushed her nose into the glass, then set it down and began to swirl the wine in circles on the table, her palm on the base of the glass and her fingers on either side of the stem. The motion to Richard seemed oddly seductive, particularly as his interest grew in the woman holding it.

"After agitating the wine," she said, "give it a few seconds to breathe, then capture its aromas again." She held up the glass and pushed her nose in again. "Look for notes of licorice, oak, tobacco, clay, or ripe red fruits," she added. "Then take a small sip."

As this was the first class in a series designed to go for five sessions, Richard was in no particular hurry to pursue the instructor for a date, but he did at least want to introduce himself at the close of the program and saw her eye contact as an obvious invitation. While most of the class dispersed quickly to other parts of the bar after thoroughly discussing the cabernet they enjoyed, Richard made a beeline for the instructor.

"This was great tonight; I learned a lot. Thank you," he said as he smiled and extended his hand to her. "My name is Richard."

"Well, that's very nice of you to say," she replied. "My name is Asha. What brings you to my class?"

"I am trying to make myself a more interesting dinner date," he said, deciding to at least signal that he was probably available. Asha nodded in approval.

"What kind of work do you do?" she asked. Richard felt it was too early to reveal that he was an FBI agent, which, when floated in introductions, often generated far greater impact than intended and changed the dynamics of the conversation.

"I'm an investor," he said, which was his go-to phrase. "I'm thinking of investing in some wines someday." Richard was proud of that second part, which once again sent the subtle suggestion that they may have more in common—at least more in theory than in reality.

"Oh, that's interesting," she replied, her voice increasing in decibels ever so slightly. "I have a few clients that are doing the same thing. I should put you guys in touch." Richard now noticed, with such little distance between them, how vibrant Asha became when discussing her favorite subject. She was also confident in herself and not at all intimidated by Richard's good looks.

Asha Chandra had introduced herself to the class as the buyer at Café Sevilla, so Richard knew he could find her again, even if he failed to close the deal for a date during one of the classes. What he saw and knew about Asha put her at the top of his priority list for a possible love interest, as he found Indian women to be quite exotic. But, playing the long game, he decided not to reveal his feelings just yet.

"I may take you up on that," he said. "I look forward to seeing you at the next session."

With that, Richard left without a phone number, but with a plan.

***

The flight from Los Angeles International Airport, aka LAX, to Haneda Airport in Tokyo was twelve hours. Tanaka tried to sleep, as by the time he landed it was 2:00 PM the following day. However, he sat in fear for most of the flight, concerned about why he was summoned by the Inagawa-kai, the third-largest yakuza family in Japan.

Even in the early afternoon, the intensity of life in Tokyo was palpably different from Los Angeles, and Tanaka was not well prepared for it. He had only visited Tokyo a handful of times as he went through the initiation to join the yakuza. On top of this, he was operating on very little sleep, and as he tried to navigate the subway system to his hotel, he couldn't help but feel overstimulated by it all. His meeting with the Oyabun was after dark, so, with a little luck, he might have been able to take a quick nap first. He definitely wanted to be in top form for the meeting and was hopeful that his remorse over the failed operation in the Bering Strait might be a suitable apology to avoid what he knew would be painful punishment.

The meeting would be held at the Shibuya Excel Hotel, which sits at the famous intersection in Tokyo where masses of people cross the street throughout the day and night, a scene captured in countless TikTok videos and Facebook reels. This was a location often used as a matter of convenience because the Oyabun's ancestral home and compound was in the countryside. The compound was reserved for meetings of the clan leadership when it was important to reinforce the Oyabun's authority. Members of all yakuza clans used fake names and identification to secure their preferred place to meet in the city, as contemporary laws were put in place to restrict their activities in Japan, and they were no longer allowed to operate in the open, nor to book conference rooms or hotels.

Tanaka took the hotel elevator up to the penthouse, where, to his surprise, a small group of men was waiting for him. A nap prior to the meeting was at that point no longer on the agenda. A stocky man in a black suit opened the door to the hotel room, then backed up to allow Tanaka to pass. As he did so, he saw three more men; two were standing at attention at either side of a hotel desk. The man behind the desk was wearing a ceremonial black robe with a large, gold, mythical dragon moving in serpentine motion up the fabric. Because the man was turned around, Tanaka could also see a long, braided ponytail flowing down his back. The other men wore black suits with white shirts and satin white ties, their arms folded in front of them.

The desk had a buffet behind it, and the man was pouring himself a cup of tea. To either side were additional rooms that were dark. Tanaka assumed one would be a bedroom and the other a bar or dining area. The main area of the room was dimly lit by ornate lamps on small tables that adorned the sides of the expansive hotel space, and there was the distinctive smell of incense in the air, but Tanaka didn't see where it was burning. In the back of the room, large picture windows revealed the lights of Tokyo's skyscrapers.

The man in the robe appeared much younger than Tanaka expected. It wasn't the Oyabun; it was Hiroshi Nakajima, the *Wakagashira*, or second in command of the yakuza and son of the Oyabun, the boss. Tanaka had never met Nakajima but was aware of his reputation. As the son of the Oyabun and heir to the head of the clan, he was determined to distinguish himself as a relentless warrior, one deserving of the respect of the elders in the clan that would be subject to his leadership when his father retired. Tanaka immediately recognized he was in deeper trouble than he expected.

As Nakajima slowly spun around in his chair, Tanaka took a deep bow, holding it for several seconds to convey his respect for the Wakagashira. Only when he heard Nakajima speak did he stand erect.

"Tanaka-san," said Nakajima in Japanese, "welcome to Tokyo. How was your flight?"

"Very well, Wakagashira," he replied, in English. "I am honored to meet you." It was understood and reluctantly accepted that Tanaka would respond in English, as his Japanese was rudimentary.

Nakajima did not stand to reciprocate any symbol of respect for Tanaka. Instead, he stared at Tanaka for some time, looking him up and down from his chair. After what felt like an eternity to Tanaka, he spoke.

"Tanaka-san," he said, "my father invested heavily in you and your family in America. He took you in as a member of this family, even though you demonstrate no ancestry to warrant it. He retired your debts from the university. He provided for your family when your father lost employment."

"I am humbly honored and deeply appreciative," Tanaka replied, bowing again, although this time simply as a gesture of recognition.

"Then, tell me, why do you make a fool of us?" Nakajima said, his tone shifting abruptly to one of scorn and anger. "Why did you play right into the American's hands when you knew they were aware of our operation?"

Tanaka expected this. He knew that his decision to proceed with the transaction in the Bering Strait was reckless when the U.S. Coast Guard was already operating in the area and had previously confiscated cargo on boats that were traveling near the maritime borders. He also knew that it was fruitless to be defensive in any meetings with the yakuza leadership.

"It was a mistake, Wakagashira, and I beg your forgiveness," he said, bowing again.

Nakajima did not immediately respond. Instead, he lifted the lid of a small, ornate box on the desk and pulled out a cigarette. His movements appeared intentionally in slow motion, as if amping up the tension in the room was even necessary. As he placed the cigarette on his lips, one of the men standing behind him leaned forward to light it. Nakajima took a long drag from the cigarette as he looked up at the ceiling and blew the smoke toward it. Finally, he lowered his head and spoke again.

"What is this I hear about some clown-like incident you arranged?" Nakajima continued, prepared to release a barrage of insults. But first, he took another drag of the cigarette and blew the smoke directly toward Tanaka.

"Breaking into our customer's home to deliver product to him? Are you not thinking of how this threatens our operation? What is this, a poorly executed magic trick?" he continued, "some kind of manifestation of your ridiculous cover?"

Tanaka realized the mock break-in could be perceived differently from the safety of the family's Tokyo headquarters. He expected to be congratulated on the creative way in which he solved the problem of getting the product to his Russian customer but could have anticipated also that Nakajima would use this as another opportunity to insult and denigrate him, lifting his image at Tanaka's expense. The other men looked on, lacking emotion.

"This was necessary because the American intelligence agencies were watching the Russian agent. He refused to accept delivery any other way," Tanaka said, trying as best he could to avoid appearing defensive.

"How do you intend to establish a sustainable operation if you cannot deal directly with the Russians?"

Tanaka was hoping the Oyabun's son would be ill-informed about his role in the family. He wasn't.

"I am establishing a route to our Russian customers through Cuba," he replied.

"Cuba!?" Nakajima said, feigning surprise. In reality, he already knew about Tanaka's latest venture. "Cuba is an unstable country. The Americans interfere with their pitiful few exports. This is the solution you offer us?"

"Wakagashira, the Russians have resumed naval exercises off the coast of Cuba and are making regular stops in Havana Bay. Getting our product on a Russian ship should not be difficult. Also, Russian customers in Cuba can take deliveries direct and fly directly to Moscow."

Of course, Nakajima was very familiar with the movements of the Russian navy in the Caribbean. But the pressure on Tanaka to demonstrate he was still capable of supporting the yakuza was the principal goal of the meeting between the two. And Tanaka appeared to demonstrate the fundamental intelligence to continue leading the family's business interests in the United

States, even though his judgment was, at times, questionable.

Nakajima refrained from speaking for some time, then rose.

"Tanaka-san," he said finally as he stood, "my father is more sympathetic to you and your family than is deserved. However, I will honor his commitment to support your operation because you are an essential part of our American enterprise. Nevertheless, your recent failures cannot go unpunished."

Nakajima motioned to one of the men standing at attention, who disappeared for a few seconds into one of the darkened rooms. He returned with a rolling cart, the style used in hotels by the room service staff. The cart had a white cloth on it, and on the cloth was a long knife, two washcloths, a bowl filled with water, and an open bottle of sake. The man pushed the cart in front of Tanaka, who looked down upon it as the man stepped back. He knew what was expected of him, a fate that he feared from the moment he was summoned to Tokyo.

The practice of *yubitsume*, the amputation of a portion of the left little finger, was somewhat rare in modern Japan and used sparingly as a form of punishment. While barbaric, the main reason for abandoning it was that it made for such an obvious signal to law enforcement that the victim was a member of a yakuza clan, providing them clues when they were attempting to detain suspicious persons or solve a crime. But insofar as Tanaka was living in the United States, Nakajima could take advantage of the practice without risk to Tanaka's cover, while messaging to the rest of the clan that he was unforgiving when members demonstrated signs of weakness.

Tanaka continued staring at the cart. The two men he saw when entering the room had moved to either side of him. He was without options and was well aware of the process. He raised the bottle of sake, opened his throat as best he could, and poured it down. Next, he leaned over the cart, made a fist, and placed his left hand firmly on the cart, leaving his smallest finger exposed. He took one washcloth and shoved it in his mouth. He next took the knife in his right hand and placed the point of the knife on the table, next to the finger.

Tanaka wanted to close his eyes but knew the importance of a precision cut, so with a combined motion pushing down and across simultaneously, he drew the knife quickly to the right with as much pressure as he could. The knife was as sharp as a knife can possibly be, and the finger snapped off just above the first knuckle. Tanaka bit the washcloth so hard that there would be a hole in it when he removed it from his mouth. He quickly took another long swig of sake, as tears flowed down from his eyes and across his cheeks.

None of the men spoke. They had all seen the traditional practice before, and in fact, the man who opened the door for him concealed the fact that two sections of his little finger had been cut off many years before. He routinely held his left hand in his right whenever he stood at attention.

Tanaka took the washcloth that had been in his mouth and covered the exposed wound on his hand with it. By making a fist, he was able to cover the wound and prevent excessive bleeding on the floor of the hotel room. With his right hand, he took the *shinu yubi*, the "dead finger," and placed it onto the second washcloth, covering it gently and creating from it a small package. He picked up the package, stepped toward the desk where Nakajima remained sitting, and, his hands still trembling from the shock, gently placed it in front of him. The distance between the two men was no more than a half meter. He bowed slightly as he stepped back.

"Tanaka-san," said Nakajima, looking down first at the washcloth containing the finger and then directly into his eyes. "I look forward to hearing about your future success in America. Have a nice flight back to the United States."

5

Richard opened his laptop at the coffee shop on Ocean Avenue, and pulled up a barstool at the counter facing outside the venue. As he settled in, he stared at the beach, which by 8:45 in the morning was now fully occupied by the Santa Monica surfing subculture. It was another warm, late summer day in the City of Angels.

Richard would have felt out of place had it not been his day off, allowing him to leave the blue suit at home in favor of a t-shirt and board shorts. He took a sip from his coffee as he reflected back on the advice he received from his mentor, Ben Klein, the now-retired Special Agent in Charge of the San Diego field office.

"Look for things that don't fit; look for patterns that are broken," he would often say to his rookie agents.

What doesn't fit? Richard thought to himself. *The wine doesn't fit,* he replied silently. *But am I saying this as an excuse to see Asha? Am I following my duty to be objective?*

As he brought the cup to his lips again, he saw McAuley standing on the other side of the Pacific Coast Highway, across the street from the coffee shop where the two agreed to meet. Richard got up to buy him a cup of coffee.

Predictably, McAuley had his surfboard under his arm, and his feet were covered in sand. He wore a tank top and flip-flops, and his shorts were still wet. He placed the board into the rack outside the shop and shook his long, dirty blond hair out in both directions, like a dog that just received a bath. McAuley was one of the few in the agency who let his hair grow out after graduating from the Academy, a practice that was tolerated for agents that might be expected to work undercover on specific operations.

"Dude, you really need to learn to surf," he said as he approached Richard. "The conditions today are sweet."

"Maybe," Richard replied as he placed a cup of coffee on the counter for McAuley, even though he had no intention of taking up the sport. Since moving to Los Angeles from New York, he had taken a keen interest in scuba diving and had quickly become certified as "Advanced." And as everyone in the beach subculture understood, a good day for surfing was generally a bad day for diving.

"All right then, what are we meeting about?" McAuley shot back.

Richard wanted McAuley's opinion on the Sisky robbery and whether he felt it was worth pursuing further.

Although McAuley could be eccentric, he had enough field experience by this time to sense if an investigation had legs, and he had produced some research on Sisky as part of a joint operation with the CIA when Richard was working on the case known as Operation Carbon Paper.

"What can you tell me about Alexander Sisky?" Richard said, as McAuley pulled up a stool next to him.

"He's the type of person you pay to carry a bag of money to someone," replied McAuley.

"So," Richard said, "you think he's bent?"

"Like the plumbing under your sink!" McAuley replied excitedly. "The CIA has been watching this guy for years. If he uses five squares of toilet paper instead of four, it goes into a field report."

"So, is he connected to Russian intelligence?" said Richard, drawing the most obvious of conclusions.

"That's not been unequivocally confirmed," McAuley said, looking behind him for anyone that might be eavesdropping on the conversation. "But he's been connected to some unsavory characters. And who you vibe with, is who you become."

***

Richard sat at the bar, waiting for Asha, taking sips from an overpriced IPA as he listened to CCR's "Proud Mary." He did not waste time calling her for a date, as he thought she could help him with the Sisky investigation. He had the photos of wine bottles on his phone, the perfect icebreaker for a wine enthusiast. He had no reason to suspect that Asha was involved in anything nefarious, but he didn't want to dismiss the possibility that she was the one to deliver the wine and accompanying note to Sisky.

Recommending a restaurant to a wine expert was a risky move, he thought originally, and he decided to be safe and suggest Café Sevilla, where she had a part-time job as a wine buyer. "I don't eat where I, you know…" Asha replied to the idea. From that point on, Richard decided to follow her lead, and the two agreed on the Water Grill at Grand Avenue, a more relaxed environment that suited both of them better.

As he waited for Asha, he found himself staring at a middle-aged woman at the other end of the bar who was clearly looking for attention. Richard had long theorized that the amount of cleavage revealed by a woman was in direct correlation to her desire for a man, nearly any man. If he was right, he thought, this woman was near desperate. She smiled directly at Richard, who reciprocated before looking down at his beer. Now was not the time for him to be playing with dynamite.

Just then, he felt someone tap his shoulder. It was Asha. She was wearing a black turtleneck and a black jacket over jeans that, combined with her shoulder-length black hair, made her look smart, classy, and just a tad intimidating to any man interested to meet her. Richard hopped off his barstool to give her a mini-hug, a movement that always seemed awkward to him but a suitable middle ground between a handshake and a kiss. A kiss on the cheek would seem patronizing, he thought, and a kiss on the lips was clearly premature. He executed the mini-hug effectively, so in his mind, the evening was off to a good start.

"Great to see you," Richard said, looking directly into Asha's dark eyes. It had been some time since Richard was with a woman who was equally successful and beautiful, and he was determined to say all the right things tonight, starting with telling the truth about the fact he worked for the FBI.

"Wait, what?" Asha said, leaning back in her chair once the two were seated. She was clearly rattled but quickly gathered her composure back to her relaxed baseline.

"Yeah, sorry I didn't make that clear before," Richard said, leaning into the table ever so slightly to avoid anything close to a public announcement.

"Oh, okay," she replied, trying her best not to appear fazed. To Richard's relief, she didn't appear to feel betrayed by the admission.

"I've never met anyone that worked for the FBI before," she said casually, now looking in both directions from her seat to verify their conversation stayed at the table.

"Well," Richard replied, wanting to demonstrate just the right measure of humility, "it's not quite like what you see in the movies. It's more like 50% drudgery, 40% paperwork, and maybe 10% fun." He was proud of how quickly he served up that response.

From that moment on, it seemed that Asha looked at him differently. He wasn't sure if that was a good thing, but he decided to assume so. He was interested to see if a relationship with Asha was possible. And he assumed that if she accepted the dinner date, there was no boyfriend in the picture.

"So," he said, leaning into the table ever so slightly, "how did you get into the wine business?"

Asha smiled but wanted to provide no more information than necessary. "My family has always been involved in the food and beverage business," she said. "My uncle owned a small bar in London, my dad owns a restaurant there, and my cousin is a wine broker." Richard was aware that England had a huge Indian community that, by all accounts, contributed significantly to the culture and economy of the island, including its share of pubs and liquor stores.

The server stopped by the table for the third time, and Richard waved him off.

"Hey," Richard said, "I want to show you something." He pulled out his phone and opened a picture of one of the wine bottles from the Sisky residence. "Do you recognize this bottle? It was in a home that I visited recently."

Asha leaned over the table to get a closer look at the picture. She knew better than to grab Richard's phone but was quite anxious to see the photos.

"Château Margaux," she said, leaning in further to tease out the vintage. She used her two fingers to expand the image. "2015, nice," she said. "That bottle would probably be worth about fifteen hundred dollars, if you can find it." She leaned back in her chair and crossed her arms, smiling.

"Really?" Richard replied, surprised. Sisky didn't seem the type of person to have built a valuable wine collection. Perhaps it was a one-off, he thought, as he swiped to reveal another bottle. "How about this one?" he asked.

Again, Asha leaned forward.

"That's a DRC La Tâche, 2014," she said quickly. "I could get that bottle for our restaurant for about five thousand."

"DRC?"

"Oh, sorry. DRC is Domaine de la Romanée-Conti," Asha said. "They are among the most expensive wines in the world. Where did you find this one?" She knew the answer.

"Oh, yeah, I've heard of it," Richard replied unconvincingly, attempting to show at least minimal awareness of the subject he was to be studying.

"What about this one?" Richard said, showing Asha the bottle that was given to Sisky by Café Sevilla. If Asha had connected the dots by this time, she wasn't giving it away.

"Oh," she said confidently, "that's the new Lost Mountain Bordeaux-blend from Virginia. My company is giving this out right now to its best customers to promote the new label. The vineyard was sold in 2022 to new owners."

At that point, Richard was convinced Asha had nothing to do with the incident at the Sisky residence and gave his phone to her to swipe through the other labels he photographed. There was always a risk that someone might scroll back farther than they should, a risk Richard decided to take. He saw Asha's eyes grow in size as she glanced at multiple pictures of rare and valuable wines.

"This is an impressive collection," she said with a slight giggle. "I'd love to be his dinner guest."

"So, these wines are rare, and there is a market for them, right?" Richard asked. "They could be sold through a broker?" If there was such value in the wine collection, it was odd that only three bottles were potentially missing. Even an intruder operating alone could have grabbed more of them.

"For sure," Asha replied, stopping at one picture and spreading the screen again to enlarge it. She put her face within a few inches of the phone.

"Except this one," she said, squinting as she spoke. "I am not familiar with this label." She finally passed the phone back to Richard.

"Vino del Mar," he said aloud. "You've not heard of it?"

"No," she said, leaning back in her chair. "Which doesn't mean it isn't a good product, but it definitely doesn't belong next to the others that have an established worldwide reputation going back, literally, centuries."

"I think we need to drink to that," Richard said, as the server returned to the table for the fourth time. "Would you like to order a bottle?" he said, fully intending to defer to her judgment.

"No thanks," she replied, looking at Richard and smiling. "I've been re-examining my relationship to alcohol," she said, adding, "I realized I am not abusing alcohol; it's abusing me."

Then, Asha turned her head up to address the waiter.

"I'll just have a dirty martini, three olives, please," she said, looking next at Richard and giving him a wink.

Richard was quick to respond.

"The same!" he said, smiling at Asha while looking directly into her eyes.

Richard believed that if Asha was not already involved with someone, he had an opportunity to pursue a romantic relationship with her. He knew this because of his effect on women in general. His last girlfriend told him he had the looks of a younger Tom Cruise with the body of Tom Brady, and many other women would agree. Many women expected or hoped for sex on the first or second date, and Richard was nearly always in a position to oblige.

But he had a habit of taking them to bed before realizing the pain that the entanglements would cause later. And he often forced himself to remember that many years before, his girlfriend Courtney committed suicide while carrying his baby. No, he thought to himself, he wouldn't be trying to sleep with Asha tonight.

***

"Good evening," Tanaka said, standing near the back of the room, his arms appearing pinned to the sides of his body. "My name is Jack Tanaka, and I am excited to join the Auxiliary. I graduated from UC Berkeley with a degree in chemistry, and I'm interested in serving my country. I recently retired, moved here to San Diego, and I plan to open a restaurant." Most of what he said was a complete lie or a broad exaggeration. The short speech, required of all guests that evening, suggested that he was either very nervous or not nearly as excited as he claimed to be.

Tanaka debated for some time about using his real name as he pursued membership in the U.S. Coast Guard

Auxiliary. In the end, he didn't trust his own ability to keep the story straight if he fabricated too much of a fake identity and felt the risk too great that he would slip up somehow and blow his cover. The Auxiliary seemed a perfect place for him to explore a new distribution system for his covert activity that would reduce his reliance on local dive charters and boat operators that could not be completely trusted.

Tanaka's attendance at the informational meeting allowed him to access the secure base known as Sector San Diego, one of the 37 sector bases from which the U.S. Coast Guard operated. The base was home to a few of the cutters responsible for surveillance of the international maritime border with Mexico and credited with drug busts and migrant crossing interdiction on a near-daily basis. It was the USCG cutter *Haddock* that had interfered with one of Tanaka's deliveries destined for the Los Coronado Islands, a delivery that had to be aborted.

"Welcome, Jack," said George Grover, the flotilla commander of Sector San Diego's Auxiliary operation. "Happy to have you here. What kind of restaurant are you opening?"

"A sushi restaurant, of course," Tanaka said, attempting to inject some humor while leveraging his obvious heritage.

"Ah, of course," replied Grover. A few chuckles were heard, and a few heads bobbed up and down.

Tanaka's story was carefully cultivated. He was aware that "Culinary Specialists" were in very short supply in the Coast Guard, and the easiest way for an Auxiliarist to get access to a patrol was to offer to serve as the crew's onboard cook. Also, he had taken an interest in cooking as a teenager and had sufficient skills in the kitchen that he wasn't intimidated by the responsibilities.

"If you are interested, Jack," Grover continued, "I can speak to the CO of the cutters here to see if they need a CS to staff the galley."

"Sure, that would be fine," replied Tanaka, concealing his relief that it would be even easier than he expected to join a crew.

The flotilla commander introduced three other guests, and after their personal introductions, the commander proceeded to discuss various community activities where the Auxiliary was expected to be present, staff officer vacancies, and ongoing training requirements. After the meeting, as the members began filing out of the conference room, Grover shouted out to the four guests, "Hey guys, would you like a tour of the base?" Three of the men stayed back for the tour, including Tanaka.

Grover led the men out of the conference room onto the base parking lot. By now, the sun had set, and the lights of the San Diego skyline began to replace daylight. The famous Coronado Bridge could be seen emerging from the downtown lights and snaking across the bay. "Best damn view of San Diego anywhere," Grover said to the men, who wouldn't disagree.

Grover walked toward the USCG dock where, among other watercraft, was the USCGC *Arowana*.

"Most of the Coast Guard cutters are named after marine wildlife," Grover said. "The arowana is a freshwater bony fish. They have long, dragon-like bodies, big eyes, and look really primitive, and they live in dark, shallow caves. If you've been to a Chinese restaurant with an aquarium, you've probably seen one there. Don't ask me why."

They are symbols of luck and prosperity, Tanaka said to himself. But he didn't volunteer the information.

Grover started saying something else, but Tanaka wasn't paying attention as he knew the other two guests were accommodating Grover's commentary. Instead, he focused his attention on the *Arowana*. At 87 feet, it was not a very large ship, but it was designed to be able to pursue other vessels and required maneuverability. It would be a challenge for him to hide an unfamiliar-looking crate on the boat, but as a Culinary Specialist, he could get provisions on the ship and, with some clever packing and labeling, solve the problem of getting his product out to a shallow drop-off location for retrieval by Gabriel Rios. The setup looked near perfect.

Tanaka and the three other guests at the flotilla meeting would become members of the Auxiliary that evening. After filling out the application and consenting to a background check, Tanaka would shortly receive his non-military ID, giving him access to the Sector base. Unlike the other three members joining, Tanaka had no intention of supporting the mission of the Guard.

6

Richard was bad at keeping promises to himself when it came to women, and Asha was no exception. No sooner had he sworn to "take it slowly" than he was making out with her in his car, outside her apartment. It was the end of their second date when he asked Asha if he could taste her lip gloss. A truly rookie move

As he ran his arm down the back of Asha's dress, his hand landed in the small of her back, above her behind, and it nearly locked into place there. Richard was amazed he could be so turned on by something that wasn't there – it was like an empty void, a concave space that was waiting for him. His hand fit perfectly in this intimate space, and he didn't want to ever pull it away. Asha decided that was enough, reached behind to grab his hand, and gently pushed him back.

"Slow down, fella," she said, smiling while making eye contact.

"Yeah, I'm sorry," Richard said, slightly embarrassed at, again, failing at the goal of setting the pace. "I'm just very attracted to you, and we have so much in common." As the words left his mouth, he realized he couldn't back up the statement.

"Me too," replied Asha, a response that didn't offer nearly as much context as Richard would have liked. The two were playing a game with unwritten rules.

Then came the line he was hoping to hear.

"Would you like to come up?"

"Sure," he replied. "And don't worry, I'll behave."

***

Richard sat up in bed, Asha's bed, and opened his phone. She lay next to him, her back turned, and her nightgown revealing that same sacred space above her behind that he felt for the second time moments before. While Richard had hoped to govern the pace of the relationship, it seemed instead that Asha was in total control of it.

For Richard, sex was still a thrilling experience, although it felt a bit mechanical with Asha, and he wondered if she enjoyed it as much as he did. Maybe she wasn't quite into him, or maybe she was protecting herself. She would have to develop a degree of self-confidence, he thought, in order to represent herself to the elites, including some of the wealthiest people in LA, that she could teach them a thing or two about wine. And if he was to succeed in linking Sisky's wine to a crime, he would benefit from her guidance.

Richard was vaguely familiar with stories about stolen wines and decided to do more research on them in the comfort of Asha's bed. The FBI case file on wine heists was substantial; this was a global phenomenon that joined stolen jewelry and art as equally subject to the laws of supply and demand, and the breaking of federal laws was on a disturbingly steep trajectory as a result. Richard clicked the folder on the FBI's secure site and began reading.

It wasn't just the fact that rare wines were being stolen; counterfeit wines were also being sold to unsuspecting collectors, and some heists actually passed over expensive yet niche wines in favor of the "easier-to-move" French standards. In some of these heists, it was established that the criminals on the ground were receiving real-time instructions from co-conspirators connected to them by mobile phone. This was the consensus regarding the heist of over $550,000 worth of wine from LA's French Laundry in 2014. Two men of Russian descent were convicted in that robbery, but some of the stolen bottles remained unaccounted for.

More recently, in 2023, a wine heist in nearby Venice at Lincoln Fine Wines caught the perpetrator on camera, who spent nearly two hours methodically pillaging the store's coveted stock, pausing occasionally to speak to someone on his phone. Well over $3 million in stolen wines were estimated to have been taken from wine collections in the LA area since the FBI began tracking this activity. Richard wondered if some of the stolen wines ended up in Sisky's collection.

As Richard continued to scroll through the classified documents on his secure phone, Asha rolled back over to face his direction. He looked down to admire the outline of her body under the sheets. Noticing this, she propped up her head with her left arm on the pillow.

"What are you working on?" she asked.

"I was reading about all these wine heists," he said. "This is big business. I wonder if some of those labels I showed you are from stolen inventories."

Asha did not want to talk about stolen wines and made this clear by removing the sheet that was clinging to her body, revealing the contours of her naked body underneath.

***

"You're gonna need to cut that off."

Takana was sitting next to the desk of Angelo Spinola, the District Officer for Culinary Services at Sector LA/LB, in Long Beach. As an Auxiliarist, Spinola didn't carry the rank of an active-duty member of the Coast Guard, but still, those in the galley called him "Captain" out of respect. Spinola was hunched over paperwork that covered nearly every inch of the desk, focused on the checklist he needed to complete to onboard a new member of the culinary team. On the wall behind the desk was posted the weekly galley menu and a series of mandatory safety bulletins from the Coast Guard, OSHA, and the FDA.

What Spinola referred to was the several strands of black hair that fell from Tanaka's chin.

"I can't have that look in my galley," he said. "And while you're at it, get a haircut."

Spinola came from a long line of families in the restaurant business and was also a former Coast Guard petty officer, first class. Upon officially retiring from the service, he cycled right into the Auxiliary and quickly earned the respect of the younger men around him. The respect came from his raw knowledge of the culinary trade, combined with the fact that he stood six feet five inches tall, weighed over 225 pounds, and took shit from nobody. In his chef coat, he had a commanding presence.

Satisfying Spinola was Tanaka's first and most significant challenge since joining the Auxiliary. A standard background check was already initiated by the Department of Homeland Security, but it would take several months before any formal report, and due to shortages, Auxiliarists were permitted to initiate training and take online exams to qualify for specific roles.

Fingerprints were also taken at the time an individual submitted an application, and remarkably, the fact that Tanaka was missing a finger did not raise any flags. But Spinola noticed it.

"And what the hell happened there?" he asked, pointing to his left hand.

"I lost it while operating a meat slicer," replied Tanaka in a response that was carefully considered and pre-planned.

Spinola stared at the hand silently. He had seen his share of galley accidents. He was also naturally skeptical of anyone who wanted to work in his kitchen, which was essentially his kingdom. And something about Tanaka didn't feel right to him.

"What do you know about culinary work?" Spinola asked. At this point, his attention turned from the severed finger back to the checklist he was completing.

"Oh, a lot," replied Tanaka, trying to appear as enthusiastic as possible. "My father owned a small bar, and my uncle owned a restaurant where I worked as a kid." He didn't bother to add that, in studying chemistry, he learned a lot about mixing ingredients, whether it was something you could create, eat, or detonate.

"Okay," Spinola said, changing the tone of his voice. "You see that there?" he said, pointing to the clock on the wall above the safety bulletins.

"Yeah," Tanaka replied.

"That clock can be your friend or your enemy," Spinola said. "We start here every morning at oh-five-fifteen and start service at oh-seven-thirty. You will work nonstop to get the breakfast service ready for when the line forms out there. THAT is the mission."

"I understand," Tanaka replied.

"If you can't make it in here," Spinola continued, "there's no fucking way you're gonna make it out there," he said, pointing outside and referring to the culinary service provided on Coast Guard FRCs, or Fast Response Cutters.

"Yes, sir," replied Tanaka.

Spinola looked at Tanaka for another moment, then spoke again.

"All right then," he said, turning his body toward the galley and pointing toward the center of the large working area. "Get yourself an apron, put on a hairnet, and go dice those tomatoes over there. Later, we'll have you make some omelets."

Tanaka rose and walked toward the counter with various vegetables staged for the meals to be prepared that day.

As he walked away, Spinola watched him, then turned back to the desk to send an email to the Auxiliary Unit Coordinator.

Lisa, please look into Auxiliarist Jack Tanaka.

His application is in review, but he's already applied to be a CS1.

I think he may have been in a gang.

By the time Spinola's message was flagged for an investigation, it was too late.

***

Richard sat in a conference room chair outside Swanson's office for at least 10 minutes before he showed up. But perception and reality can be quite different, and Richard was about to bail on his boss when Swanson finally walked into the outer office with the Los Angeles District County federal prosecutor, Paula Williams.

"O'Brien," Swanson said in a voice that had an air of superiority in it. "Come on in."

Richard and Williams followed Swanson into his office on the 19th floor of the Federal Building. They took their seats opposite Swanson, who immediately reclined his office chair and placed both hands behind his head.

"So, O'Brien," he started out. "What've you got? Please don't tell me I brought Paula here on a witch hunt."

"Sir, there is something about this case that merits our deeper involvement," Richard said. "Local law enforcement is withdrawing from it and not investigating further."

"Right," Swanson shot back. "Because there was no crime. It was a petty theft exercise that failed."

Swanson enjoyed intimidating his agents and Richard, whose good looks and emerging reputation threatened to eclipse Swanson's domination of the water cooler conversations within the agency.

"Agent O'Brien," interrupted Williams, who could sense the tension in the room, "if no crime has been committed, or even suspected, we need to tread very carefully here. As I'm sure you're aware, the CIA has had surveillance on Sisky for the past 4 years, ever since he left the embassy. We don't want to invite a harassment charge and the resulting media circus that would follow."

Richard expected this to be a tough sell. If he was able to open an FBI investigation but was ultimately wrong about Sisky, it could be a career-limiting move for him. But his instincts about human behavior were well honed, and combined with the observations made by Sgt. Schaeffer and Agent McAuley, he decided to go for it.

"Sir, Sisky is hiding something," Richard said as he shifted his weight in the chair to ensure he was making eye contact as needed with both members of the jury. "And the so-called break-in was a poorly executed skit, a distraction."

"Distraction from what exactly?" said his superior officer, who was now taking his hands from the back of his head and placing them firmly on the desk.

"That part is unclear, but look," Richard replied, "the man has a lifestyle that cannot be explained. The CIA hasn't gone beyond visual surveillance which won't prove a crime if he's been careful. And he may very well have in plain sight a collection of stolen wines in his living room."

Richard realized that his last point was a huge reach, and he regretted blurting it out. He wasn't close to proving the wines were stolen, even though he had the labels photographed and could have easily cross-referenced them to inventories at the French Laundry, Lincoln Fine Wines, or other sites that had reported a recent heist. He was counting on the stolen rare wines to tap into Swanson's sense of adventure. Evidently, it worked, with an assist from the federal prosecutor and an eccentric wine collector in an exclusive enclave of San Diego.

"I saw the labels you photographed in your report," Williams said. "I don't know too much about wine but, you know, we all have friends that do. I know a collector down in La Jolla, an eccentric pathologist that passed the sommelier exam. He tells me these wines wouldn't be found in most collections due to the cost to acquire them."

At this point, nobody spoke, but both Richard and Williams looked at Swanson for his reaction. He looked straight ahead, between the two, his left hand running slowly up and down his right cheek as he thought about the situation. He was somewhat trapped: He loathed giving Richard what he wanted, but he was still on a professional honeymoon in his new role as assistant director in charge, and it wouldn't be a good look in front of Williams if he denied support for ambiguous reasons. But if Richard was wrong, he at least had a scapegoat.

"All right," he said finally, then letting out a sigh. "What exactly are you proposing?"

The FBI has a range of tools to support investigations, and most of them are deployed before the perpetrator even realizes he or she is being targeted. Some of these activities would require a court order, such as wiretaps, subpoenas, and search warrants. But investigating financial records fell in a grey area that was often viewed by the court as below the threshold for them to be involved, accepting instead a formal written request. Richard believed these records could give the FBI enough information to go beyond "reasonable suspicion."

"I'd like to get access to his bank statements for the past three years," Richard said. "That should tell us if he is involved in anything potentially nefarious."

Swanson looked at Williams who nodded just enough to demonstrate her agreement that the ask was reasonable and justified.

"Okay, go for it," Swanson said. "I'll clear the request through legal on this side. Paula, you're good with this?"

"Yes," she replied. "I'd support the move."

All three stood simultaneously.

"Well then," Swanson said, determined to reinforce his seniority, "let's see what this bastard is hiding."

***

Tanaka held the empty crate in his arms and then dropped a large bag at his feet, rolled up the orange door at the Public Storage building at Pico and Crenshaw, and pushed the bag inside with the side of his foot. In the bag was his Coast Guard uniform, cap, and boots. He had just returned from Sector San Diego, the Coast Guard base across from San Diego Airport where he finished up paperwork on his membership, purchased his uniform, and had his picture taken for his Auxiliary ID card. His request for appointment to Sector San Diego ensured he would be close to the international border for any deployments.

Due to the shortage of Culinary Specialists available to staff ships, the base was willing to fast-track the onboarding process for him. The background checks on him revealed nothing of concern. He simply needed to complete the Personal Qualification Standard, or PQS, along with some other online courses including Basic Sanitation, Airborne Pathogens, and Risk Management. In the coming days, he would be meeting with the XPO, the executive petty officer of the USCGC *Arowana*, for an orientation to his duties in anticipation of going underway for a 4-day deployment.

He put the empty crate on his long desk and began to shake a can of spray paint. He placed a stencil template on the crate and proceeded to spray in long, even strokes a diagonal message on the side of the crate. In large green letters, it read "PERISHABLE."

The empty crate would test Tanaka's ability to bring onboard cargo under the presumption it contained vegetables for use in the galley. It could be lettuce, tomatoes, or virtually anything that would typically be taken onboard for use by the cook. If an inspection was required on the docks, Tanaka would simply feign confusion as to why the crate was empty. If he was able to get it onboard without an inspection, he was well on the way to creating an effective distribution system that no longer depended on dive boats that could be intercepted by the Coast Guard or Mexican Navy. And he could retain the money that would otherwise be paid to them.

He removed the crate from the desk and placed it outside the storage unit to dry. Then, he stepped back inside the unit and pulled down the door. Should the test prove successful, he needed to prepare for his next shipment. This time, the customer was the Ministry of State Security, the CIA-equivalent in China.

Tanaka bent down in front of the gray shelving unit. He counted four bottles that would represent $4 million USD to be paid by the Chinese government, and one bottle offered to a private Chinese businessman for

$95,000. The Ministry assured the yakuza that they had an extensive spy network in Cuba and that both tankers and warships made regular stops in Havana Bay, and Tanaka's obligations for delivery would be satisfied once the bottles were collected there.

He returned to his desk, sat down, and leaned over to open the small file cabinet that was underneath. He pulled the manila file folder titled China and laid it on his desk, opening it to reveal the contents. There were several sheets of paper inside, and each sheet followed the same format. To an unobservant person, each document might look like a resume or job application.

Tanaka laid out the first few pages from the folder on the table, each document next to the other. The last page was an order paid for by Dennis Spence. If Richard had been looking over Tanaka's shoulder, he would recall Dennis Spence had committed suicide in Hong Kong several months before, because he was there to witness it.

7

"Well," Swanson started, "that was awkward."

Swanson put the phone down and stared blankly at David Brooks, his second in command.

"Go on," Brooks replied.

"That was Director Pritchard. The department is asking us to assist in investigating how an agent in Havana was unmasked."

"What was our agent doing in Havana?" Brooks asked.

"Not FBI, CIA," Swanson said.

"Wait, what . . . where is the agent now?" Brooks asked.

"He's dead," Swanson replied. "An apparent assassination."

"Oh." Brooks looked down at his lap, recognizing the gravity of the moment. Agents lost in the line of duty, no matter the branch of service in which they served, were a rare occurrence and a grave matter.

Since the CIA's founding in 1947, one or two agents were killed in the line of duty every year, but in recent years the number of agents killed had increased exponentially, with 6 killed in 2017 and 8 more in 2021. While the agency would typically recognize the loss of agents in a ceremony honoring them, the identities of the agents lost more recently had been kept confidential, a testament to the sensitive nature of the work they were doing at the time they were murdered. They served their country in anonymity and would remain so even in death.

"There's not much precedent for this," Swanson added, referring to the prospect of an FBI/CIA collaboration. "But the agency believes the increase in fallen agents is due to a single perpetrator group, or possibly a cartel."

"What I don't get," Brooks said, "is that we lost 24 officers in 2021 from premeditated ambush or other unprovoked action, and we continue to lose officers in the double digits every year, but the Director wants us to focus on the CIA."

Brooks had a point. The Law Enforcement Officers Killed and Assaulted (LEOKA) Report was a closely watched series of metrics that examined every facet of law enforcement officers killed in action, including the specific circumstances, weapons used, and even the range from which a firearm was shot before striking the officer. What the report didn't attempt to track was when the ambush or unprovoked action might qualify as a targeted assassination. And a fallen FBI agent included in those statistics was as important as a fallen CIA agent.

There was another problem with the Director's request. The fraught relationship between the CIA and the FBI was legendary for those in the law enforcement and intelligence community. While the FBI's collection of intelligence was designed to support a prosecution, the CIA's use of intelligence was to inform where to get more intelligence. Hoarding of sensitive information on the FBI side created distrust on the CIA side. But protecting intelligence was often necessary to protect the sources behind it.

Occasionally those walls would come down, but that didn't mean outcomes improved. The CIA was convinced that Russia interfered in the election of Donald Trump in 2016, but the FBI disagreed and didn't investigate until years later when Russia was already sowing doubt among American voters in the 2020 election. And before this, the CIA, FBI, and National Security Agency were all severely criticized in congressional hearings and commissioned reports for the lack of cooperation and information exchange that could have prevented the loss of life on 9/11. Historians argued that J. Edgar Hoover intentionally set up a competitive environment between the agencies to bring out the best in each.

"If the CIA is asking for FBI assistance, it might indicate that they recognize the potential for a mole in the agency," said Brooks, a conclusion already reached by Swanson.

"I just worry about us getting sucked into the next big news story on CNN," Swanson replied. "Anyway, it looks like the large branches are being pulled into the investigation: New York, Miami, DC, and LA."

"What do you want us to do?" Brooks asked.

"Pull together a team here for a briefing at 1400 hours tomorrow," Swanson said. "I'm expecting the case files in the morning, and I'll press them to send me details on any persons of interest. And see what you can find out about Gregory Zukov in the meantime."

"Sir?"

"He's the CIA asset that was murdered in Havana."

***

He understood the assignment. There was nothing unusual about it.

It would come as no surprise that the fraternity of competent and successful assassins was, in contemporary times, very small. A few of the better ones were on the permanent payroll of certain governments. But Steven Daniels was not one of the better ones. He was still climbing the learning curve as new business rolled in from the dark web and from his clandestine contact within the CIA.

Daniels was a former Navy SEAL on the operation that killed Osama bin Laden in May 2011, along with Robert O'Neill, Mark Owen, and three others on what was known as SEAL Team 6. They followed up that victory in 2019 with a botched attempt to plant listening devices in North Korea, barely making it out alive and creating a story the administration tried desperately to keep secret from Congress and the general public. Those two operations marked the beginning of the end for Daniels' career in the Navy.

The Navy SEALs receive their orders from the Special Activities Group of the CIA, a tactical paramilitary agency that takes action when diplomacy and visible military commitments are impractical, and deniability is potentially important. Their Latin motto, *Tertia Optio*, or third option, could as easily be "final option."

After the successful mission that eliminated bin Laden, debate continued for some time about which Navy SEAL deserved credit for actually killing him. In follow-up interviews, O'Neill claimed he fired the fatal shot while expressing frustration that he lived "paycheck to paycheck" on his salary of $2,500 every two weeks. Meanwhile, Owen was roundly criticized for appearing on *60 Minutes* to promote his version of the story.

The truth about who really pulled the trigger to kill bin Laden was never made clear. But one thing was clear: Daniels carried with him the sum of all resentment from Owen, O'Neill, and others in the military who felt unappreciated and marginalized. On top of the grievances levied by his peers, Daniels was intensely introverted and socially awkward, perfectly competent to take orders, but not comfortable to express his opinion.

Because of this, Daniels was satisfied to remain in the background during his time in the service. But in doing so, he kindled jealousy that he wasn't able to attract the military recognition or later media attention of his peers. After an honorable discharge, he found himself not only without the meager financial support of being in the Navy; he was without friends or family to carry on. Daniels suffered many months of depression seeking a path for his future.

He eventually turned to freelance work in the security industry, providing security to dignitaries and diplomats, before learning about the existence of the dark web. There he found a near-perfect marketplace for his skills: forcibly repossessing goods or collateral from people who failed to repay "hard money lending," spying on behalf of suspicious husbands, wives, and romantic partners, and, ultimately, contract kills. The contract killing paid better than any other service he could provide, and while he had multiple kills as a Navy SEAL, he had far less experience as a mercenary.

At 195 pounds and six feet five inches with a shaved head, Daniels was an imposing presence. He was only twenty-eight years old and as fit as an Olympian. His tattooed bicep muscles pushed through virtually any clothing. He was trained in jujitsu as a child and became an expert marksman in the Navy. If ever there was a killing machine, Daniels met the specs.

He decided early on that his "red line" would be the assassination of an American, and he made this clear to those seeking to retain his services. In spite of his ambiguous moral compass, he didn't want to threaten the viability of his relationship with the CIA and any business it might offer him.

But as luck would have it, most of the contract killing gigs offered were focused on American and British covert agents, and so when he got an offer to kill British agent Geoffrey Moore, he capitulated and accepted the assignment; he needed the money.

He found Moore at the Metropolis Bar, just down the block from the Secret Intelligence Services building in the Vauxhall section of London. The SIS building served as the official headquarters of MI6, Britain's counterpart to the CIA. Moore was not particularly difficult to find if not on an assignment. Daniels simply asked for him at the self-proclaimed "spy hangout," the Morpeth Arms Public House on Millbank, directly opposite the SIS building. Daniels thought such a blatant inquiry about Moore was safe as he definitely did not see him anywhere in the bar. Endlessly deciding between "safe" and "unsafe" was the curse of anyone in Daniels's profession.

Between 2023 and 2025, Moore nurtured a source in the Iranian Revolutionary Guard, Colonel Amir Farhadi. Farhadi knew the specific coordinates of the underground Fordow Uranium Enrichment Plant. With the promise of sanctuary, protection, and potential citizenship for himself and his family, the young officer produced a dossier of valuable intelligence that guided

U.S. efforts to bomb Fordow and two additional sites in June 2025. After the attack, the Iranians discovered the leak and summarily executed Farhadi after forcing him to reveal Moore's identity. The rest of Farhadi's family went into hiding.

Moore was next on the list. While most contract kills required the assassin to make a body disappear, the Iranians made no such demand of Moore's killer. They preferred to put their work out for display as a warning to Western powers not to meddle in their affairs.

That particular night was cool and crisp following a light rain shower earlier in the day. The sound of police sirens pierced the tranquility of the Thames nearby. Around the bar, fallen leaves mixed with small puddles, making pedestrian navigation a challenge. On spotting Moore at the bar, Daniels lit a cigarette and leaned against a light post. He was in position.

In anticipation of fulfilling the demands of his contract, Daniels had followed Moore at a safe distance for several days to establish his patterns of movement and decide when he would be most vulnerable. Moore made himself slightly more unpredictable by going home after work either by bike or boat. The Uber boat was a good option, but Moore usually preferred the far more economical and healthier alternative of riding his e-bike from the SIS building to his flat on Ferry Street, located on the other side of the Greenwich Foot Tunnel.

Daniels watched Moore stumble out of the bar and step squarely on a puddle that anyone else was likely to spot. He pulled his bike from the rack and started cycling down the Albert Embankment. Daniels understood that Moore's flat was a thirty-minute ride from Vauxhall. He grabbed a rentable cycle outside the bar and started his pursuit. Daniels would catch up to Moore in time, and there were enough other riders in the cycle lane that he would not attract any unwanted attention.

In all of New York, there are an estimated forty thousand security cameras, which would sound like a lot. But in London, there are close to *one million* CCTV cameras, taking surveillance to a whole new level. Daniels understood this and, while not overly concerned about being recorded by a camera, he would certainly do what he could to avoid it. The best way to avoid being recorded in the course of committing murder in Greenwich was in the tunnel.

The Greenwich Foot Tunnel opened in 1902 and is crossed by four thousand pedestrians daily. There is nothing remarkable about it; it is simply a cast iron tube lined with white glazed tiles running 1,215 feet under the River Thames. The day before, Daniels counted twenty-two cameras across the entirety of it, including six devices at each end where a spiral staircase created space the cameras could not reach. If Moore were to leave the tunnel, he was too close to his flat and with too many cameras for Daniels to act. So, it would have to be done in the tunnel or in the staircase.

Moore guided his bike down the spiral staircase because the lift was predictably out of order. Once he was in the actual tunnel, he followed the safety ordinance requiring that cyclists push their bikes the length of the tunnel. He was only slightly inebriated, enough to feel satisfied as he pushed the bike forward a couple of hundred meters from his home.

When he reached the midpoint of the tunnel, he heard two bicycles approaching rapidly behind him and turned around to see two young men riding side by side in the tunnel. This rankled him.

"Get off the fucking bikes," he yelled as the young men passed him.

"Piss off," one of them replied.

Moore's training as an agent required him to maintain a high degree of self-awareness, and despite his condition, his powers of observation were barely blunted. When he turned to see the two cyclists, he also saw Daniels about ten meters behind him.

Moore had too much pride to consider asking for help, and the tunnel at 9:50 PM was essentially deserted. But he was alarmed by Daniels's intimidating presence and realized he might be in trouble. He reminded himself that once he exited the tunnel, he was only five minutes from his front door.

Moore reached the end of the tunnel and the beginning of the stairs. Had he not been determined to protect his bike and bring it home, he might be alive today.

"Let me help you with that, mate," said the voice behind him.

"I can manage," he replied, continuing to look at his feet to avoid tripping.

But it was too late. As soon as Moore reached the dark spot that cameras couldn't reach in the spiral staircase, Daniels came upon him and shoved a knife into the side of his neck, pulling it back quickly to sever the carotid artery and jugular vein. Blood that jettisoned from Moore's neck hit the wall of the staircase. The attack would become one of his signature moves as a professional contract killer.

Moore dropped the bike, but remarkably, Daniels was able to throw Moore's left arm around his shoulder while Moore's legs continued their march slowly up the stairs. Any camera that would pick up this movement could presume Daniels was helping a drunken buddy to get home in one piece.

Once outside, Daniels continued to guide Moore to the embankment overlooking the River Thames. He rolled Moore's body over the railing, where it fell about twenty feet onto the muddy embankment below. His body was found next to the water the following morning.

The ensuing investigation would connect the dots to confirm the murder was that of a professional assassin. And that is why it was immediately reported to the head of MI6, Audrey Delaroche.

8

Richard and Jeff McAuley sat on opposite sides of the table in the FBI conference room on the 17th floor of the Federal Building. Each had a laptop open and a cup of coffee to their right. Richard was staring at a spreadsheet with hundreds of lines of data. McAuley's screen showed "Surfline," the popular website providing real-time updates on tides, swell, and other conditions that would determine the best places to engage in the sport.

The spreadsheet contained the wines stolen from the last three major wine heists in Los Angeles County over the past ten years. Looking at the screen made his eyes hurt, but he fortunately remembered enough about how to use Excel to make the job minimally efficient and had persuaded McAuley to assist him with cross-referencing the wines to those photographed in Sisky's wine rack.

Richard highlighted the spreadsheet's contents and sorted the wines by "Product," which collapsed all the same wines into the same portion of the spreadsheet. This way, all the "Domaine de la Romanée-Conti" wines would appear in the same section of the sheet, and all the other bottles were now organized in alphabetical order. Meanwhile, McAuley had separate photos of the wines that Richard photographed while in Sisky's residence. On each photo was the essential data to identify the vintage of the wine and the year the grapes were harvested.

"Okay," Richard said, his eyes still glued to the screen. "I'm ready. Give me the first one."

McAuley pushed his face closer to his laptop in order to read the label.

"Shat, O, Margoks," he replied.

"Château Margaux," Richard said, offering up the proper pronunciation. McAuley would never have expected to get it right anyway. "Okay," Richard added, "I got a hit."

"Three bottles were stolen from The French Laundry wine heist," he continued. "What is the vintage of Sisky's wine? Look for a year."

McAuley squinted again at the photo. "2015," he said.

Now Richard was leaning into the laptop. "Nope," he said. "The bottles stolen were from 1982."

"What's next?" Richard asked.

"D-R-C La Totch," McAuley offered. "2014."

"Hmmm, La Tache," Richard replied, scanning the sheet. "Got it."

Two bottles of DRC La Tache were stolen from Lincoln Fine Wines and three from The French Laundry; however, none of these wines were the same vintage as what Sisky owned.

On a whim, Richard googled the price of the stolen La Tache and found that their values were multiples higher than Sisky's. He began to wonder if Sisky's collection was all that special.

Richard and McAuley repeated the process for all the wines he photographed until he got to the bottom of his alphabetical listing.

"Here's the last one: VDM," McAuley said. "Oh wait, it says Vino del Mar below that."

Richard scrolled to the bottom of the sheet. There was no VDM wine listed as stolen. Richard recalled that Asha had never heard of the wine either.

"Let me see that photo," Richard said. McAuley spun his laptop around. Richard took a closer look at the photo.

The bottle had an elegant label, with lots of words in Italian on the front label that he didn't understand. It appeared to be imported from Malta, one of the smallest wine-producing countries in the world. Richard googled "VDM wines."

The website that popped up showed a video clip of a scuba diver pulling a bottle of wine from a metal crate resting on a coral reef in the ocean. According to the website, "Vino Del Mar," or "Wines of the Sea," was one of many companies capitalizing on the growing movement to ferment wines in the ocean. Underneath the video explaining the novel winemaking process was the phrase "The wines and this website are under construction."

"Well, that's pretty cool," Richard said, watching the diver. "They are fermenting wines in the ocean now."

"Why are they doing that?" McAuley said, unimpressed.

"Hell if I know," Richard replied, "because there's a fool born every minute, I guess."

***

It was a warm and pleasant Saturday morning when Richard and Asha arrived at the wine fair in Temecula, about an hour's drive south from Los Angeles, and home to about 50 wineries. Spending Saturday at an outdoor event was totally contradictory to Richard's fall routine, when the anticipation of a Michigan football game would typically hijack his thoughts. Ever since his alma mater won the National Championship in 2023, Richard would go out of his way to catch all games that were televised, often meeting friends at a local sports bar to scream at the suspended TV screens whenever appropriate, which was most every play.

One of the first things Richard noticed was how quiet it was all around him, in spite of the fact that people were wandering around. While the event was surrounded by nature, it felt surreal to him.

"What do you think?" Asha said as the two walked slowly toward a tree-lined street lined with booths. As they walked, fallen leaves slid under their shoes. Richard was looking down at his phone, checking on the game. There was no score yet in the first quarter. Michigan was playing a non-conference opponent and expected to dispense with them early. Richard just needed to confirm it.

"It's pretty here," he replied, pushing the cell phone back into the front pocket of his jeans. "Are you involved with any of these wineries?"

"Not the ones exhibiting today," she replied, "but I do buy from some of the others, you know, for the restaurant."

As the two continued down the lane where an additional ten booths lay waiting, a series of other people approached them from the opposite direction, stopping at booths on the other side of the small road, which was closed off to traffic. Richard didn't feel comfortable holding her hand, but the two walked side by side along the right side, below the protection of the shade trees.

They stopped at a booth, and Asha took a small paper cup, the kind often seen at grocery stores offering samples, and sipped the contents. If she found a variety that she liked and that was unrepresented in her cellar at Café Sevilla, she might take a card from the vendor. Richard elected not to indulge. He was more of a beer drinker anyway and decided it best to play the role of designated driver.

"How is it going with the stolen wine investigation you're doing?" Asha asked as the two moved on to another booth.

Richard knew better than to reveal too much about an active investigation, even to a trusted love interest, but he also knew a few nuggets would be harmless and that Asha's feedback could be useful.

"I'm just at the beginning of this one," Richard replied, thinking carefully about what he could put out there that might return a valuable response.

"Hey, remember that wine, VDM?" he added, looking at Asha as they walked. "Did you know they ferment that stuff underwater?"

Asha continued casually to take a sip from another booth, choosing not to respond immediately. She gently moved the wine around in the front of her mouth before swallowing.

"No, I told you I don't know that company," she said. Then after a short pause added, "But I've heard about underwater fermentation. It's a niche market, really.

Serious wine enthusiasts haven't embraced it. They wouldn't be worth stealing."

As the two continued to the next booth, Asha made eye contact with somebody. He was walking in the opposite direction while carrying a case of wine without labels. It was Jack Tanaka.

***

Richard had told Asha that the life of an FBI agent was boring ninety-five percent of the time. He longed to experience the remaining five percent, but that wouldn't be happening on that particular day. As he sat at his desk filling out an expense report, a clerk came in and dropped a large, heavy envelope on his desk. It was from HSBC Bank, and it contained the information they supplied on the accounts of Alexander Sisky.

Richard decided he couldn't wait. He set aside the expense report form and pulled the envelope by one corner toward him. He flipped it to the other side and used a letter opener to cleanly open it, dropping the contents on his desk. There were multiple statements included, plus three individual alerts that the bank had issued in compliance with the Bank Secrecy Act.

The Bank Secrecy Act requires financial institutions to assist government agencies in detecting and preventing money laundering. They are required to keep records of cash purchases or negotiable instruments, file reports of cash transactions exceeding $10,000 to the IRS, and report "suspicious activity" that might assist in a criminal investigation. Banks would do the minimum to comply while protecting the identity and activities of their customers. It was not in the bank's interest to attract any attention to themselves.

Richard had seen the standard Form 8300 used by banks to record large cash transactions, but he had never seen so many in one place and wondered how this activity went unnoticed. However, the "don't ask, don't tell" attitude of the banks, combined with lax enforcement, would explain how Sisky flew under the radar all this time. The forms did not conclusively prove Sisky had done anything wrong, and Richard understood that it was common for Russians to prefer dealing in cash.

Richard set the reports aside. The next series of documents represented old bank statements. The statements showed a fairly consistent balance of about $85,000 from month to month. Richard scanned each document, looking for large transactions. Then, in November of the prior year, he saw wired funds of exactly $2 million in that month and a check written for $1.8 million in December. Richard's heart began to race. How could Sisky be so careless as to write a check?

"Please, please, please…" Richard said aloud as he thumbed quickly through the multiple pages of activity for December. There, at the end of the month's reconciliation of activity, were copies of the checks that Sisky had written. And among them was a check for $1.8 million written to "VDM Enterprises," based in Malta.

Got you! Richard said to himself. He picked up the phone to call McAuley.

"This would either buy a shit-ton of wine," Richard said to McAuley, "or what we have here is a case of money laundering."

"Or," McAuley replied, "maybe those stolen wines from the French Laundry heist are being relabeled and introduced to the black market under a new label to avoid detection." McAuley was always one to see an angle that was oblivious to everyone else.

But then Richard, fully embracing the spitballing exercise, said something that would put the investigation on a new trajectory.

"Or maybe," he said, "whatever is in those bottles is not real wine."

9

Fireworks illuminated the horizon of northwest Palermo, with enormous starbursts of red, green, and white exploding from a single dot in the sky before slowly disintegrating. Residents of the Sicilian capital had become used to these displays, in this case a celebration that a scamming operation scored a big payday from an ignorant American retiree. The poor soul was conned into handing over a significant sum of his life savings to an AI-generated bot posing as a lonely and sexually deprived woman in her mid-50s.

The audacity with which the scammers glorified their illegal accomplishments no longer surprised anyone in this gritty underbelly of the city, where a vacant lot on Via Castello provided the perfect base from which to operate with impunity. After all, Sicily had evolved from a haven for organized crime to a cottage industry for cybercrime, thanks to a combination of lax regulations and an economy that rewarded little else. Tens of billions of dollars flowed through various banking systems as money was scrubbed of its origins or taken directly from naïve and vulnerable people.

Giuseppe Rizzo did his best to concentrate on the digital display in front of him as chrysanthemum fireworks exploded overhead, and M-80s caused the building to shake. Windows had long since been shattered or removed in the vacated building where he sat at a desk facing the festivities outside. After several months in its current state, it was uncertain if the building would ever be remodeled.

Wiring fell gracefully from above through exposed steel girders from what used to be a ceiling and might someday be connected to modern lighting and electrical outlets. Without air conditioning, the most Giuseppe could hope for was a cool breeze to combat the ubiquitous heat and humidity of a Sicilian summer. Instead, he smelled smoke floating in from the pyrotechnic display outside the window that was not there, adding heat where it was not needed.

Giuseppe was ironically grateful for his circumstances. His job as a scammer paid relatively well by Sicilian standards. He arrived in Palermo at the age of fifteen from a mountain village in the center of the island. His parents gave him his first computer at the age of nine, and having no interest in football, he spent hours on the internet every day, learning how to hack into websites. As a result, he was able to reduce his parents' bill for utilities, redirect purchases made by others, and stream movies for free.

Recruited by a mafia crime family and placed in a shell company called "Calabria Venture Capital," or CVC, Giuseppe earned enough to send money home from time to time. This was because he paid no rent; in exchange for living under the protection of the mafia, he became an indentured servant, forced to move from time to time to evade authorities. Presently, he was squatting inside the abandoned apartment building, sleeping in the darkest corner he could find on the seventh floor.

While Cosa Nostra ruled much of Sicily for nearly two centuries, they had more recently been weakened by the combined efforts of law enforcement and NGOs determined to destroy them. In 2023, the legendary godfather of the organization, Matteo Messina Denaro, was arrested after 30 years on the run, and the organization proceeded to reinvent itself, often cooperating with a previous rival on the Italian mainland known as 'Ndrangheta. Today, most members of 'Ndrangheta are between 20 and 30 years old, and many have learned to bend the internet to their advantage, running a variety of schemes designed to separate unsuspecting individuals from their hard-earned money.

As Italian authorities and international law enforcement encroached on their illicit activities, they would change their name, nexus of operations, and the hundreds of bank accounts they owned to support their brisk business. Law enforcement agencies were forced to engage in a form of whack-a-mole with the many corporations engaged in money laundering, identity theft, and other forms of cybercrime. Every time they were successful in shutting down one operation, several others would pop up.

A money laundering operation might conceal revenues from illegal gambling or drug trades, inflate construction invoices to pay for protection, or create fake balance sheet entries for the purposes of tax evasion. For stolen property, they would sell the goods privately in order to "launder" the cash before spending it.

While this was the bread and butter of the mafia's business for most of their existence, young recruits pivoted the organization's activities toward cybercrime, which was regarded as much safer. There was the expectation this group might eventually break from 'Ndrangheta and create their own *cupola*. Giuseppe certainly hoped so, as it would represent an opportunity for him to become initiated as a member. Until that day, the young men would be referred to as "Giovani Soldi," or "Young Bucks."

Giuseppe's main job included the production of fake profiles. Using ChatGPT or similar AI apps, he would launch profiles on a variety of social media platforms, but mostly LinkedIn, TikTok, and Facebook. On TikTok and Facebook, he would combine photos of attractive young women with obscure philosophical musings of a person that didn't exist. It wasn't his concern when lonely men in developed countries would pursue these ghosts; that was the responsibility of another team. His quota was to maintain 100 fake identities and to keep them current with a series of non-sequiturs that would improve the likelihood of engagement with an unsuspecting victim.

On LinkedIn, Giuseppe would launch fake profiles of professionals in the IT industry. Giuseppe enjoyed this work more than the creation of profiles to ensnare lonely men because it allowed him to imagine himself as one of these accomplished professionals, and he learned a lot of IT terminology in the process of creating them.

The IT profiles were essential to the organization's newest venture: placing IT helpdesk professionals in roles that provided access to sensitive information that could be sold. This was a greenfield opportunity with many new players across Sicily and parts of Eastern Europe, racing to exploit the opportunities.

The scam went like this: A person with IT experience on LinkedIn that was clearly unemployed, and preferably desperate, would be offered an opportunity to interview for a position on an IT helpdesk by one of Giuseppe's supervisors, posing as a recruiter and speaking perfect English. Giuseppe would then create a more impressive version of the candidate's online profile, something they called a "boosted profile," which might include certifications and experience the candidate did not possess. Others on the team would next assist with scheduling an actual interview with a potential employer.

Because these were remote jobs, interviews were also remote, and the supervisor would guide the candidate in real time (by listening in) to ace the interview. Once the candidate was hired, Giuseppe's team would install software on their employer's laptop computer to control it. A somewhat intimidating nondisclosure agreement would keep the candidate sufficiently in the dark and compliant until it was too late for them to back out. They were already in too deep.

As Giuseppe was posting a nonsensical poem to a fake profile on Facebook, he got a ping from his supervisor, requesting a boosted profile. The candidate's name was Katrina Evtushenko. Katrina would ultimately assist the FBI to make all the dots connectable.

***

Richard rolled out of Asha's bed early. Her back was turned to him as he quickly pulled on the pants draped over the chair nearby. He had enough time to swing by his place and change before the morning briefing in the Federal Building.

As he left the apartment, he was conflicted about the situation with Asha. She was smart and attractive, but she was not an inspiring partner sexually, rarely initiated anything, and didn't come close to satisfying his fantasies about what a new partner could bring to his bed. And he couldn't even get her in his bed! She always insisted on him staying at her place.

Richard had a habit of obsessing over women, and Asha gave him much to obsess about. The night before, they had just finished a very quick and perfunctory sex session in the missionary position, where Asha barely moved and did not climax. Richard tried to lighten the conversation by suggesting it was a great coincidence to meet Asha due to her knowledge of the wine trade. She replied dryly,

100

"There is no such thing as a coincidence." This comment made his head spin.

However, there was a lot to like about the relationship. He was always very attracted to exotic-looking women, and now that he was in LA, it seemed they were everywhere. But most LA women seemed determined to remain in their own subculture of city life. Asha, on the other hand, was quite interested in the work Richard was doing and asked about the Sisky investigation every time they got together.

All these thoughts about Asha occupied Richard as he proceeded on autopilot to drive home, change into fresh clothes, and head to the Federal Building. Once there, he persuaded himself to set his feelings about Asha aside, at least until lunch.

***

"Okay, people, listen up," Swanson barked as the agents were still settling into their chairs in the 17th-floor conference room. Swanson walked past them to the front of the room as he spoke.

"We've been contacted by the Justice Department to assist in an investigation surrounding the death of a CIA agent, an apparent assassination," he said. "We will be coordinating with some other agencies and branch offices on this, and this will be a priority of this office until we understand what is going on, and preferably, have the perpetrator in custody."

The phrase "other agencies" signaled a case destined to be complicated. It was well known that federal agencies often failed to cooperate productively. There was rarely a case where the whole was greater than the sum of its parts.

Swanson allowed only a few seconds for the announcement to sink in before continuing.

"I want a team of agents back here at 1300 hours for a meeting to organize ourselves on this operation. So, if you aren't currently working on securing an indictment for cases assigned to you, I'll see you here later today."

"Sir, what are the rules of engagement on this? I mean, what if we don't get, you know, CIA cooperation?" The question came from Special Agent Tara Johnson, a veteran agent who had experienced her share of frustration in advancing cases where inter-agency coordination was necessary. Swanson was sympathetic.

"We'll burn that bridge when we come to it, Johnson," Swanson replied. "In the meantime, move with purpose. We won't be the branch accused of dropping the ball and fucking this up. Let's show them what we are capable of."

Special Agent Johnson appeared satisfied with Swanson's direction.

"Moving on, then," Swanson said, "does anyone have anything else?"

Richard raised his hand.

"O'Brien?"

"Sir, I'd like to give an update on the Sisky investigation we initiated a week ago."

"Proceed." Swanson realized if Richard hadn't done his homework, at least one of the agents would call him on it. Richard stood in front of his seat and organized his notes for easy reference. He was well aware of the pressure he had put himself under as he had the least amount of experience of any agent in the room.

"So as many of you know, we joined the LAPD in investigating a break-in at the residence of a former Russian diplomat," he said, moving his eyes across the room to ensure the other agents were tracking.

"We suspect the break-in was staged and are considering a variety of theories. Since then, we've obtained bank statements on Sisky and found some huge transactions, including a deposit for 2 million and a payment for wine that would appear well in excess of its value."

The agents stared at Richard and appeared unimpressed. But Richard was ready with a narrative to get them engaged.

"So wine is not something that we've found as the basis of a money laundering scheme – yet – but we know that the mafia, Mexican cartels, and private investors have all used art to launder dirty money. And the value of stolen wines that could be resold at multiples of their legitimate value, in LA County alone, is in the hundreds of millions."

There was a brief silence, then an agent spoke from the back of the room. It was Special Agent Miguel Morales, a veteran originally from the San Antonio branch.

"Yeah, in 2012, our office in Laredo busted a crime ring involving the Las Zetas Mexican cartel," he said. "They were buying and selling racehorses in the United States and inflating the value of transactions to launder drug money. At one point, they owned over 300 racehorses in the U.S."

The story of how the Las Zetas cartel established a money laundering operation in the U.S. became a huge story and eventually the subject of multiple documentaries, but most agents in the room were not even in high school at the time. At the height of their operation, the cartel owned a farm in Oklahoma for quarter horses and maintained hundreds more across the Southwest. According to the IRS, they shielded over $4.2 million in drug profits through the buying and selling of racehorses.

To conceal their identities, the cartel threatened successful businessmen and demanded they act on behalf of the cartel. In some cases, they would beat them up or kidnap members of their families. To avoid further harm, these men would travel to the U.S. to write the checks and purchase the horses; in many cases, they were required to actually use their own money. Should they refuse to cooperate, Las Zetas would put them in a petrol barrel, douse them with gasoline, and burn them alive.

Morales then said the important part out loud for anyone not following.

"So art, horses, wine, it doesn't really matter. So long as the true value of the product is ambiguous, it can support the laundering of ill-gotten gains."

Richard was close to consuming all of the three minutes he was allowed at the briefing when another hand was raised. At this point, he wasn't sure what he was hoping for from the opportunity he was given to speak. Then, he got his answer.

"Are you aware of the wine confiscated by the Coast Guard up in Alaska?" said Agent Johnson. "It's sitting in a warehouse in Anchorage. Might be worth looking into. I heard it includes a dozen bottles. Something called VDN, VDM, or something like that."

***

"Hear me out," Richard said to Asha as he shoved the tuna poke and rice in his mouth.

The two were having lunch near the Federal Building, a rare treat for Richard to see her in the middle of the day. He persuaded her to meet him because he was so excited to talk about his latest discovery in the Sisky investigation. The two sat at a picnic table with the poke bowls they purchased from a nearby food truck.

"So, I don't know," he continued, "I am not sure this is a money laundering case. I mean, it might be, but I can't help but think those bottles might contain something other than wine."

Asha was not speaking, just listening. And she made minimal eye contact with Richard, focused instead on the poke bowl in front of her. Richard was sharing more than he probably should with Asha, but inasmuch as she was always asking about the investigation, he felt she might offer him some added perspective on the case.

"What's happening with the wine in Alaska?" she finally asked.

"We've requested the Coast Guard to send it here. I am going to have it examined in the laboratory to see what's inside."

"What makes you think it's not wine?" she asked.

"Well, it could be," he replied, "but look, this VDM company, they make ocean-aged wine. This is a new thing. The average bottle costs no more than a few hundred dollars." Richard paused to take another scoop of poke, chewed, and swallowed, then continued.

"There is no way Sisky bought nearly two million dollars of wine worth two to three hundred dollars per bottle. It doesn't make any sense. He'd have crates of it stacked to the ceiling. The CIA would have noticed. He'd have been tagged for an investigation into money laundering a year ago."

"What else could be in the bottles?"

"Dunno," Richard said, swallowing again. "The most logical candidate is drugs: fentaryl, meth, coke," he said. "The cartels are very creative these days what with unmanned narco subs and all."

Asha didn't respond; she just looked down and poked around at her poke.

"Hey, know what's the most expensive liquid in the world?" Richard interjected, hoping to get Asha's attention. "Scorpion venom! Especially the Palestine yellow scorpion. For real, I looked it up! But I don't think they can fill many bottles with that."

The comment fell flat. "So, what are you going to do now?" Asha replied.

"Well, the money laundering angle is the one I can sell to the prosecutor and to a grand jury," he said. "It's the easiest narrative to explain and understand."

"And what happens after that?"

"Well, among other things," Richard said, "a search warrant. And the records we could collect from a raid on his home will allow us to identify all his business associates."

What Richard failed to realize was that Asha was already a few steps ahead of him.

10

Richard sat at the back of the conference room with his attention half-focused on the presentation that Assistant Director Swanson was making. The other half of his brain was still trying to comprehend why Asha appeared so distracted during lunch. He now regretted not asking her about it directly.

"We have a good understanding of how we've lost agents going back to 2015," Swanson said, standing at the front of the room. "At that time, we discovered a data breach that revealed a trove of sensitive documents, including the identities of government contractors and agents. We lost four agents in the three years following that breach." A PowerPoint slide on the screen summarized his comments while showing a map of the last known locations of each agent.

Many agents in the conference room were taking notes. Richard was not.

Swanson continued. "Then, in 2021, Wikileaks dropped a file of agents operating in China. Three agents were quickly imprisoned and four others went missing," he said, pausing to allow the agents to keep up. "But since that time, we've lost eight more agents without understanding how they were unmasked."

Swanson next projected a map on the screen showing the last known location of these agents. Three dots were in China, two in Russia, one in Iran, and one in Cuba.

"Last month, Gregory Zukov, a CIA operative in Havana, was found in his hotel room. He died from massive coronary arrest, triggered by Novichok poisoning."

Novichok is a lethal nerve agent developed by the Soviet Union in 1971 and a common substance used by the Russian government to eliminate dissidents, investigative journalists, the leaders of opposing political parties, and, when practical, foreign agents.

"It's been suspected that Novichok could be used by other adversaries, so the presence of it in Zukov's blood isn't necessarily a smoking gun implicating the Russians," Swanson added.

All CIA and FBI agents were familiar with the risks of Novichok poisoning. In his training, Richard learned how to disinfect his body if he felt he was exposed to it.

"There is one common theme to all these presumed murders," Swanson said. "Most of the agents involved were working as 'knocks'—nonofficial cover—and assigned to gather intelligence on countries hostile to the United States."

"But isn't that pretty much all they do, all the time, anyway?" said McAuley, who, along with Richard, had no indictments pending.

"That's a good question," Swanson replied. "And an opportunity to clear up some possible confusion with regard to our sister agency."

It was a fair statement to say many in the FBI were clueless about how the CIA operated.

"About one-third of the CIA's twenty thousand employees are working under some form of cover. Without getting too technical, know that most of the agents working undercover are in an embassy somewhere in a diplomatic capacity while serving as a resource to U.S. intelligence agencies," he said.

"But some agents are working in multinational corporations overseas, with identities carefully crafted to protect their identities—all the way down to fake passports, falsified tax returns, and even fake payroll checks. This is a much smaller number of agents. These are the agents that are at greatest risk because they don't have diplomatic immunity. And these are the ones getting assassinated."

"How are they being identified?" came a question from the audience.

"We don't know," Swanson replied. "Cover is like a puzzle; every piece must be protected because you don't know what piece the perpetrators are missing. Somehow, it seems that lately they have been finding all the pieces."

As Swanson continued to field questions from his team, Richard's phone lit up in front of him. It was a text message from Asha. It would have been against every known protocol in the FBI to use your phone for non-agency business during a meeting, other than to say, "Honey, I'll be late," but Richard couldn't resist. While feigning attention to Swanson's presentation, he slid up the screen on his iPhone to reveal the message.

Richard,
I don't think we should see each other anymore.
I'm not ready for a relationship.
Please don't reach back.
Take care, Asha.

Richard's heart sank, then it began to flutter rapidly, and he couldn't stop it. He could tell something was bothering her but had written it off as Asha's melancholy outlook when the two were alone together. He had presumed until now that her gregarious nature in front of large crowds was a projection, something she mustered from within in order to succeed as a respected sommelier. Now, he wasn't sure of anything, other than he had just been dumped. Did he do something wrong? Was he tone-deaf around something specific?

"Okay, people," Swanson said, grabbing Richard's attention. "That will be all. Sandra will get on your calendars to schedule our next briefing; I am obtaining a file on current persons of interest. In the meantime, consider all inter-agency boundaries will cease to exist."

The screeching sound of chairs backing up from the conference room tables filled the room. Richard sat there, still processing. Then, he felt a gentle hand land on his shoulder.

"Dude," McAuley said, "what's up?" Richard didn't bother to look up.

"I think I've just been dumped."

***

McAuley snacked on tortilla chips with salsa, barely managing to get them in his mouth without leaving a bit of salsa on his chin. He and Richard were on the patio of a Mexican restaurant not far from the Federal Building. Richard had managed to get through the rest of the afternoon by finally completing his expense reports. He cradled a tequila with two hands as McAuley washed down the tortillas with a pint of Lazy IPA.

"Dude," McAuley said, "I didn't know you liked tequila!"

"I don't like tequila," Richard replied. "I need it."

McAuley looked pensive for a moment. He saw the look of disillusionment on Richard's face.

"So, have you ever been dumped by a girl before?"

Richard had to think about that one. There were a lot of relationships and boxes he had to check mentally. He looked up at the sky for answers.

"No," he replied finally, "no, I haven't. I've never been dumped by a woman, ever."

McAuley continued to speak, but Richard was busy litigating every encounter with Asha from the time they first met. Her suggestive look in his direction at the wine tasting intentionally drew him in. She later invited him into her apartment, and they made love together several times in one weekend. She invited him to a wine festival. All of these signs pointed to a level of interest in an intimate relationship.

But then there were the red flags, signs he ignored. She didn't seem attracted to him sexually. She went through the motions in bed but never went down on him. She seemed distant at times. And then there was the comment "there is no such thing as a coincidence," which at the time he presumed was an outlook informed by her religious upbringing. Did she mean something else?

"I'm swimming against the current here, man...." Richard said, borrowing a line he learned from McAuley, one of his favorite nautical metaphors.

"Well, whatever you do," McAuley said, leaning closer to the tortilla chips, "don't show up at her apartment unannounced."

That idea wasn't on Richard's mind until he heard it.

***

Richard pulled up to Asha's apartment and threw the car in park while it was still crawling, causing him to lunge forward. It was around 6:45 p.m., and the street was dark due to overgrown maple trees, but her building was well lit, and he had a clear view of it. He sank back into his seat to consider his options.

Her unit looked out on the other side, so Richard couldn't look into her windows for any clues of what might be inside. Since the text he received from her, he spun up a half dozen theories of what might have happened. Perhaps he offended her with some sarcastic comment. Maybe she or her family was involved in something illegal, and she got spooked because he worked in law enforcement. But most likely, he concluded, she ended a relationship just before they met, and her boyfriend persuaded her to return.

Richard conceded to himself that the relationship was probably over. But he didn't want it to end on the basis of a text message. He deserved an explanation, and he was going to get it. Then, he told himself, he would walk away with his head held high. He was never without a love interest for very long, and as McAuley said that afternoon, "you'll have another girl by Monday."

He started brainstorming possible opening lines when he saw her walk out the double doors of her property. She was dressed for the evening in a skintight short dress. She looked amazing, and Richard instantly wanted her. *Where was she going?* he thought. More theories enveloped him, and he could feel his heart beating within his chest.

At that moment, Richard lost his moral compass. His eyes followed her as she walked down the sidewalk, got in her car parked on the side of the street, and drove away. Seconds later, Richard was following her. He had training on how to follow a suspect, and it kicked into gear, though he had no grounds to suspect Asha of anything in particular. He maintained his distance as the two cars proceeded through the neighborhood.

Once on the freeway, Richard had more options for concealing the fact that he was following Asha by traveling a lane or two away from her. Throughout the drive, he berated himself for allowing the behavior that led to him stalking a woman, but he had come this far, and it was too late to turn back.

Asha exited the freeway at Cienega Boulevard, and Richard allowed a car to get in between them. He could look through the windows of the car in front of him to see the rear taillights of Asha's Tesla as she proceeded down the street. She pulled into the right lane and put on her turn signal, so Richard drove on while looking at the parking garage she was about to enter. His heart rate accelerated again when he saw the sidewalk sign, "Largo at the Coronet - Hollywood Improv Tonight." None of this made sense given what he knew about her.

While attending a comedy club seemed out of character for Asha, Richard thought perhaps it was a "girl's night out" scenario and her friends wanted to console her on the loss of a promising boyfriend. Then Richard realized he never met any of Asha's friends. Was she meeting a date here? Richard turned his car around and parked in the garage close to Asha's vehicle. He no longer cared about the possibility that Asha might see him, but he also no longer planned a confrontation. He waited a few moments in the car to ensure that Asha would have enough time to get inside the club and sit down.

Largo at the Coronet was a cultural landmark in Los Angeles, and many popular comedians started their careers there. Although it sat on the edge of Beverly Hills, the neighborhood could be described by some as sketchy, with a few bars, cannabis shops, and the store "Trashy Lingerie" in screaming hot pink next door to the club.

As he approached the entrance to the club, Richard noticed two security guards standing outside. The last thing Richard wanted was to create a scene where the guards might be called upon to remove him. He walked past them and into the club. Once past the entrance, he found himself in a courtyard with small ornamental trees around the perimeter, a large room off to each side, and the theater toward the back. The courtyard displayed many posters of past performers, and nearly every visitor would recognize at least one of them who went on to national fame. Many people were standing, talking, and holding drinks in paper cups that they purchased upon arrival. The sun was beginning to set, bringing darkness to the courtyard. Even so, Richard felt exposed simply because he was alone.

To his right, he noticed the room had a long bar and tables scattered about, with vintage items from the entertainment industry—a violin, ukulele, and film reel—adorning the dark red walls. There he got a glimpse of Asha, sitting alone on the far side of the room at a small, round cocktail table. He backed off and walked across the courtyard to the other side, where another bar was offering beer, wine, and water.

"What can I get you, buddy?" said the bartender, breaking Richard's concentration, even as he was staring right at the man. Richard hadn't thought this entire time about how much alcohol could improve the situation.

"I'll take the Guinness please," he said, noticing that glasses of the beer were lined up on the bar for quick access.

"I'll have to empty that into a paper cup if you want to take it into the theater," the bartender said as he slid the drink in Richard's direction. Richard decided that wouldn't be necessary and proceeded to empty the glass.

He placed the glass back on the bar and walked across the courtyard to peer into the room where Asha had last been seen. There he saw a man standing at the edge of her table, looking down and speaking with her.

The man was wearing jeans and a loose t-shirt, revealing several tattoos running down the length of his arms. He was probably close to two hundred pounds and overweight for his height, which Richard put at about 5 feet, 9 inches. Richard didn't consider the man to be Asha's type, and yet no one else had shown up to join her. But then she abruptly stood, shook his hand, and started to walk out of the club. She was not there for the performance. Richard dispensed with another idea: that Asha was there to support a friend or relative taking a shot at stand-up.

Whatever Richard had witnessed didn't fit any previous theory stored in his memory. He was back to square one. As he left the building, he stopped to look at a poster showing the evening's entertainment and a picture of what would be his next obsession. It was the man speaking to Asha moments earlier who performed under the stage name of Jack Tobacco.

11

Tanaka sat down the following morning in his storage room, allowing only ambient light from two tiny windows on one side of the room to illuminate the area. He had a cup of coffee from Starbucks to his right and a protein bar in his left hand. It was an important day, so he flipped up his laptop and got down to business.

Tanaka did not like most of his customers, and he was particularly irritated by Alexander Sisky. Sisky was a stubborn old man who refused to conform to the protocols of business, even though he served at the pleasure of the Kremlin. His insistence that the wine be delivered to his home, combined with his refusal to pay for it through untraceable means, put Tanaka's operation at risk. However, the fact that he lived in the Los Angeles area did offer a level of convenience. In this case, no wine had to be dropped in the ocean for retrieval later.

Tanaka didn't trust the Russians in general, but his disdain for the Chinese trumped the Russians, Iranians, and all other customers. The hostility that China and Japan exhibit toward each other is legendary and dates back to ancient times. But the Chinese represented his most profitable customer, so instead of ignoring them, he took pride in taking their money on behalf of the yakuza.

And so, apart from the business he conducted with Sisky and the local Chinese spy ring, all other transactions Tanaka conducted were over the dark web. The "Vino Del Mar" website available to the public would forever be "under construction," while the real marketplace for Tanaka's wine was accessible only on a TOR browser. TOR, also known as "The Onion Router," was the most direct way to access the dark web, and Tanaka was about to list his latest products there.

In 2014, the FBI, working in collaboration with Europol, the Department of Homeland Security, and Immigration and Customs Enforcement, shut down over 410 websites on the dark web. But this didn't stop the proliferation of sites engaged in nefarious activities. Even today, as sites continue to be closed down and perpetrators brought to justice, it's possible to purchase recently stolen merchandise, a forged passport, and even a fake death certificate to access a decedent's pension. A visitor can acquire various poisons and other banned substances, hack a social media account, or arrange for a kidnapping. One site offers an anti-tank rocket launcher, and for .05 Bitcoin, you can also livestream a purported torture room in Russia used to extract intelligence from Ukrainian prisoners. What they all have in common is that they accept payment in various cryptocurrencies to conceal any trace of their commercial activities.

The dark web, for those with access, allowed the Vino Del Mar website to exist in plain sight without the risk of raising suspicion among law enforcement agencies because it simply sold bottles of wine. Even the fact that the wine was listed at ridiculously high prices wouldn't trigger any attention because, as it was well known, there were many people willing to pay exorbitant amounts for products of ambiguous value that no reasonable person would consider worth it. And the FBI had many more suspicious and concerning leads to follow, with its bandwidth limited to the number of agents available to take on new cases.

Tanaka rolled his office chair over to the left side of his desk and opened his file drawer, pulling once more the file with the name "China" on it. He knew that his customer would be waiting for the listing of wines he had available. China is Cuba's second-largest trading partner after Venezuela, and if the shipment he arranged to be loaded on a Russian warship was successful, then he could be confident his new trade route would be a success, and he would never again need to deliver one bottle at a time.

He next rolled his office chair over to the gray shelving units where several bottles of unlabeled VDM wines from his last trip to Temecula were standing on the bottom shelf. He moved three of them to the table, setting them down gently. He then grabbed the labels sitting on his printer and began to apply them to the bottles. Once the label was applied, he sprayed the bottle with a silicon-glue spray to protect the label from being disturbed underwater.

He took a picture of each bottle individually with his cell phone, paying particular attention to the serial number displayed on the back label in the bottom right corner. Once he photographed the bottles, he rolled back to the center of the table where his laptop was waiting and uploaded each picture individually to the VDM site so that each would display a thumbnail to the site's users, along with the serial number. A QR code was present but blurred out so that it couldn't be activated from the website.

The serial number corresponded to the specific details on each bottle, information already shared in advance with the buyer over "Threema" by yakuza operatives selling the information. Threema is a secure messaging app that doesn't require a registered cell phone number in order to create an account. The platform is just one of several encrypted apps that facilitate communication among nefarious actors that don't want to be found by the agencies hunting nefarious actors. Even the Chinese Ministry maintained an account there.

Each bottle was offered for the equivalent of $950,000 USD in cryptocurrency, with the exception of a few "value-oriented" wines offered for a fraction of that amount, only $95,000 each. The site would accept only Ethereum cryptocurrency.

When he finished the process of uploading the photos, Tanaka closed the TOR browser and cleared his browsing history. He then put the contents of each file for which a label was made into the paper shredder, including any photos. Finally, he closed his laptop and prepared to change into his new ODU, or "On Duty

Uniform," for the trip to Sector San Diego. It was almost time for his first deployment on the USCGC *Arowana*.

He stood in front of a small mirror hung from the metal shelves at eye level, then reached down into the paper bag containing his navy-blue Coast Guard uniform. He watched himself in the mirror as he pulled the heavy fabric across his large frame. Over his left breast, it said "US Coast Guard Auxiliary," and over the right, simply "Tanaka." As his hands pushed through the coarse sleeves, he was cautious not to rub too much against the severed pinky finger on his left hand. He looked down at the portion of the finger that was no longer there. It would strengthen his resolve to overcome obstacles to the success of his mission.

Looking back at himself in the mirror, Tanaka admired how the uniform rested on him and how it conveyed an image of respectability that he rarely felt at any other time. He caressed the few long strands of black hair growing on his chin and pushed back the thick black hair on his head. He understood that if he was to remain in the Auxiliary, he would need to get a haircut.

Then he reached back into the bag for the cap and pulled it across the back of his head so that the bill rested just above his large, bushy eyebrows. He liked the look and felt the bulky uniform actually hid some of his excess weight.

After another brief moment of staring at himself in the mirror, he reached down again, this time to pick up the crate he would be loading onto the USCGC *Arowana* for his "dry run." He stepped outside the storage unit, pulled down the heavy orange door, which came down with a loud thud. He locked the door and carried the crate with both hands down to his car for the trip to San Diego.

As Tanaka pulled away from the storage facility, drove down the street, and merged onto Interstate 405, he didn't realize he was being followed.

***

"Davis, it's John Swanson. How are you?"

"I was doing great until I picked up the phone," said Davis Delmatoff, special agent in the Criminal Investigations division of the Internal Revenue Service.

Delmatoff was regarded as something of an oddity within the IRS, a man in his 50s with gray, shoulder-length hair that he wore in a ponytail. He drove a 1989 fire-engine red Porsche 911 Cabriolet that he purchased from a man being prosecuted by the agency for tax evasion. Well known as an eccentric personality and wine connoisseur, he also had the best conviction record of anyone else in the agency during his tenure there, which was why he was a "go-to" resource for Swanson.

"Very funny," Swanson replied. "Look, I have something here for you."

Davis had come to recognize these words as a smokescreen for something that would take a considerable amount of his time, include more than a little aggravation, and result in an audit that would yield minimal benefit to the division. Still, if there was anything that might result in a true adventure worth pursuing, it would be something out of Swanson's office.

Swanson decided Richard had enough evidence on Sisky to escalate the case. In most situations, following the money would inevitably answer a lot of questions about criminal wrongdoing while revealing most of the perpetrators.

"We don't yet know where the money is coming from or where it is going," Swanson said to Delmatoff. "We also don't know who is behind the operation, but I think we're getting close. We don't think that Sisky is directing it, but it smells like money laundering to us."

"There is someone behind everything; you just need to know where to look," Delmatoff said philosophically. "Okay, send me what you have. Sometimes you've got to take a shot, or nobody will."

Delmatoff was hoping that, at the very least, he'd eventually be able to buy rare wine at fire sale prices.

***

Money laundering is the process of illegally making a large amount of money and then transforming it to make it look like it was generated from legitimate sources. If the wines were being purchased well in excess of their true value and the source of the money was obtained illegally, then a case could be proven, particularly if the perpetrators were selling back to themselves, as was the case involving the Mexican cartel. HSBC Bank was already at the center of multiple money laundering investigations and had paid out nearly $2 billion in fines, so their potential involvement in the current FBI investigation was not a surprise.

And why not wine? thought Davis. After all, precious art was already a familiar vehicle for money laundering, and it was found that the racehorses purchased by the Las Zetas cartel shielded several hundred thousand dollars' worth of drug money.

But what concerned Davis was that there was no clear integration of the wine back into the economy—once paid for by Sisky, it did not appear to be returning for sale anywhere, meaning those who paid for the wine were not recovering anything—other than relatively cheap wine that may have spent a few months underwater. It was entirely possible the wines were being taken outside the U.S., but, unlike rare art used for money laundering, their provenance wouldn't attract much interest from investors. Simply put, the money laundering charge was premature, and in Davis's mind, no more attractive than a cheap bottle of Pinot Grigio.

Then he remembered the FBI's raid in 2024 on the exclusive wineries in Napa Valley. He immediately picked up the phone and dialed Swanson's secure line.

"I think you may have something here," Delmatoff told Swanson over the phone, excited to discuss the money laundering investigation that fell into his lap.

"Go on," Swanson replied as he leaned back in his office chair. It gave way, creaking loudly on its way down.

"So, you may be aware of this," he started, "in 2024, the San Francisco FBI field office subpoenaed a laundry list—no pun intended—of high-net-worth investors in various wineries across Napa Valley. There were 40 individuals in all."

Swanson popped back up in the chair. At the time of the FBI inquiry, he was still based in the New York field office, so he wasn't aware of the investigation, led by Katherine Ferrado, a veteran agent with experience investigating complex financial crimes.

"Well, it was covered extensively in the *San Francisco Chronicle* and other papers up there, but they planted a false narrative to avoid tipping off the investors," Delmatoff said. "They leaked that the Napa County Supervisor was potentially involved in a bribery scandal, but that's not what they were looking for. They just didn't want to tip off our target."

Swanson had a bit of trouble understanding where Delmatoff was going.

"What were they looking for?"

"Okay, so hear me out," Delmatoff said, getting excited at his own powers of deduction. "After we shut down the money laundering scheme of the Las Zetas cartel and dispositioned all those racehorses, we suspected the drug money might be coming in another way. It would be reasonable to expect the cartel wouldn't have given up."

Swanson was beginning to make the connection. If a gang member could own a farm, buying and selling racehorses for inflated values to conceal drug money, then a gang member could own a winery to engage in the same scheme. They could also bribe, coerce, or threaten existing owners to serve as their shell company and operate with impunity south of the border.

"So," Delmatoff added, "they started following the money of all the investments coming in. The CEO of the Napa Valley Farm Bureau committed suicide as all this was unfolding. By the way, you can Google this; it's all there."

Swanson made a note to do just that.

"Did they find anything?"

"Yes," Delmatoff said excitedly. "But it wasn't the Mexican cartels. It was the Japanese mafia."

12

The yakuza, known colloquially as the Japanese mafia, faced an existential threat. Dating back to the 17th century, the yakuza was a powerful collection of families involved in a range of illegal activities and earning the label on Wikipedia as a "transnational organized crime syndicate originating in Japan." But their numbers were declining, and the elders were concerned.

In 1991, Japan passed the Act on Prevention of Unjust Acts by Organized Crime Groups. The legislation, combined with other laws that followed, further fueled the stigma against the yakuza and stifled their ability to operate in the country. This, combined with the fact that new generations of young men and women found gainful employment in professional fields, led to the erosion in yakuza membership. In 1963, there were over 184,000 members of various clans. Today, fewer than 20,000 remain.

The yakuza craved legitimacy, and if they couldn't have it in Japan, they believed they could perhaps establish it somewhere else. Their traditional tradecraft involved cheating seniors out of their savings, dealing drugs, and engaging in sexual exploitation and human trafficking. But in 1989, they started investing in public companies with a $255 million investment in the Tokyo Kyuko Electric Railway. From there, they invested in 50 more companies, and in 2008, the FBI verified they were actively laundering money in U.S.-based businesses.

In 2018, the Department of Treasury's Office of Foreign Assets Control took action against two companies and four individuals associated with the Yamaguchi-gumi, the largest of the yakuza syndicates, accusing them of money laundering activities to conceal their illicit operations, effectively blocking their ability to engage in certain commercial activities in the U.S.

Undeterred by obstacles to operate in the U.S., a yakuza leader, Takeshi Ebisawa, was charged in 2024 for conspiring with a network of associates to traffic nuclear materials, military-grade weapons, and lethal narcotics. The radioactive materials were offered for sale along with other products on the dark web, showing a Geiger counter reading next to various substances to demonstrate their potency. A DEA agent, posing as an Iranian general, agreed to purchase materials in a meeting in a Bangkok hotel room. He was shown a radioactive substance in yellowcake form, but before other samples could be presented, agents flooded in. The materials were seized and the participants arrested.

"As the yakuza fade from relevance in Japan, their crimes here and elsewhere have become more and more brazen," Delmatoff said to Swanson, "so in comparison to some of their other criminal activities, their involvement in the wine industry would not at all be a surprise. It's a perfect front for them, given the proximity to our own wine industry."

As much as Swanson loathed the idea of giving credit to Richard, he had a lot of respect for Delmatoff and was convinced some of the resources of the agency should be directed to work with Richard on this as-yet-to-be-named operation. The timing was not ideal given the priority established by the Director to investigate agent disappearances and assassinations, but in the FBI, the concept of "good timing" was a misnomer.

"Thanks, Davis," he replied, "I think we need to expose this activity to a larger audience."

***

Richard pulled ahead of the late-model silver Toyota Corolla as Interstate 405 became the I-5 freeway, a stretch of road that ran the length of the western United States from Canada to the Mexican border. He settled in the right lane but never took his eyes off the car that Tanaka was driving. By alternating between being in front of or behind the Toyota, Richard expected Tanaka would never suspect he was being followed.

At least a half dozen times, Richard looked at an off-ramp and questioned yet again whether his obsession with Asha had clouded his judgment. He was operating on little sleep after following Tanaka to his storage unit, where Tanaka slept the prior evening, leaving Richard to doze off in his car. He also wondered how far Tanaka was planning to travel. Once out of the city, this stretch of highway afforded many opportunities to be "unconsciously competent," driving on autopilot and daydreaming. Richard had no reason to suspect Tanaka was one of the "bad guys." After all, he mused, how many stand-up comedians would moonlight as criminals?

As Tanaka approached the city of San Diego, Richard straightened his back and prepared for whatever might come next. After a time, it was apparent that Tanaka was taking the exit to San Diego International Airport, at which point Richard realized he would have to make a decision. There was no way he could justify surveillance of Tanaka, so boarding a flight with him seemed out of the question.

But as the two cars slowly edged their way to the departures ramp at the airport, Tanaka crossed several lanes of traffic to enter the left turn lane, away from the airport. Richard couldn't respond in time and saw that Tanaka was in the lane to turn into the U.S. Coast Guard base, also known as Sector San Diego. Richard stopped at the same traffic signal across from the base and watched as the man in the Toyota flashed a badge to the guard and proceeded through the gate.

He took the next left turn, at the entrance to Harbor Island, an artificial island built from dredged soil that today houses multiple marinas on the edge of San Diego Bay, across from the Naval base on the island of Coronado. He guided his car to a parking lot along the bay, with a view of sailboats, aircraft carriers, and other watercraft slowly edging their way across the calm waters. He threw the car in park and fell back into the car seat, confused.

What was Tanaka doing at a Coast Guard base? What business was this guy in anyway?

Richard thought back to the night before when he saw Tanaka with Asha at the comedy club. The two appeared somewhat friendly toward each other. Asha was in the wine business. The Coast Guard had confiscated wine from the waters off Alaska and sent these to the base in Long Beach for analysis. Now, this stand-up comic shows up at another Coast Guard base over one hundred miles away. Just then, Richard had an epiphany.

Tanaka and Asha were intelligence agents working undercover on the same case as the FBI.

This was the only explanation that made sense to Richard, and it wouldn't be the first time he was fooled by an attractive woman who later turned out to be a CIA agent. Memories returned of Emma Lee, the double agent who helped bring down the Chinese plot to build an army of cloned soldiers in Operation Carbon Paper.

And it *definitely* wouldn't be the first time that two agencies were secretly working on an investigation at the same time and on a parallel course.

Richard ruminated on this scenario for some time, trying to poke holes in it or to contrive some other explanation for why an apparent stand-up comedian would have business in the Coast Guard. He put his car in reverse and allowed the car to crawl to the entrance of the lot. He didn't have sufficient cause to talk his way onto the base and feared making something out of nothing, eroding his credibility within the agency. He had a long drive back to consider how he might validate his theory.

As he merged back onto the interstate, he was tempted to call Swanson to complain that he wasn't informed about the CIA's interest in the potential money laundering operation, but he knew that one of two things would happen: Swanson would respond that he didn't know, or he'd ridicule Richard for attributing so much significance to the activities of an amateur comedian. Or both.

***

Tanaka parked his Toyota as close to the docks as he was permitted, then went to his trunk to load a crate of "perishable vegetables" on a foldable handcart that he kept in his trunk. The crate was packed with lettuce, cabbage, and corn; in the future, it would carry the wine he intended to deposit in the shallow waters off Point Loma. To anyone else on base, he was just another uniformed servicemember going about his business.

Once at the dock, he carried the crate to the top of the steel staircase that would allow a sailor to climb on board, putting the cart down at the top to salute the American flag that flew off the stern of the boat. He then realized that negotiating the stairs down to the galley while carrying the crate was going to be a lot more difficult than he anticipated. Most men would turn around and hold the guardrails on the way down, but that wasn't an option with the crate.

"Here, let me help you with that," said a young man who came out of his berth. Tanaka couldn't even see him down below with the crate in his hand, and he panicked briefly at the prospect of handing it off.

"Oh, thanks," he replied, realizing he had no choice. He handed the crate down to the crewmember, who put it directly into the galley for him. Tanaka would need another approach when that crate carried several bottles of wine.

The rest of the crew would be arriving soon, and the boat would be going underway early the next morning for a day-long drill. Tanaka retreated to his berth. If the crate was left undisturbed the next morning, he would consider the trial a success.

***

The all-hands meeting started with a lecture in the Federal Building's auditorium, where about one hundred twenty agents, mostly dressed in blue suits, sat facing the speaker. Their guest was a professor from UCLA who studied the practices of the yakuza clans in Japan and followed the migration of their illicit activities from Asia to the United States and beyond. The slides behind him showed a map with dots indicating previously confirmed criminal activity. A cluster of dots was concentrated in San Francisco and Los Angeles.

"The members of the yakuza adhere to a strict code of conduct," he said, "and identify with their clan through a series of tattoos across most of their bodies."

The professor was specifically asked to assist the FBI in detecting where the yakuza was operating on U.S. soil and how to safely approach them. Being a certified member of the yakuza, he explained, was not illegal in Japan, and so it was insufficient grounds to detain a member simply because he was a suspected member.

This presentation was long overdue given the increase in activity that the FBI tracked among yakuza clans. Swanson used the call with Davis Delmatoff as the reason for finally arranging it. He had not concluded the yakuza was connected in some way with the CIA assassinations but did not want to rule that out either.

"And another thing..." the professor started to say. But at that moment, he was interrupted by the sound of about fifty cell phones buzzing. The buzzing cell phones were joined a few seconds later by many more that were chiming, and pretty soon, it seemed like all phones were doing something to alert their owners, creating a cacophony within the auditorium and a palpable sense of panic among the participants. Agents began to get up and proceed in single file out of the row in which they were seated, one after another. The professor looked on, confused.

Richard was daydreaming at the time, still replaying in his mind what he observed at the comedy club, when his phone also started to vibrate. He looked up to see his colleagues rushing out of the auditorium as if there was a bomb threat. He then pulled his phone from his pocket and looked in horror at the news alert.

KABC-TV News: FBI Agent in San Diego Murdered

The agents had good cause for returning to their desks immediately. There would be secure messages, top-secret bulletins, and office room gossip offering more details about what exactly happened in San Diego that day. Many would want to check in with their families to let them know they were okay. There would be tributes to send and flowers to order. There would be an investigation and a detailed report. There would be a funeral.

But for Richard O'Brien, there would be an additional layer of grief as he read the story behind the headline.

The FBI agent murdered was his friend and mentor, Ben Klein.

***

Richard and Jeff McAuley didn't speak much on the drive down the I-5 from Orange County to Fort Rosecrans National Cemetery, located at the tip of the Point Loma peninsula in the city of San Diego. This was the second time this week he found himself driving down south to San Diego, and he avoided feelings of resentment, which would have been shameful given the circumstances.

With over 120,000 interments of soldiers and federal personnel, the cemetery had long been closed to new interments, with exceptions made for servicemen and women killed in the line of duty and on a space-available basis. As a veteran of the 3rd Battalion, 9th Marine Expeditionary Brigade serving in Vietnam, Klein was assured a place there and was known to say, "When I'm gone, I'm gonna have a fantastic view."

The cemetery was one of his favorite places to visit when he needed to escape the pressure of his job as assistant director in charge of the San Diego field office. From the grounds on one side was a limitless view of the Pacific Ocean. From the other side was a panoramic view of San Diego Bay with the island of Coronado in the foreground and downtown behind it.

Ironically, Klein was supposed to be retired, so there was some additional paperwork to verify the Agency's "killed in the line of duty" claim. He was eligible for retirement at the end of his last mission, code-named Operation Carbon Paper, a case he worked closely on with Richard. The operation resulted in the destruction of China's capability to create an army of cloned soldiers, a science the Chinese had perfected at a state-owned company called BioSplice. Had the FBI not succeeded in destroying the lab and disabling the clones, that synthetic army would have invaded Taiwan, and the entire balance of power in the South China Sea would have shifted in China's favor.

But retirement is a tricky thing for someone of Klein's energy and character, and it didn't last long. He was soon back at the FBI as a contracted consultant, training new agents, lecturing, and presenting case studies, including a recap of Operation Carbon Paper so that the Bureau was always prepared for the possibility that another rogue nation might attempt a similar approach to regional domination.

"Well, at least this will take your mind off that Asha chick," said McAuley, finally breaking the silence as Richard drove. McAuley, who was not as close to Klein as Richard, realized as the words left his mouth that the statement was not helpful.

After another couple of miles, Richard spoke. "What I don't get is, why Klein? The man had no enemies and wasn't working any cases."

Details about the incident were still flowing into the agency. There seemed no doubt that Klein's murder was premeditated, a targeted killing. Cell phone footage from a handful of witnesses showed him removing the charge cord from his vehicle at an outdoor strip mall. A man in a ski mask exited a vehicle on the aisle across from Klein's car. He walked up to Klein and shot him point-blank in the temple as Klein was bending over to replace the charge cord. The assailant's vehicle drove up, the man got in the passenger seat, and the car sped off as Klein lay dying. According to the videos obtained, which began after the shots were fired, there were no license plates on the car.

"A revenge killing?" McAuley speculated. It was a sensible theory.

As Richard's car reached the end of Point Loma, the gravestones started to appear on both sides of the road. Bright white stones stood erect as far as the eye could see, side by side, in perfect lines, facing the water, row after row after row. Thousands of them. The symmetry and solemn nature of the grounds would grab anyone's attention and not let go, a reminder of the ultimate sacrifice made by thousands of men and women who defended democracy for wars that were necessary and some that were not.

"There it is," said Richard. A line of cars made clear where Klein's burial site would be, and Richard slowed the vehicle to park directly behind the last car in the line. The funeral was scheduled to begin at 10:00 in the morning. Richard and Jeff were a bit early as they walked up to a small crowd of mourners all dressed in black.

It was a typical day in San Diego, few clouds, temperatures in the mid-70s. It could have been winter, summer, or spring, and the description of the weather would be about the same. A light breeze caused the fronds from queen palm trees to sway back and forth. As Richard walked up to the crowd, he wasn't prepared for what he saw. It was Sarah Goodman, an FBI special agent whom he once asked to marry. She was as beautiful as the last time they were together. He walked directly up to her.

"Sarah," he said breathlessly while embracing her, "it's good to see you." McAuley smiled in Sarah's direction and understood the best course of action was to steer a course away from the two.

"Hello, Richard," she replied, smiling as if she was about to receive a sum of money that was owed to her.

"I didn't know you and Ben were close," Richard said, using all his powers of observation to take in the view of the most significant love interest of his life so far. She was wearing a white blouse under a black blazer and long black skirt, quite appropriate for the occasion. Her long brown hair rested on her shoulders. Her blue eyes were concealed behind a large pair of designer sunglasses. She looked like she walked right out of a glamour magazine.

"I was tagged to join the task force investigating the assassinations of agents," she replied. "How've you been, Richard?"

"Good, good, damn it's good to see you," said Richard. As far as he knew, Sarah married a federal prosecutor back in Detroit where she was stationed, but he noticed immediately that there was no ring on her finger.

"You're married, right?" he continued.

"Shortest marriage in the history of law enforcement," she replied. "Turns out my husband had a drug habit that he didn't disclose up front. I gave him an ultimatum, and I guess he prefers cocaine over me."

Richard nodded instinctively. As a former user, he could see the situation with great clarity, but he didn't dare signal anything that would suggest a level of understanding. Also, he was quite certain he would never choose a great high over sleeping with Sarah, having experienced both. Still, it was abundantly obvious that Sarah, a law enforcement officer, couldn't be in a relationship where her partner used contraband.

"That's crazy," he said. "I'm so sorry. Will you be in town for long?"

13

Nothing created in the digital world is ever completely erased. That's why the Sicilian scammers were successful in penetrating the security infrastructure in place to protect covert operatives and other high-value targets. With the right tools and approach, they were able to establish a comprehensive file on how to identify and locate them. Giuseppe was one of the best identity detectives in the business due to his methodical approach. When he wasn't scamming people or creating boosted LinkedIn profiles, he was digitally hunting people who did not want to be found. As a result, his desk was littered with cell phones from all manufacturers to test and support a full range of nefarious activities.

Giuseppe would begin by trying to acquire a "fullz" package of the target. A fullz file is a complete set of personal information that can be purchased on the dark web. This might include social security numbers, credit card information, security codes, medical history, current and past addresses, etc. If this didn't yield all the information needed for one of his customers, he would turn to commercially available apps like Eyezy, Minispy, or Detectico to track the target's cell phone and location without their knowledge. If the target was oblivious to this risk, finding them was easy. If they guarded against detection by disabling location tracking or Bluetooth, or operated their phone on airplane mode or a VPN, then the effort reverted to more advanced methods.

If he didn't have a cell phone number but had an email, he could drown the mailbox with seemingly unrelated outreach and offers, each featuring an "unsubscribe" link in the top right corner, masquerading as a legitimate offer to remove the recipient. Clicking any such link would take the target outside the safety of their email and into the hands of the scammer, who could install malware or extract additional personal information.

Of course, anybody worth following, blackmailing, or assassinating would probably have a bodyguard or assistant managing their email and phone, especially if they were a political rival of a dictatorial government. Such situations required a multi-faceted approach.

At the time he received instructions to locate and develop a profile on Ben Klein, Giuseppe was experimenting with a homemade Stingray device, which was producing good but often inconsistent results. The device, used principally by law enforcement agencies, mimics a wireless carrier tower in order to force all nearby mobile phones to connect to it. When the targeted phone connects to the device, its location can be immediately pinpointed. The legality of these devices was contested in the United States as an invasion of privacy, but in Sicily, the government turned a blind eye to the activity.

If all else failed to this point, Giuseppe's next level might involve conducting a reverse image search for any photos found on social media accounts, including posts that the target might have believed to be deleted. Any previous locations might be combined with public records of license plate or driver's license registrations, patterns of travel into and out of areas that use photo readers for registered drivers or automobiles, and facial recognition applied across hacked security footage, compared to photos in the public domain.

His final approach, merely to verify any prior findings were accurate, could involve a seemingly innocuous ping to their phone or social media accounts to tease out their location in real time. One of Giuseppe's favorite strategies was to call out the target on a social media account they were known to use and congratulate them on a distinction they didn't earn, perhaps posting an old photo of the target at the same time. This would often precipitate a reply, and that was all he needed to triangulate his target with the cell phone and location.

With the help of an IT programmer, Giuseppe built a brilliant application whereby he could assume the identity of his target and, using both the Stingray device and "Find My Phone" feature, enable his customers to identify the person's location in real time. Once the target's cell phone, residence, photo, next of kin, and other protected information were gathered and verified, Giuseppe would place the details in a zip file along with a link to the application, send it to his yakuza client, and receive enough compensation to feed his family for a month.

***

The drive from the Federal Building to the IRS headquarters was a short distance east on Interstate 10, but at 10:00 a.m. it might as well have been across the county. Richard's appointment with Davis Delmatoff was at the instruction of John Swanson, who was preoccupied with the investigation into the recent CIA, and now FBI, assassinations.

It didn't matter that the CIA Director wanted to focus on the men he lost; Swanson was going to throw Klein's assassination into the mix of CIA agents recently murdered, even if it meant complicating the investigation. Klein was beloved in the department, and while he never met the man, he knew that many in the LA and San Diego branches had worked with him. It was to Swanson's benefit politically to do everything within his power to champion the investigation.

There was another reason Swanson directed Richard to work directly with Delmatoff. He was not convinced the theory about money laundering through the wine industry had legs, and he wanted to insulate himself from being the target of criticism if the theory was wrong.

However, all Richard could think about as he stared at the bumper in front of him was the encounter with Sarah the day before. He still had feelings for Sarah and also regret that the relationship fell apart after his admission of an affair with Harmony Hutchins, the young woman with whom he was held captive during an investigation into The Center for New Beginnings, a facility operated by Dennis Spence. Thoughts of Sarah effectively pushed Asha out of his stream of consciousness, and he was excited that she accepted his invitation to dinner the following evening.

As Richard parked his car in the massive lot at the IRS building, he noticed a bright red Porsche 911 Cabriolet parking among the reserved spaces. Emerging from the convertible was a fifty-year-old bespectacled man sporting a ponytail. Richard mused he must be there to contest an audit until he saw the vanity plate, which read "AUDIT-OR." Then he remembered Swanson's description of the legendary IRS agent who successfully exposed multiple financial schemes and brought several white-collar criminals to justice.

"Mr. Delmatoff!" he called out. Delmatoff didn't hear him and continued walking, so Richard galloped a bit to catch up.

"Good morning, Sir," he said once he was side by side with Delmatoff.

"Yes, and you are…?" Delmatoff was often hounded by the local media for stories about white-collar crime, either recent or historical, and he had a policy of not speaking about any ongoing investigations.

"Special Agent Richard O'Brien, Sir," Richard replied as the two walked in sync toward the building.

"Oh yes, O'Brien," Delmatoff replied. "I came into the office just for you." Delmatoff spent most of his time working remotely, a privilege he earned from decades in the Service.

The two men entered the building and engaged mostly in small talk until they arrived at Delmatoff's office, which looked like it had been struck by a tornado with selective vengeance. Documents littered his desk to the point that its surface couldn't be seen below them. Small stacks of paper defined each corner. They were organized in various piles across the credenza, on the small coffee table next to the guest chair, and on the floor. Yellow post-it notes hung off the 90's era CRT monitor that faced him. There were even post-it notes that were camped on top of each other on his desk's telephone with various reminders he managed to forget. Richard had to wonder what it might look like in his home kitchen.

"Here, let me get that," Delmatoff said as he scooped a stack of papers off the chair facing his desk, then laid them on the only space he could find on the credenza, which was on top of another stack. He pointed to the seat, indicating it was available to Richard.

"So, Agent O'Brien, what makes you think this VDM company is engaged in concealing a crime?"

Richard explained the growing interest in ocean-aged wines and the fact that VDM wines were not available for purchase on the internet because the company website was under construction. He added that a bottle was found in a collection of other rare wines and that the owner paid nearly $2 million to the company the year prior. Much of what Delmatoff heard was already shared by Swanson.

This by itself, combined with his preliminary research, wasn't persuasive to Delmatoff. The company could have been a broker of rare wines, working through an established network of collectors, perhaps also creating a private label the way Costco and Trader Joe's produce their own wine. Then Richard added that VDM wines were confiscated by the US Coast Guard and on their way to the base in Long Beach. This was news that had not yet reached Delmatoff.

"That's right," Richard added. "We hope to get a look at the wines tomorrow."

Delmatoff looked at his lap for a moment, then stood up. "Follow me," he said, grabbing a key from inside his desk drawer.

Richard followed Delmatoff down the hallway to another room. He opened the door with the key and flipped on the fluorescent light. The room was very small, with a desk you might find in an elementary school, and a computer terminal. In front of the desk were two chairs.

"Have a seat," he said to Richard.

Richard knew where they were sitting. The computer was set up as a type of air-gapped system. While an air-gapped system is unplugged from any networks where it might be vulnerable, this computer was disconnected from all federal applications with firewalls preventing it from allowing any intrusion beyond the circuits in the physical system, while allowing it to access The Onion Router, or TOR, for browsing sites on the dark web. As an extra measure of security, the computer used a virtual private network, or VPN, to conceal that it was operating on a server owned by the federal government.

Delmatoff took the seat directly in front of the computer screen, and Richard sat off to the side, like a schoolboy about to get a lesson that he already knew. Within a couple of minutes, Delmatoff found what he was looking for.

"Hello VDM," he said, "AKA Vino del Mar. Pleased to meet you. Why are you hiding here?"

"Well, I'll be damned," Richard said, staring at the screen. He took his phone out of his jacket's inside pocket and took a few pictures of the screen. Delmatoff didn't object.

"They want to keep their products out of the public's view," Delmatoff said, as Richard took one final pic. "One reason may be that a market value cannot be established. That certainly supports the money laundering angle."

"However, in the art world, a painting could be sold for $10 million in illegally acquired funds, placed in an airport warehouse, and sold in the future for anywhere above or below the cost. Once sold, the proceeds become legitimized," he said. "I'm still not clear on why anyone is paying such huge sums for a wine that doesn't have an established reputation or following. It doesn't make sense."

Richard and Davis stared for a moment at the computer screen showing thumbnail photos of 18 bottles of wine, organized in three rows of six bottles each. Then Richard hatched an idea.

"Let's buy one."

Delmatoff giggled as he pointed to the bottom right corner of the screen.

"Son, you wouldn't get the agency to cover that expense," he said, "and frankly, you couldn't even afford the shipping and handling with a full month of your salary."

Richard focused on where Davis was pointing. There, running across the bottom of the screen, was a banner that read "All purchases subject to shipping and handling fee of $USD 12,000."

"Twelve thousand!" he said, laughing aloud, "is this some kind of prank? Who or what is the target market for this?"

That, of course, was the million-dollar question. Most observers would be forgiven for dismissing the site as a scam or hoax. Neither Davis Delmatoff nor Richard O'Brien had that luxury.

***

The USCGC *Arowana* pitched gently from side to side in relatively calm waters off the coast of Point Loma, drifting slowly in a current running at 270 degrees south/southwest. The ship's engine was quietly idling; it was not anchored in case it was called into action and a rapid response was necessary. The deployment called for the crew to patrol an area of the Pacific where migrant crossings and attempts to land were occurring with regular frequency.

On the bridge, the crew monitored heat-sensitive radar to detect disproportionate heat signatures that would be emanating from bodies on boats. Three petty officers were on duty there as the captain slept. They sipped coffee and talked about everything from cars to women to politics. There was nothing on the water that merited any attention.

Tanaka stood outside at the stern, looking out at the lights of Tijuana some twenty nautical miles away. The lights demonstrated just how sprawling Tijuana was compared to the relatively compact downtown of San Diego. He hoped that the Bonine he took earlier would be sufficient to prevent him from becoming seasick.

The moon was in its waning crescent phase, so barely visible, and a blanket of clouds prevented any light that might reflect off it from illuminating the area. The bellowing foghorn from the Zuniga Point jetty, at the tip of San Diego Bay, was the only sound that pierced the night. The crisp air was unlike anything on land; it demanded to be noticed because, apart from the periodic interruption of the foghorn, there was so little else. The serenity of the scene was not lost on Tanaka, but he still had work left to do.

The rest of the 12-man crew was below deck, either playing cards in the galley or in a berth, streaming movies on their phones. Tanaka wanted the crew to become accustomed to his presence at the stern of the boat so that they would not become suspicious of his actions back there later on. He had already served the crew their dinner in a series of three shifts. The crew was quite impressed with his culinary skills, which included a range of sushi, poke dishes, and fried fish. Many suggested that the cuisine on the *Arowana* was better than anything they could expect back home. Tanaka's acceptance by the crew was critical to what would happen next.

He lit a cigarette and leaned on a barrel at the back of the boat, looking relaxed. Smoking was generally discouraged unless on a break, and Tanaka had completed his assignment for the day. He listened carefully to the activity below, waiting for the card game to wrap up and for the crew to retire to their respective berths. Some of them would be relieving the bridge crew in the coming hours, so Tanaka had to move with purpose to avoid running into them later.

He went below to collect the crate and backpack that he had placed in the kitchen area. When he reached the crate, he kneeled down, opened the backpack, and pulled out a line and buoy, which he then tied to the crate. He carried it up to the upper deck, relieved to find it was far easier to get up the deck with a crate than it was to go down.

Tanaka was confident that the only active members of the crew would be on the bridge. He returned to the stern of the boat. Leaning over the edge, he slowly lowered the crate into the water, being careful not to create any noise that might attract attention. The crate was quickly absorbed by the waves and dropped the rest of the way down, leaving the buoy to mark its position. Any mariner would assume the buoy to be a lobster trap and leave it undisturbed.

Tanaka returned to the galley to warm up coffee he would bring to the bridge to replenish the crew. The *Arowana* would soon drift away from the buoy.

"Hello, gentlemen," he said, smiling as he entered the bridge with a thermos. "Who needs a fill-up?"

"Tanaka," said Chief Petty Officer Varela, "you're a life-saver. Get over here." The two other crewmen looked on with amusement.

Tanaka went straight to Varela and poured coffee into his mug, looking into the chief's eyes as he did so.

"How is it going tonight?" Tanaka asked. "And where exactly are we?" Tanaka intentionally moved in the direction of the onboard GPS monitor.

"Can you read one of these?" said Petty Officer Lewis. "This shows our exact position."

"No, not really," Tanaka replied. "Is it OK if I take a picture of it? My family would be really impressed."

The chiefs looked at each other. Varela shrugged his shoulders.

"Sure, go for it."

Tanaka grabbed his phone and took a picture to identify the location of the dropped shipment. The GPS read "32.54° N, 117.39° W."

"Thanks, gentlemen. You have a good night," said Tanaka as he backed himself out of the bridge.

Tanaka returned quickly to the stern. He could still see the buoy, but the ship was already several yards away. He pulled out his cell phone and opened a text to Gabriel Rios, his contact in La Bufadora, Mexico. He attached the screenshot of the GPS coordinates and hit "Send."

Tanaka watched anxiously to see if he was within range of a tower that could relay the message. The progress bar moved slowly, then seemed to be stuck. Finally, the word "Delivered" appeared on his phone. He silently thought to himself, *Mission Accomplished*. The most error-prone phase of his distribution system was significantly improved.

Tanaka retired to his berth with a great sense of satisfaction, relief, and even a bit of pride.

14

"We will help you get an IT job, pay you an additional retainer, and provide you a bonus for buying a home in America," said the man with a thick accent on the Zoom call with Katrina. The words continued to resonate in her head months after hearing them when she finally realized what she would be giving up by giving in.

Katrina Evtushenko arrived in the United States from Ukraine eleven months before the call, and nearly four months after the end of her contract job, which enabled her to immigrate with her two young children. In Ukraine, she worked as an IT consultant for Vodafone, one of the largest mobile phone carriers in Europe. Now unemployed, she was anxious to find work and frustrated by her diminishing prospects.

Katrina was escaping an abusive relationship with her husband, but the conflict with Russia meant she would not be returning anytime soon. Her H1-B work visa would allow her to remain in the United States, but she desperately needed work soon, or she would find herself seeking government assistance or receiving a visit from the Department of Homeland Security. She worried most of all for the welfare of her children.

Finding vulnerable yet talented people for Calabria Venture Capital's needs was exceedingly easy using various forms of social media. LinkedIn identified all the credentials necessary to find the resources they needed, and complementary searches were conducted to verify their level of desperation. The Trump administration's termination of thousands of federal workers in 2025 created a rich pool of resentful talent that they could exploit. In Katrina's case, it was simply a matter of ignorance that made her attractive.

What Katrina lacked was a documented work history in the United States, something easily remedied with a few dishonest entries on her profile and resume. Giuseppe Rizzo and others from CVC were responsible for setting up fake profiles and people to occupy them all over the world. They would later guide Katrina on how to further optimize her profile in anticipation of her first virtual job interview over Zoom. Katrina would easily pass any security clearance required for employment, were it to get to that point.

During the interviews, Katrina was coached by Giuseppe's boss, another young man with a significant IT background, who was listening in. On a couple of questions, she had to ask for a moment, whereupon the instructions were texted to her on how to respond. Some of the questions dealt with competencies that she didn't have, but based on the coaching provided, the employer was satisfied that she could do the work, and she ultimately received an offer from the Internal Revenue Service to provide remote-based technical support to IRS employees using government-issued computers and laptops. Katrina was soon in the workforce with a laptop shipped directly to her apartment in a working-class suburb outside Pittsburgh. She received training on how to create a secure environment, how to remain compliant with privacy laws, and other policies and procedures unique to the agency.

It was eventually time for her to satisfy the terms of her agreement. As she signed in one day for work and examined the support tickets from users that had been received the day prior, she could see a remote agent deploying a tool to view her screen. She was breathless at the efficiency of the hack and stared at the screen in horror. Her work environment was no longer secure, and the violation of her privacy made her feel nauseous. Worse than this, the hackers could go directly into the IRS systems to take whatever information they required.

They downloaded the personnel files of all government employees, separated them by agency, and put the FBI and CIA employees into a dedicated file. And there was nothing Katrina could do to stop them.

***

Richard selected a restaurant far enough away from Asha's apartment and the comedy club that there would be little risk of running into her, but when Sarah arrived, he easily forgot that Asha ever existed. In fact, his heart began pounding as if he were a prepubescent teen laying eyes on a celebrity pin-up. Sarah remained the undisputed champion that owned his heart and soul.

She wore a white blazer over a blue top and designer jeans. Her silky brown hair cascaded down in equal measure on either side of her shoulders. Whatever makeup she may have been wearing was undetectable, apart from red lipstick that completed the classy, understated look.

"Over here!" he called out to her as he stepped back from the bar so that the two could find a table.

Richard decided against any white tablecloth environments for fear it would send the wrong message to Sarah, even though his intentions were the same. As she took her seat opposite Richard, she arched her back to remove her blazer, displaying the spectacular figure that Richard remembered distinctly from their time together. He felt himself getting hard and wasn't sure he could last the evening without making a fool of himself. He sensed the eye contact and other nonverbal cues from Sarah indicated she was willing to take him back, at least for one evening.

"How is Swanson treating you?" she asked. It was well known across the agency that John Swanson and Sarah Goodman had dated while in the Bureau, a situation that explained why Swanson looked to make life difficult for

Richard once he arrived and showed interest in her. In New York, Swanson was a Special Agent and Richard a translator. Now Swanson was his boss, a more challenging dynamic.

"He's harmless," Richard replied, determined to demonstrate that Swanson was not a concern. What was a concern to Richard was Sarah's feelings about how their relationship nearly ended, shortly after learning that he had slept with another woman while drugged in a psychiatric hospital.

"Say, about us," Richard said awkwardly. He had his eyes locked on Sarah's, looking for clues to her state of mind.

"We're good," she replied, smiling, giving the impression that Richard was forgiven for a crime he didn't commit. He swallowed a sigh of relief to conceal just how elated he was at that moment.

"Okay," he said, deciding it best to pivot away from any discussion about the past, "what do you know about ocean-aged wines?"

The rest of the dinner date went by quickly, with Richard and Sarah covering a range of topics including the money laundering case, Klein's murder, and the investigation into agent assassinations. Richard decided he didn't want to waste any more time to get what he ultimately wanted.

"Would you like to come back to my place," he said bravely, "for an after-dinner drink?"

Sarah just stared at him, then smirked.

"An after-dinner drink, really?" she said, sarcastically. "We can have that here."

"Well," he replied, "mine comes with a little umbrella. C'mon, don't make me beg."

Richard's car was parked on the top of the parking structure, and since Sarah took an Uber to the restaurant, she accompanied him. The evening air was cool, and the lot was empty. A few tall street lamps provided the only light available, but Richard's car wasn't under one. As Sarah approached the passenger door, Richard moved ahead to open it for her. Then he swung around, put his hands on her waist, and moved in for a kiss. Sarah obliged.

Within seconds, the two had their hands all over each other, Richard anxious to feel her breasts again and Sarah moving her hand down Richard's side, just to the left of his groin, demonstrating her intent, but equally intent to tease rather than satisfy him. Richard guided himself down to the passenger seat and pulled her inside, on top of him. Then he reached over, pulled the door shut, and reached beneath him to release the seat and allow it to fall back as far as possible. The seat shot back quickly due to the weight upon it, hitting the end of the rail with a loud thud.

Sarah held his cheeks as she kissed him hard, and in between a passionate kiss, he lifted her shirt over her head. She unzipped his pants and released his penis. He pulled her panties to the side and was quickly inside her. She rocked on top of him as he cradled her bra. Sarah was breathing heavily; Richard groaned. The whole session lasted no more than two minutes, but it was the most raw and intense sex that either had in a long time.

"I missed you," he said as she collapsed on top of him, trying to catch her breath.

"I know," she replied.

"What now?" Richard asked, clearly recognizing he was still not in control of the relationship's trajectory.

"Now," Sarah replied, still gasping for air as she pulled her bra strap back on her shoulder, "you drop me at my hotel."

***

Swanson stood to the left of the screen at one end of the large conference room, his back to the row of windows facing west. On the screen was a slide with photos of three suspects, but Richard wasn't paying attention to it. His mind was still in the past, in the car with Sarah, rocking back and forth on the front passenger seat. It didn't help that she was sitting across the room from him in the same meeting.

As a temporary transfer from the Detroit office, Swanson made a special point to introduce Agent Sarah Goodman to the group at the beginning of the meeting. From that point on, Richard wasn't the only one having difficulty concentrating. She was one of a few women in the room, and thanks to her mature demeanor, she stood out as the perfect "MILF" fantasy for many of the young men in attendance.

"Our brothers in the CIA have narrowed their search down to four suspects," Swanson said, "any one of these guys may be involved in the assassinations, or maybe it's all of them," he said with a hint of resignation in his voice. "Everything we have on them will be available on the shared drive, but I'll tell you now, it's not much."

"What about the fourth suspect?" an agent asked.

"Thanks for that setup," replied Swanson. He advanced the slide while making prolonged and direct eye contact with her as well. The next image was the black silhouette of a man's head with a large question mark within it, and underneath the suspect's name, "Febri Irwansyah Djatmiko." To the right of the headshot were bullet points summarizing everything known about him.

"We don't have a photo of this man," Swanson said, returning his attention to the rest of the audience, "but the CIA believes he also may be a central figure in this. His surname is a tongue twister, so they call him simply 'Febri.'"

Swanson paused to look at the slide himself. "As you know, the CIA doesn't maintain a 'most wanted' list," he added, "but Interpol has a red notice out on this man. They call him 'the Ghost.'"

"Febri was raised in Indonesia as a laborer," Swanson said. "He was hired in 2013 by his employer, Chia Kee Chen, to travel to Singapore and murder the man having an affair with Chen's wife. The victim's body was brutally beaten and mutilated, with every bone fractured from his eye sockets to his jawbone, neck, and shoulder."

"Both Chen and Febri were charged with capital murder in a Singaporean court. Chen was taken into custody and sentenced to death in 2018, but Febri escaped justice and disappeared, first returning to Indonesia and, from there, to Shanghai. He probably assumed he could never go home."

Around the time of Febri's disappearance, China resolved to shorten a long-term project when they dismantled the CIA presence on Chinese soil, capturing or killing nearly a dozen sources in a 24-month period. The Ministry of State Security was in the middle of this campaign when Febri presented himself to them. He was quickly taken in, given a new identity, trained, and put back into the field. His ability to quickly leave Singapore resulted in him going off the grid with no photos in existence to corroborate his identity. He was indeed a ghost.

China's decision to outsource killings came when the Ministry realized that Chinese nationals were simply incompetent at assassinating anyone. One incredibly hard-to-believe story made the point. In 2013, a Chinese man hired a local contract killer to eliminate a business competitor, who, in turn, outsourced the job to another man, retaining a portion of the fee for himself. The man receiving the job outsourced it yet again, retaining a portion of the fee he was offered. This process was repeated four times before all five men, and the original client, were caught and sentenced to up to five years in prison. It was revealed the final assassin actually met with the target and offered to help him fake his own death, an act that caused the entire plot to unravel.

The CIA eventually concluded many of their agents missing or murdered in China were possible victims of Febri, whose talent as an assassin grew further in his service to the Chinese. And as the Chinese were quite committed to the task, it was reasonable to expect they would expand their operations beyond their borders – so an operation in Cuba would be plausible, and it was well established that China had agents operating there.

"Febri has been rewarded with a relatively safe and comfortable environment, free from the risk of extradition back to Singapore, so long as he remains useful," Swanson said. "We need to find out if there is any record of him being in Cuba."

That implied directive from their boss caused many of the agents to take down notes on either their iPad, notebook, or phone. Richard also was working on his phone, but not for the same reason. He sent Sarah a text message while staring straight at her from across the room.

How are you feeling today?

He wanted to keep the message innocuous but indirectly reference the night before. Sarah looked down at her phone and read the message. She showed no emotion and did not look up to acknowledge Richard, but she did type out a response, lay down her phone, and then return her attention to the slideshow.

I can't believe I forgot to pack panties.

Richard read the message and felt a rush of adrenaline. Sarah's text was particularly difficult to square with the fact that she was clearly wearing underwear the night before. If Richard had any hope of tracking with all the intelligence being shared by Swanson, it was now lost. As he looked up, he noticed Sarah very slowly uncross her legs and cross them again the other way. She never looked in his direction.

***

Swanson moved the deck forward again, now displaying a map of the United States and its telecommunications infrastructure. Hundreds of straight lines running in all directions across the map would cause one to wonder the point of the image, other than to say it was busy. But Swanson's intent was to take the discussion in a new direction: identifying how the assassins were able to obtain protected information on their targets in the first place.

"In addition to their capacity to eliminate American agents through traditional means," he said, "criminal syndicates are improving their ability to hack into the telecommunications infrastructure of adversaries to the point that nobody in our government is completely safe."

A few months prior to the meeting, hackers from a group known as "Salt Typhoon" were able to access the personal communications of high-ranking officials and expose the identities of a handful of intelligence employees, no matter where they lived and worked. The organization, widely believed to be an instrument of the Chinese Ministry of State Security, extracted the telecommunications companies' call data records, obtaining detailed call history and associated phone numbers of all users within the network.

Then there was the "massive counterintelligence disaster," as one official put it, when in 2025 the Trump Administration demanded a list of CIA agents with up to two years' experience to be shared with the White House in an unclassified memorandum. While the leak provided a bonanza of intelligence to anyone paying attention, it was unlikely any of the relatively newer staff were already deployed in a covert operation. However, as Swanson put it, this careless exchange of information was "destroying careers before they even started." Indeed, it seemed sometimes that sensitive data was leaking from a sieve.

"Sir," said an agent in the room, "how do we square the assassination of Chief Klein with all this? I mean, he was never a covert agent. In fact, he was retired."

"That's a fair point," Swanson said, pointing directly to the agent. "Klein's murder was either an outlier or unrelated to any hidden pattern in the most recent assassinations."

Then there was the fact that Klein's murder was on U.S. soil. Swanson would have to fight traditional bureaucratic silos to get the CIA to agree that Klein's murder was part of the same emerging pattern. One thing was certain: now that he was tapped by the Director to lead the investigation, he didn't want to wait for another assassination, even if it meant scoring additional clues.

"We've lost as many agents as the CIA," said Swanson, as he advanced the slide again to the end of the presentation and laid the remote on the conference table. "Five of our agents were assigned to Chinese counterintelligence; the others were assigned to Russia, North Korea, and Iran. Klein's last operation was Carbon Paper, so he was focused on China."

Swanson assumed all agents in the room were already familiar with the operation involving China's production of an army of what came to be known as "synthetic soldiers." Certainly Richard was, and hearing the phrase "Carbon Paper," the operation he named, successfully rescued him from the stream of consciousness that he was drowning in to that point.

"Sir, we have been studying the recent activity of APTs in Sicily," said Agent Tara Johnson. "They are now trafficking in information that includes federal employees, and we believe they are as advanced as the

Chinese." APT was shorthand for "Advanced Persistent Threat," a designation applied to criminal organizations that penetrate and exploit the IT systems of governments, financial institutions, and large corporations.

Agent McAuley was next to speak.

"If a hacker can get into those databases that, you know, have the highest level of threat protection," he said, "then what's to stop them from identifying our agents working undercover?"

Richard looked on, impressed with how much McAuley had grown into his role since joining the agency, able to challenge conventional wisdom without losing his eclectic personality as a West Coast surfer dude. He wanted to contribute to the discussion, but he was still too far behind in understanding it all. Instead, he was thinking about how best to connect with Sarah after the meeting.

"That information would be pretty easy to sell," McAuley said.

"Yeah, but where would they get the information to connect a covert agent, operating under an alias, to his or her real identity?" asked another agent, turning to McAuley who was sitting on the same side of the room.

"I dunno," said McAuley, "HR?"

McAuley was closer than anyone would have realized. Then, he nailed it.

"Or… payroll?"

15

"Wanna go on a field trip?" Richard offered to McAuley. "Lunch is on me."

Richard had just got the word that the crate of wine confiscated by the Coast Guard off the coast of Alaska had arrived at the "Los Angeles/Long Beach Sector" base, about a thirty-minute drive from FBI headquarters.

"Can we get fish tacos?" McAuley replied. "I know a place."

The US Coast Guard base in Long Beach is sandwiched between narrow waterways serving the ports of Los Angeles and Long Beach that together comprise the largest port in North America. As Richard and his partner left the freeway and drove slowly over the bridges en route to Terminal Island, they entered a world that many residents of LA would never see: dozens of huge cranes scattered among stacks of shipping containers, each the size of a school bus.

"There must be a couple thousand of those containers," McAuley mused as Richard inched the car closer to the entrance of the base, winding through lines of trucks that would soon be loaded up with containers. The actual number of shipping containers was not on Richard's mind. What he was worried about was the reception and cooperation he could expect from the Coast Guard active-duty personnel.

It was no secret that the FBI and Coast Guard had a rocky relationship. It started with the fact that the FBI falls under the Department of Justice and the Coast Guard under Homeland Security. But where the friction manifests itself is in maritime law enforcement, where both agencies claim a degree of jurisdiction. The publicity around any conflicts is like catnip to the media, and so Richard had reason to be concerned that he may not have been welcome on the base. Those concerns were erased when Chief Petty Officer Chris Aaron met him at the gate.

"Good afternoon, sir," he said, smiling, "we've been expecting you."

Aaron pointed to some parking spaces just off the entrance, and walked behind the car as Richard parked it. The three shook hands, exchanged a few words about the weather and local traffic, and then Aaron led them down the long road along the perimeter of Deadman's Island, to a warehouse behind the USCG Exchange. As they walked, they passed at least a dozen fast boats, cutters, tugboats, and other watercraft that served the needs of the Guard.

Aaron led the men through the warehouse to a cavernous air hanger sheltering a small fixed wing aircraft and a Jayhawk helicopter. The size of the aircraft in the hangar made it difficult to focus on anything else, but there, in the back and lying next to a mechanic's toolbox, was a wooden crate the size of a sofa ottoman. The crate was made of pine, and it was clear it had absorbed some sea water on its extended journey.

"Here you go, sir," said the Chief Petty Officer, extending his arm in the direction of the crate. "You're welcome to take it into evidence, just sign here please." Aaron handed Richard a three-part form on a clipboard. The inter-agency paperwork released the crate to the FBI's possession.

"Thank you, Chief," Richard replied as he signed the document, while leaning over the crate for a closer look. He then had a delayed reaction, and stepped back, standing erect.

"You've tested it for radiation, right?" Richard asked, hopefully.

"Yes sir, for sure," Aaron replied. "That's SOP for anything we remove from the maritime environment."

Richard was immediately impressed with the professionalism of his host.

"There are low levels of Uranium and Cesium-137," the officer added.

McAuley instinctively took two steps back while looking on.

"Seriously?" he blurted out. Richard looked back at McAuley who had the same reaction.

"Yes sir," Aaron replied, calmly. "But you should know, this is not uncommon among wines," he added.

"Say more about that," said Richard, feeling like he was about to receive an education. He was right.

"Yes sir, so as a result of the atomic age, atomic bombs, testing, and what-not, traces of radioactive materials have fallen on the grapes that end up in the wine. And a host of other fruits and vegetables we consume, I might add. It's totally harmless."

"Well, that's good to know," Richard replied as his spine relaxed and he passed the signed document back to the officer.

"Thank you, sir," Aaron replied. "I'll let you take it from here." He walked away.

Richard walked completely around the crate, looking down on it as if it might confess its sins, while McAuley turned away to admire the Jayhawk helicopter. The Coast Guard had removed one panel of the crate to reveal the contents, but not enough to remove any bottles. Richard turned back to the mechanics' toolbox which stood nearly 5 feet tall. He grabbed the largest screwdriver he could find and pulled back another slim panel of wood, allowing him to remove a bottle.

The VDM wine bottle looked like any other bottle of wine that Richard had seen before, however, the details on the back label were sparse. While most mid-level wines would have a detailed description of the grapes, regional characteristics, spices, and resulting notes to help align its target market with its product offering, the VDM bottle simply said:

> *Each bottle of VDM, filled with the finest wine from the vineyards of Malta, is submerged in the Mediterranean Sea for up to 12 months, where pristine conditions, stable temperatures and gentle agitation evoke a truly transformative experience. The result is a wine that is smoother, more complex, and vibrantly flavorful.*

Except, Richard thought to himself, these bottles were recovered in the Pacific.

In the lower left corner of the back label was a serial number that appeared to be added after the wine label was created, and in the right corner was a QR code. Richard remembered the labels he saw on the VDM website, and these were no different. Instinctively, he held the wine in his left hand and pulled his cell phone from his jacket pocket to scan the QR code. He waited about 5 seconds before his phone returned a screen with nothing but a blank data entry field, with the three words above it:

Enter security key:

Richard believed at this point that VDM wines were probably not wines at all.

***

Malta made sense for so many reasons.

As one of the smallest countries with a winemaking industry, it could produce wine products without raising suspicion. It existed in the shadow of Sicily, but protected from the reach of Italian law enforcement. And exporting regulations in Malta were more lax than in its neighbor to the north because it joined the European Union much later and sought to compete with much larger and economically powerful partners. Malta certainly made more sense than any place in the United States, where regulators were far more aggressive in enforcing labeling requirements for domestically-produced wines.

Malta made sense also because it served as the mafia's second "home office." While the bulk of the mafia's personnel continued to operate out of Sicily, they saw Malta as a practical alternative. The tiny island nation became particularly attractive when, in 1996, the Sicilian government made good on a threat to confiscate the wine-producing land of mafia clans and distribute plots to community co-ops that would carry on the wine making tradition and related business legally.

In contrast to the Hollywood portrayal of the mafia as urban criminals, the organization actually has its roots in agriculture. Their genesis can be traced back to the 19th century, when a proto version of the Sicilian mafia began to take care of land owned by noble families, including land dedicated to the production of grapes for wine production. By the dawn of the 21st century, the mafia was actively involved in using their investments in the wine industry to conceal their money laundering activities.

In 2019, it was reported that the mafia had "taken over" the business of Fuedo Arancio, known as one of the cheapest wines in the industry, producing an $8 pinot grigio that was highly regarded by sommeliers. While the Guardia di Finanza fraud police put forth a compelling case to implicate members of the mafia, the judge ruled in favor of the deal, suggesting the case had "no basis in fact." It was immediately speculated that the judge was compromised.

Another advantage of bringing in bottles from overseas had to do with labeling. If produced in the United States, the FDA would provide oversight of the bottles and require certain formatting, information regarding ingredients, and a long list of disclosures. If imported, they could enter the U.S. to an authorized distributor, and Tanaka could collect them as they arrived in Temecula. And if the alcohol content of the product was less than 7 percent, there were no labeling requirements at all. The prerogative of what actually went on the label fell exclusively to Jack Tanaka.

***

Richard was excited to see Sarah for dinner again and to share the status of his investigation into VDM wines. He was definitely more relaxed with Sarah than Asha, and not feeling the least bit insecure that he was, in fact, ignorant about wines. Instead, he was practicing his tolerance of whiskey in the form of an Old Fashioned, while Sarah had a Cosmopolitan.

"Where is the wine now?" Sarah asked, clearly intrigued by Richard's new case.

"I dropped it at the Court of Master Sommeliers in Santa Barbara," Richard replied. "We don't have a lab that can evaluate liquids of unknown origin."

Sarah next stated the obvious. "Should they be drinking this stuff if they don't know what's inside?"

"Beats me," Richard confessed. "I assume they do some testing before tasting it."

The Court is responsible for establishing the training and examination requirements for Master Sommeliers, of which there are less than two hundred in the entire United States. Richard counted on the likelihood that the organization could assist him in securing the services of a seasoned sommelier in the LA area, other than Asha, and he was right. This was just the type of project that a sommelier would generally find to be a great challenge. "It's what we live for," was the comment made when Richard came calling.

Although the Court wouldn't be able to determine the exact provenance of the wine, they could test it to ensure it was safe to consume, and offer subjective judgment on its overall quality and probable market value. Richard advised them of the radioactivity readings, which they dismissed as a common characteristic of modern wines, particularly those manufactured in North America.

"So, is it a case of money laundering, or transportation of some illicit substances?" Sarah asked.

"Honestly," Richard replied, "I'm not sure. I've just got this feeling that there's something there."

An intelligence agent's "sixth sense" was often the trigger that moved an investigation forward even when no clear evidence was present. Richard's intuitive powers were still developing, and he recognized the potential for the investigation to eventually hit a dead end. If that were to happen, he'd have to pray for another investigation to sufficiently distract attention from him wasting agency time, energy and resources.

It was time for Richard to change the subject, and he leaned in as he did so, making direct eye contact with Sarah.

"Listen, Sarah," he started out, about to make a pitch for them to get back together. In the back of his mind Richard felt it was an opportunity to settle down with an amazing woman.

"Richard," she said, cutting him off while repositioning the napkin on her lap, "I'm not interested in anything serious."

He listened carefully to her reply, noticing there was no "right now" attached to "anything serious."

"Didn't you feel we had something, you know, a powerful connection?"

"I did," she replied. "But I'm not ready to be tied down again."

"You want to see other men?"

What Richard was missing was that Sarah carried the pain of a failed marriage, and used that experience to redefine her expectations from men generally. Above all, she wanted to put an end to the dynamic where men viewed her as an object to conquer, rather than an equal partner to respect. Sarah needed a simple way to recalibrate Richard's expectations about her current outlook. She didn't consider her position to be all that unique among women, especially those that had recently divorced.

"It's a feature, Richard, not a bug."

Richard leaned back into his chair, confused by the situation but not wanting to press his luck any further. Still, he wasn't about to let the date end prematurely. He continued to stare at Sarah, considering his next move.

"Okay, fine," he said finally, accepting the end of the debate but not quite willing to give up the fight.

"So, do you want to go to a comedy club tonight? I know a guy performing there. He goes on stage at ten thirty."

***

Every veteran intelligence agent and law enforcement officer has his or her ghosts. This was among the seldom acknowledged occupational hazards of the job. Richard wasn't alone in this regard, having survived a couple missions that challenged his physical and mental limits, so he was always on guard for any threats to his safety that might be around the next corner. In this case, he was determined to confront the threat proactively.

So, on the way to Largo at the Coronet, he debriefed Sarah on the whole matter, although he left out the part about sleeping with, and obsessing over, a petite young woman named Asha. He explained the visit to the comedy club in the context of following a delivery of possibly stolen wine from a Russian diplomat to a stand-up comic, then followed the suspect to the US Coast Guard base in San Diego. He got it backwards but was not far from being right.

Sarah had no reason to question the veracity of the story, and besides, the idea of a stand-up comic being involved in a money-laundering scheme sounded too irresistible to ignore.

"Who would've thunk it, right? A comedian?!" Richard said, as they pulled into the lot of the club.

"Never underestimate the man that overestimates himself," Sarah said dryly as they walked toward the club.

Richard purchased tickets in the theater where the performances were held, just behind the lobby and lounge areas. The club was in-between acts allowing Richard and Sarah to continue discussing the money laundering investigation. Meanwhile, Tanaka was backstage preparing for his act.

Tanaka had arrived directly from the Coast Guard base in San Diego. He despised the long commute up and down the I-5 freeway, but Sector San Diego was the only base that would come close enough to the international border for Tanaka to drop his shipments. The base in Long Beach, which was much closer to his apartment, was simply not an option. He had to remind himself of this every time he completed the 90-minute journey. That and the fact that 90 minutes on LA freeways was common even when traveling across town.

He had removed his uniform blouse in the parking lot before leaving the car. In the clothes that remained, the t shirt and blue cargo pants, he could simply say he was painting a home, or doing other chores, without giving away his role in the Coast Guard Auxiliary. The fewer details of how he spent his free time that he had to discuss, the less likely he could be caught in a lie.

In the backroom of the club, he changed into a long sleeve shirt and blue jeans. He took a quick look in the mirror to confirm most of his tattoos were hidden from view, and to push back his thick black hair with pomade. As he did, he could hear the announcement from the stage microphone. He had no time to get into character.

"Hello everyone and welcome to another great night of comedy. Next, we have a regular here at the club," the manager declared, "you all know him as Japanese Joker, we know him as Jack Tobacco. But in spite of his name, remember, no smoking in the club! And now, heeeere's Jack!"

The reception was muted, as always, as Jack galloped on the stage, approaching the microphone in the center. Richard held his phone in an inconspicuous manner, and snapped a few photos of Tanaka as soon as he stood still at the mike.

"Hey everyone, I'm sad tonight," Jack said as he took the microphone from its stand, displaying an exaggerated frown. "My Chinese friend died recently. His name was So Yung." Tanaka hung his head down, feigning grief. A few people chuckled but most were talking to each other, or ordering drinks.

Then, he picked up his head with a smile and started pacing on the stage.

"Speaking of odd Asian names," he continued, "why can't two Asians make a white baby?"

He paused to see if anyone was actually paying attention, and was satisfied to see a few people waiting on the punchline.

"Because 2 'Wongs' don't make a 'white.'"

After a few moans and chuckles from the crowd, a young man in the back yelled "you suck!"

Tanaka ignored the insult and continued, unfazed.

"Another buddy of mine from America asks a pretty Japanese girl for her phone number and she says, 'Free, sex, free, sex, to-night.' My buddy is very excited, but I had to tell him that what she means is three, six, three, six, two-nine." This has little more impact than the last couple jokes.

Tanaka had a carefully curated routine that would start with two to three one-liners, followed by a longer story, and finishing with a singular one-liner that would signal the end of his act.

As he started out on his prepared story of a Buddhist that decided to convert to Judaism, he noticed Richard sitting in the audience and recalled seeing him in Temecula with Asha. The sight of Richard rattled him, and he mustered all his powers of concentration to tell the story while suppressing the panic, not knowing if Richard posed any kind of threat. He instinctively moved the microphone from his left to right hand, and put his left hand in his pocket. But it was too late. Sarah noticed it.

"Well," Richard asked, turning to Sarah after Tanaka finished his act. "What do you think? Could he be an intelligence agent working on a case that required a visit to the Coast Guard?"

Sarah continued staring at the stage, somewhat befuddled. Then, she started to giggle.

"If you bring that idea to John," she said, "you know how he will react."

"Yeah, I know," Richard responded quickly, "he will laugh me out of the building."

"Did you notice his pinky finger was severed?" Sarah asked. "I doubt he is CIA, but he could be a gang member."

Richard was dumbfounded. He never noticed the severed finger and, even if he had, he may not have made the connection to organized crime. Sarah's raw intelligence and skill never ceased to amaze him. He found it oddly seductive.

16

David Rosen was excited to engage with the FBI, so when he heard they were seeking the counsel of a sommelier he made certain to offer his services. Growing up, Rosen would pretend to be a secret agent and interrogated all house guests that would visit his family in the bedroom community of Calabasas. But at UCLA he joined an intellectually-oriented fraternity with a wine club, obtained a degree in culinary arts, and after many years in the restaurant business, ended up as Executive Director of the Court of Master Sommeliers.

Richard recognized the call coming in from the Court on his cell phone.

"Agent O'Brien," Rosen said, "You'll never guess what's in those wine bottles."

"Okay," replied Richard. "Then I won't even try."

"It's wine."

Richard was silent as he processed the news. About half his theories about the nature of any crimes involving the bottles evaporated. Rosen continued.

"We tested everything, including the cork, and sampled several bottles. The bottles are not vintage, and neither is the wine."

Richard had one remaining theory to pitch.

"Mr. Rosen," he said, "I'm grateful to you for your assistance. Tell me, is it possible the bottles contain wine of significant value that might have been transferred from other bottles, you know, to conceal the actual contents?"

"That's unlikely," said Rosen. "The wine is rather pedestrian. It's not even twelve percent alcohol, which is considered average. Actually, the industry average is 11.6 percent, to be exact."

"Really?"

"There's more," Rosen said, "there are no particular notes in this product that would distinguish it from a commercial perspective. To provide an analogy, if this wine were a car, it would be a Ford Fusion. No disrespect to Ford owners."

At this point, Richard settled into the reality that there was nothing nefarious about the contents of the wine, and he was trying to think of any other questions worthy to ask, when Rosen spoke again.

"There was one thing that caught our attention," he said.

"What's that?"

"Well," he said, "the labels make the product appear to be legitimate, but they fail to capture all the labeling requirements for sale in the United States."

"Please, tell me more about that," said Richard, hoping for inspiration of where to go next.

"There are several required elements that need to be disclosed on a wine label, presuming the wine is produced in the U.S. You know, things like the type of wine, alcohol content, and the government health safety warning," Rosen said. "A few more elements are required for wines that are imported, or those that have artificial coloring."

"One of the required elements for wines containing either cochineal extract or carmine is that they disclose this information on the brand label," he said. "These wines contain carmine. It's a red pigment found in many wines, but it's not disclosed. So, the bottles do not meet the requirement for sale in the U.S."

"That's interesting," was all that Richard could think to say.

"There's something else," Rosen was anxious to add.

"What's that?"

"Well, there's no bar code, just a QR symbol. I don't know of any retail outlets that can determine price from a QR code. Virtually all products sold in the U.S. will have a bar code somewhere on the item."

The fact the bottles could not be legally sold in the United States was not necessarily an issue if the bottles were sold only through private transactions. This simply meant they couldn't be offered in stores without risk of exposure. But the careless handling of this aspect fed into the narrative emerging that the bottles were somehow connected to illicit activities beyond the concerns of the FDA.

Richard was processing this conclusion as Rosen continued to speak.

"Agent O'Brien, what do you want us to do with the rest of the wine?"

"We will have someone collect them, thank you. Please keep the bottles in a secure place for now."

"I'll keep them here in my office for safety," Rosen said. "Is there anything else we might assist with?"

Richard decided his next step would be to interview the captain of the boat that carried the wine. He had never been to Alaska. But then, he had an epiphany.

"Actually," he said to Rosen, "there is something that I'd like you to do for me."

***

Rosen could barely contain his excitement about working with the FBI but he knew that this was not the time to be cavalier or immature about it. He looked up the phone number for Asha Chandra in his membership database and pushed the speaker on his desktop unit to place the call. Although Richard did not request it, he recorded the call on his cell.

The phrase "Wine Court" popped on Asha's phone.

"This is Asha Chandra," she said, presuming the call was related to membership dues, which she had yet to pay.

"Asha, David Rosen, how are you?" Asha had met Rosen at a recent wine tasting event, but the Court of Master Sommeliers included several hundred members with many concentrated in Southern California, so a call from the Executive Director was indeed uncommon.

"Oh, hello, I'm good. How are you?" she replied, spinning theories simultaneously about the nature of the call. If it was the Executive Director calling then it was certainly not about paying her dues.

"All is well in the wine world," Rosen said. "Asha, I wonder if I can ask a favor. We are a bit shorthanded at the moment and we've received an interesting product that we'd like to have analyzed. Can you help us out?"

It was not uncommon for the Court to involve members in assessing wines; however, it was usually part of a structured event like a sponsored wine tasting for the general public, a feature in a magazine, or some other media-related activity. And Asha had not been a local member for that long, having relocated to the U.S. less than a year ago.

"What's the event?" Asha asked. Participating in events was a great way for sommeliers to break free from the constraints of their restaurant, and to network with colleagues. They also often paid handsome honorariums. Any member would be honored to be consulted.

"Actually," Rosen said. "This is more of a one-off. A diver brought the wine to us. He found several bottles sunk off the coast somewhere. We don't know too much about it. It has a label 'Vino Del Mar' but nobody here has heard of it."

Asha's heart fluttered. She was at a loss for words, and the line went silent for several seconds.

"Oh, I know what you're thinking," Rosen added. "It's safe. We tested it for radioactive elements and I actually sampled some of it. I'd just like a second opinion. I reached out to Jerry Kolins who works close to our office but he's overseas. You're next on the list. This could make for a fun and interesting story."

"Uh, okay," she replied. Asha would decide after the call how to deal with it.

"Great," Rosen said with a dose of authentic enthusiasm. "I'm here all week so just send me a calendar invite when you can make the time. It will be great to see you, Asha."

After the call, Rosen immediately reached out to Richard to confirm the meeting.

Asha reached out to her superior officer. She would finally get a good look at the bottles she had been pursuing since her arrival in the United States.

***

Finding the crate of wine that was intended for his customer at the Ministry of State Security would have been near impossible had Tanaka not joined the Coast Guard Auxiliary as a Culinary Associate. When he was notified by the Alaskan fishing vessel that the Coast Guard boarded the boat and confiscated the wine, he knew right away that he had a problem. Not only would he have to replace the shipment, but he would have to recover the confiscated bottles before they could be fully examined. As a Culinary Associate, he had the perfect excuse for tracking them down.

He prepared a mental script, then dialed the Public Affairs office in Kodiak from within his public storage unit in LA.

"Good afternoon," he said using his most professional tone of voice, "Jack Tanaka, Sector San Diego. I'm the Culinary Associate here." In reality, there were a half dozen Culinary Associates associated with the base, but by introducing himself as "the" CA, he counted on eking out a tiny bit more credibility.

"Yes, sir, what can I do for you," said the third-class petty officer answering the line. Tanaka was lucky, he was speaking to a young recruit that wouldn't think twice about sharing what was clearly not classified anyway.

"Yeah, well, you're not going to believe this, but somehow a shipment of wine we ordered for a change-of-command reception here ended up on your base."

"Is that so?" said the young man. "How did that happen?"

"I've no idea, we were told about it by your CO. Look, we will just go and get this wine from somewhere else. Our incoming CO has a particular vintage in mind, I just want to know what you plan to do with our wine up there, so I can report back to the galley here and we can account for it. You know, the Coast Guard drowns itself in paperwork, no pun intended."

"Sure," said the petty officer, mustering a chuckle out of respect for the weak attempt at humor. "Hold on."

Tanaka waited a few minutes, hoping the ruse would go undetected. Then, he got the answer he wanted.

"Hi, thanks for waiting," said the petty officer, "we've already shipped it out to something called 'The Court of Sommeliers' in Los Angeles. Does that make sense?"

Tanaka wrote down the name. He was not familiar with the organization.

"Oh yeah, perfect, thank you. We will get in touch with them."

"No problem, sir. You have a good rest of your day."

Tanaka took a deep breath, then looked to his left where he had a shelf containing a wide range of materials to build an improvised explosive device, commonly referred to as an IED. It was time to put that chemistry degree to use.

***

"Hello Asha."

Richard was waiting for Asha in the lobby at the Court of Sommeliers.

"Richard, what are you doing here?" she said, her eyes bursting to their full potential.

"Well, you know," he said, looking directly into her eyes for any signals she may give off, "we are still investigating the possible money laundering operations involving rare wines."

"Oh right," she replied nervously, "how is that going?" Asha's eyes started to dart about in case there were more surprises in store for her, like uniformed policemen holding a pair of handcuffs. At that moment, David Rosen entered the lobby.

"Asha," he said, loud enough to fill the space of the cavernous lobby, "good to see you. Thanks so much for coming." Rosen noticed her positioned opposite Richard and so he added, "I see you've met Agent O'Brien."

The space between Asha and Richard was filled with so much tension at this moment that it would be impossible not to notice. Rosen did, but he had no knowledge of how deep the relationship was between Richard and Asha. He merely assumed Asha was involved in something potentially nefarious, but did not go so far as to assume she was even aware of it.

"Please," Rosen said, his arms outstretched in the direction of his guests, "let's go to my office. I have the wine set-up in there."

Richard took one last look in the direction of Asha to see if her demeanor would give off any clues about her culpability in the as-yet-to-be confirmed money laundering operation. She avoided eye contact with him, but he realized it could have as much to do with their failed romance as any illicit activities. He reminded himself it wasn't a crime to dump your boyfriend.

Richard and Asha walked behind Rosen and into his office, which was behind the front desk in the lobby. It was an impressive room with mahogany paneling, a plush sofa, guest chairs and a large L-shaped oak desk. In a corner of the room was a round cocktail table that rose to above the waist, and on top was a bottle of VDM wine, along with several long-stemmed wine goblets.

"Here we are," Rosen said, directing them to the table. "Asha, as I said on the phone, we'd like your opinion of this product that was collected by some divers off the coast. Agent O'Brien here suspects the wine may be of a rare vintage and valued by collectors." Asha gently nodded.

Asha knew that her only objective in visiting the Court was to photograph the back label of the wine. But even if she had the presence of mind to do so, explaining her actions in front of Richard would potentially have consequences. The three took positions around the small table, staring at the bottle. Rosen reached for it.

"May I?" Rosen said, looking directly at Asha. The bottle had been opened just prior to their meeting to allow it to aerate.

"Yes, of course," she replied, "I'm excited to see what you have here." Her monotone voice communicated otherwise.

Rosen slowly poured the wine into a glass and handed it to Asha.

"Agent O'Brien?" he said, pointing the bottle in his direction.

"No, thank you," Richard replied, staring all the while at Asha as she took a small sip and began swirling it in her mouth. She followed this with a large draw from the glass, turned it up, and nearly emptied it.

Both men looked at her, waiting for the verdict. She had her eyes closed as she considered the product. After a few moments, she spoke.

"Well," she said "it reminds me of Fontanafredda Barolo 2018 from the Piedmont region of Italy. I taste red cherry with a hint of leather and tobacco. However, I think it's a bit light on the alcohol content."

"That's really interesting," replied Rosen, who was thinking of a different comparable product, but preferred Asha's assessment.

"So, it's an expensive wine?" asked Richard.

"It's drinkable," she said. "But it's not great. You can get a bottle of the Barolo for about $35 on wine.com. And in Italy it would be much less than that." Then, she saw an opening.

"But," she said, "do you mind if I take a pic of the label, you know, for my files?" Asha snapped a picture of the label with her phone. Unfortunately, she completed only half the job.

Richard was awarded another opportunity to dispense with a theory driving his investigation. The wine bottled by VDM did not conceal anything of significant value. So, it was unlikely to support a money laundering operation because the contents were not in demand, as was the case for high profile art or race horses, unless the perpetrator tried to sell the products back to themselves. The Mexican cartel attempted to do this with their own race horses, but it did not work out well for them.

Authorities soon pounced on the operation, shut it down, and made several arrests.

"All right," said Rosen, interrupting the thoughts of his two guests. "I suppose we are in agreement that the wine is not likely some rare vintage, and it's not colored water either. But it was a fun little project while it lasted. Agent O'Brien, do you have any other questions?"

Richard continued staring in Asha's direction as Rosen announced the performance was over. She continued to look in the other direction.

"Agent O'Brien?" Rosen repeated. Richard snapped out of his momentary trance.

"Yes, thank you Mr. Rosen. Ms. Chandra, may I walk you out to your car?"

Asha was without a sensible objection. And even though she wasn't walking out with one of the bottles, she had the picture, which was just as important.

Just before leaving the office, Richard had the presence of mind to make one more request of Rosen. He turned back to face him.

"Oh say, do you mind if I take one of those bottles with me?"

"Of course, they belong to you," replied Rosen. "What should I do with the rest of it?"

"Please hold on to the bottles and I'll have someone from the agency collect them."

Asha and Richard walked silently into the parking lot, Asha walking one step ahead. Richard was like a coiled spring at this point, trying his best to avoid a full-scale verbal assault on Asha, in spite of the feelings of anger and resentment that he had pent up inside him. He decided to try the magnanimous approach. The only problem was that the distance between them was increasing.

"Asha," he said, "wait up."

She slowed down and turned toward him, then briefly looked up at the sky, as if it might provide an exit strategy.

"So, how have you been?" he said.

"Fine, and you?" She crossed her arms as if impatient, then quickly released them. She did her best to muster an inauthentic smile.

"Look," Richard said, doing his best to avoid the perception of an interrogation, "I'd like to ask you a few questions about a person-of-interest in our investigation."

"Do we have to do this here?" she replied. Any delay in the conversation would give her more time to craft a believable story. Richard could see he had no choice but to accommodate Asha's request. He would have to wait a bit longer for answers.

The "old" Richard would have used the opportunity to suggest a romantic dinner. But given that he was now trying to rekindle a romance with Sarah, he thought otherwise.

"Sure," he said. "What works for you?"

Asha definitely did not want the stress of meeting at the FBI building, and she also didn't want to send the wrong signals to Richard by suggesting they talk over a meal. As it turns out, she didn't have to offer either, as her cell phone began to ring.

"Excuse me," she said, reaching into her purse. "Yes, hello?"

Richard stood there like a child waiting for permission to go play.

"Oh, thank you, okay, I'm coming," she said. She then put the phone back in her purse.

"Everything okay?" Richard asked.

"Yes, I guess I was supposed to sign something in the office for David. I'll message you some options to meet later today."

And with that, Asha turned back and began walking briskly toward the building, not revealing the fact that the call was a recorded reminder from her dentist about an upcoming appointment.

As Richard watched Asha walk back toward the building, Asha noticed Tanaka's car leaving the building at the opposite end of the lot. She walked quickly back toward the building, hoping to discover his purpose in being there.

She would regret that decision moments later.

17

When the bomb went off in the corner of Rosen's office, he was at his desk responding to the many emails he had received throughout the day. Shattered glass from wine bottles became lethal projectiles, destroying everything in their path. Fire quickly consumed many cardboard boxes stacked to the ceiling, filled with varieties of wine. Whatever wine bottles did not burst were burned beyond recognition. A cloud of thick, black, acrid smoke rose from the cratered structure, and could be seen for blocks.

At an elementary school nearby, the bomb caused windows in the classrooms to buckle and, convinced the effect was from an earthquake, children instinctively hid under their desks. Within moments, traffic helicopters abandoned their surveillance of the freeways to get footage of the structure fire for the 24-hour news cycle's next local broadcast.

The bombing created a blaze that kept the LA Fire Department busy for nearly six hours. The news reports immediately suspected arson based on the obvious clues left behind, including evidence of an IED, and the presence of incendiary chemicals.

Rosen died almost instantly from the blast in a gruesome scene: whatever parts of his body were not charred from the fire; shards of glass shredded the rest. The few other employees that were in the building at the time: a receptionist, bookkeeper, and membership manager, were all hospitalized with second degree burns. Fortunately for them, they were nowhere near the wine bottles that were stored, or the bottle containing the bomb, and were evacuated before the structure began to crater.

Tanaka anguished over the fact that his wines did not reach their intended destination, but eventually concluded that trying to recover them without getting caught would have been too dangerous. So, he decided the safest thing to do was to destroy all the bottles, which would have served as evidence of his operation, and start over.

Tanaka had no intention of adding to the body count associated with his activities, but he was about as effective a bombmaker as he was a comedian. He built an IED with easily sourced chemicals from a swimming pool supply store, cutting into a wine bottle around its midsection and sliding it inside. Separately, a timer in another bottle would determine when the blast would occur. He had intended that time to be 2200 when the building was expected to be vacant, and did not realize that instead he had set it for 2:00 pm in the afternoon. He added a card to the case to indicate the wine was a gift to be delivered directly to the Executive Director.

The case was resting on the edge of Rosen's L-shaped desk, waiting for him to open it. It was not at all uncommon for him to receive bottles and cases as gifts or promotions, and part of his daily ritual was to open one of these bottles at the end of his day to enjoy something new.

Richard was sitting in traffic on the I-405 interstate when he saw the black cloud rising above the low-lying buildings to the east, just a few miles away. He turned on KCRW to see if the incident was being covered by local public radio. He caught the story already in progress.

"….believed to be from pool sanitizer, which contains hydrogen peroxide, the necessary chemical to make an explosive known as triacetone triperoxide," said the reporter. "We've learned this explosive compound goes by another name among amateurs: Mother of Satan, because it's so dangerous to handle. It was used in another high-profile bombing in 2017, in London, killing 29 commuters in the subway system. We don't yet have a motive for the bombing, but we know the building is the site of the Court of Master Wine Sommeliers, an organization that trains and certifies individuals in the wine industry."

Richard felt his heart racing. This had to be related to his investigation, and he felt a sense of redemption that he was already so close to confirming "there was something there, there." Then, his excitement turned to horror.

"The Executive Director of the organization, David Rosen, was in his office when the blast occurred, and is presumed dead. Five more have been taken to UCLA Medical Center. We don't have information on the extent of their injuries but will be covering this story as we get more details."

Richard had been speaking to Rosen just twenty minutes before, now he was dead. Had Richard set the appointment with him and Asha later in the day, he'd also be dead, and perhaps he was actually the target. This was Richard's first thought, then his thoughts turned to Rosen. Instead of taking the rest of the afternoon off, he changed freeways and headed to the FBI Building, and was immediately summoned to Swanson's office.

"Shut the door, O'Brien," Swanson said. Richard was accustomed to Swanson's talent for drama, and his penchant for acting like he had information, or even merely a perspective, that nobody else was privy to.

"So let me get this straight," he said, as Richard took a seat opposite him in his office, "you made an appointment to see Rosen this afternoon, just before the blast?" Swanson was already sifting through status reports on the fire in anticipation of his office joining the local police on the investigation.

"That's right," replied Richard, sitting erect and still quite amped up over the unfolding drama. While he felt awful that Rosen was a casualty, his focus was on persuading the agency to get behind him and offer more resources to the investigation.

"And you were there to have him sample this wine collected by the Coast Guard Base in Kodiak?"

"That's correct," Richard left out the fact that he had another civilian involved in the visit.

"Do you have any reason to believe that you were the target?" Swanson asked next, his eyebrows coming closer together and his gaze sharpening on Richard's face.

"No sir, I do not." That wasn't entirely true.

"But Rosen was not a person-of-interest, correct?"

A "person-of interest" in law enforcement jargon is the label given to a person before there is enough evidence to make them a suspect in a criminal investigation.

"No sir."

"Was there anybody else with you on this visit," Swanson asked.

Richard did not like where this line of questioning was going. Without a partner to corroborate his story, he was vulnerable. Agents were expected to partner whenever practical. Also, it forced him to reveal Asha's involvement in the visit.

"Sir, I asked a respected wine buyer to attend the meeting, just to get a second opinion, but I was also attempting to gather intelligence from her for the investigation."

When Swanson heard "her" he immediately saw Richard in a different light. A bias he had nearly abandoned in the years since Richard started dating Sarah Goodman, a fellow agent that Swanson had also been dating, had returned full force. Richard was a womanizer in his view, the man that "stole" Sarah from him.

"Is this woman Asha Chandra?" Swanson demanded.

"Yeah," Richard replied, surprised by Swanson being so well informed. "How did you…"

"Ms. Chandra was one of the casualties taken to UCLA Medical Center. According to the reports we received, she suffered only minor injuries. She'll be fine."

Richard looked back at Swanson in stunned silence.

Swanson's eyes narrowed further as he knew he had Richard trapped. And while Richard initially felt the bombing confirmed his suspicions around the wine being at the center of a money laundering operation, he now considered for the first time that Rosen's murder, and Asha's injuries, were potentially his fault.

"O'Brien, you've really fucked up this time," Swanson said, leaning back in his chair. "What were you thinking?"

"Sir," Richard replied, "I'm not sure where you are going with this." But he did. And he knew he was in trouble. Swanson's anger was palpable.

"O'Brien," he snapped back, "I'm suspending you from the agency pending an internal investigation. Leave your badge at the front desk and deliver your firearm to the locker."

"Sir?"

"It's clear to me O'Brien that you've taken unnecessary risks, risks that may have led to the death of a civilian and significant collateral damage in the community," Swanson said sternly, "we will conduct an internal investigation to determine your role in precipitating the incident. You will wait out the results of the investigation - outside this building."

Richard sat with a look of disbelief on his face. He was frozen still. And so, Swanson spoke again.

"You are dismissed, Mr. O'Brien," intentionally leaving the term "agent" out of his demand.

"Get out of my office."

***

Richard walked out of the FBI building a defeated man. Although his colleagues were not yet aware of his suspension, he avoided eye contact with anyone and headed straight for his car. He sat for a moment behind the wheel, his head facing down, running the whole scene from the day through his mind. Then, he pulled out of the lot and drove back to the building where the Court of Sommeliers once stood.

On arriving, the scene was still chaotic, but the fire was extinguished. Thin and narrow wisps of smoke rose up from various parts of the structure where embers continued to burn. A row of five red fire engines were parked, bumper to bumper, directly opposite what was the front entrance to the building. Men in oversized fire-retardant uniforms walked back and forth in front of the scene, pulling hoses with them. Police cars were scattered around the scene, their red and blue lights flashing. One of them was pulling a long yellow tape along the perimeter of the blast scene which included most of the building's parking lot. A few local news outlets had vans parked nearby, and journalists were filming footage for an upcoming broadcast.

Richard had to park across the street to stay clear of all the activity at the scene. He still had his FBI badge which he neglected to turn in. As he walked across the street toward the scene, an ice cream truck slowly passed in front of him, playing its whimsical music. The irony was not lost on Richard, who had to navigate behind the truck in order to reach the lot.

Richard was not entirely sure why he was there, but he would have to act quickly in the event other agents were dispatched to the scene. At some point the jurisdiction of the various law enforcement agencies would have to be decided with regard to any ongoing investigation into the fire, to determine if it was arson, an accident, a terrorist attack, or something else. But Swanson already seemed convinced that the FBI would be involved.

As he approached the taped off perimeter of the scene, a uniformed officer left a small group of police men and women, and approached Richard to cut him off.

"Afternoon," Richard said in a nonchalant manner, while pulling his badge from his inside coat pocket. "Quite a mess you have here."

"Yes Sir," said the young officer. "Please be careful and watch your step."

"Copy that," Richard replied, as the officer spun back around and headed to rejoin his comrades.

Richard walked slowly through the wreckage. He pulled a handkerchief from his coat and put it over his mouth to guard against inhaling too much of the smoke that continued to envelop the area. He stepped over glass, fallen ceiling tiles, wooden beams, and overturned furniture as he walked deeper into the infrastructure. He stopped when he got to the point where Rosen's office would have been. Rosen's body had already been collected by an ambulance, along with others that were injured, and transported to LA General Medical Center for identification.

Richard surveyed the ground, looking for fragments of the wine bottles that he had sampled earlier in the day. Some of the glass had melted into unrecognizable shapes due to the intensity of the fire. But there, on the floor at his feet, was a curved piece of glass that had remnants of a wine label still attached to it, tenuously hanging off the side. Richard looked back at the firefighters. None of them were monitoring his movements. He took the handkerchief and used it to pick up the shard of glass. He wrapped it up in the cloth, and shoved it in his suitcoat pocket.

Then, he drove to UCLA Medical Center.

18

Nick Sabian had arrived on time, but she always kept him waiting. He was due in at noon, and now it was ten past. It rankled him every time. His slightly over-caffeinated mind wandered so as to ignore the wall clock above his boss's secretary, who sat working at his desk and ignoring Sabian with great skill.

The interior of the headquarters of MI6 - officially known as the Secret Intelligence Service (SIS) - at 85 Albert Embankment in Vauxhall, London, was as dissimilar to the cliched version of it found in films as the life of an SIS officer like Sabian was from the lives of certain well known so-called "secret agents."

The term always made Sabian smile, likely because it connoted a glossy, sexy version of his office as foisted by film makers and fiction book writers on the public, which was seemingly addicted to anything in the genre.

He didn't smile now. To distract himself from himself, Sabian dwelt for a moment on the banality of the interior in which he now waited to be seen by Audrey Delaroche – his superior at Six, as this branch of SIS was known colloquially by certain media, film makers, and some of its 'inmates,' as Sabian claimed himself to be.

There was little to differentiate the place he was in from any number of functional urban interiors across London and the world. The only difference was that to be in here, your security clearance had to be very far beyond watertight. This exclusivity wasn't visible in what Sabian saw with eyes that had seen too much for his still tender years (*is 37 even old?*, he mused), as he glanced around to ignore the old-fashioned wall clock ticking on another minute beyond his agreed meeting time with the formidable Delaroche.

What of his fellow workers? How did they feel about the "privilege" of being allowed in here, where prying eyes are so very unwelcome, and so few belonged?

He watched an admin junior come and speak to Delaroche's secretary, who glanced at his watch, then at Sabian, as he responded. In that microsecond, Sabian chose to return the secretary's glance with bullet hole eyes that said, *Yes. I'm pissed off. I don't like to be kept waiting. But we all know this is a power game, and we all have to play.*

The quality of Sabian's glance made the secretary look away quickly. The secretary was used to being safe in this fortress of banality. This eye-contact was something the secretary did not wish to be involved with. It frightened him. Sabian frightened him. That was as it should be.

215

A green light flicked over the door behind the secretary's desk. Sabian was already moving by the time the secretary moved his mouth slightly as a way of inviting Sabian to go through that door into Delaroche's minimally decorated office. Moments later, Sabian was standing in front of Delaroche's busy but ordered desk. She always made him stand there for a moment, but that day seemed different.

"Sit down, Nick," she said without looking up.

The use of his first name was new. Somehow, too, was the texture of her voice – a voice honed by private education and a finishing school somewhere in the Alps. Sabian sat. Delaroche finished writing something on her profoundly encrypted Mac.

"What do you know about 'Mother of Satan'?" she asked, eyes still down.

"She's a real bitch, ma'am."

His quip made her look at him. The subtext - that she was a bitch, too - made her hold his eyes. He immediately regretted saying it. They both knew he had huge admiration for her.

"Triacetone triperoxide," said Sabian levelly, his eyes softening slightly to apologize tacitly for the "bitch" comment.

"I'm sorry to have kept you waiting, Officer. How's that?" she said.

'Officer.' That's more like it, he said to himself. Back to business.

"That's more than I deserve," Sabian found himself saying. He didn't like it when his subconscious stole a march on his conscious mind, as it just had. He prided himself on his self-regard, but took pains to remain humble, as he was brought up by humble parents.

"Triacetone triperoxide," Sabina continued, "the stuff killed what, twenty-nine people on the Tube back in twenty-seventeen didn't it?"

"It's nice to know I'm not the only one who reads the Evening Standard," Delaroche replied. Her tired eyes flickered with the memory of humor as she said this. Now they were all square.

"Well first reports suggest that the stuff has just been used to blow up the Court of Master Wine Sommeliers in LA," Delaroche continued, suddenly devoid of emotion.

"Someone didn't like their Pinot Grigio?"

"You know the saying," she replied, "when America sneezes, the whole world catches a cold." Sadly, despite the best efforts of the US government, this is still the case. A case of wine, actually.

"Forgive me for asking ma'am," Sabian interjected, "but what does this have to do with us?"

It was a fair question and the reason why she trusted the situation to Sabian, who would let little stand in his way for king and country.

"We lost contact with one of our agents who was investigating a case of money laundering in the wine industry," Delaroche said. "I believe you know Asha Chandra."

"That's correct." Sabian remembered Asha favorably. She was a sharp operator, and in many other ways, unforgettable. "Ma'am?"

Sabian was still processing all the information. The operation would have obviously been under tight wraps if a British agent was sent to work undercover on American soil. Such situations could produce an unwelcome response from the Director of the CIA, if discovered.

"Chandra was admitted to the Burn Unit at UCLA Medical Center," Delaroche said. "We frankly aren't one hundred percent sure that she hasn't switched sides. Go there. See what she knows. Extract her from the operation. Pick up the pieces and report back to me; you know the drill."

"Understood," Sabian said, pivoting instantly from curious to committed. "What more can you tell me about what she was working on?"

Delaroche let out a sigh, then pushed her wheelchair back from her desk slightly to deal with him straight-on – the way that she dealt with, Sabian sensed, life in general. God knows how she dealt with Multiple Sclerosis like that, or with the future it mandated. For now, Sabian found himself moved to observe, her fire burned bright and defiant. He couldn't imagine such courage.

"Our intel suggests the Japanese yakuza and Italian mafia have partnered to penetrate the intelligence apparatus of the US and UK, and to sell protected information off to the counterintelligence agencies of rogue nations," she said, as she turned away briefly to gaze outside the window behind her desk. "We may have lost an agent or two as a result, you may recall Geoffrey Moore was found dead on the banks of the Thames earlier this month."

If Sabian looked at all comfortable to this point, that moment had passed. He understood that, to Delaroche, all covert agents were her children.

"We aren't clear on how the wine business is related," she continued, "that is what Chandra was working on. She studied for the role."

"So we are, for now, *not* working with the Americans?"

Sabian was troubled by the implied challenge that was being revealed at that moment. Delaroche was aware. She was priming one of her best weapons: Nick Sabian. She secretly favored doing this, but it worried her. It worried her what Nick Sabian was capable of doing when there was nowhere left to run. And there were already multiple foreign governments and agencies that would like to dispense with him altogether.

"Officer, in so many ways the Atlantic no longer exists," she replied in a measured tone. "But for now, we will pretend that it does, and make ourselves scarce once on the other side."

Sabian understood the pretext.

"Ma'am. I have no desire to reinvent the Atlantic."

"That's good to hear. How is your daughter?"

That caught Sabian off-guard. The fortress of his face threatened to crumble.

"While you're gone, she will have the full protection and safeguard of the Ministry."

All he could do was nod his gratitude. A moment of strangely pleasant silence followed, and was ended by her.

"That will be all, Sabian, keep me up to speed," she said, curt and mechanical again. She twisted her wheelchair back again to work on her Mac. He stood.

"Speed it is, ma'am. Good day."

As Sabian exited, his feet silent on her plush, burgundy colored carpet, she managed a smile. He closed the door behind him.

"And the warrior whispered back, I am the storm," she said to herself.

And work owned her again.

***

Due to burn victims from local wildfires, Los Angeles Medical Center was at capacity. And so, instead of being taken to a facility that struggled to provide quality care for the indigent, Asha was taken to the comparatively more comfortable UCLA Health Regional Burn Center. She was sitting up in her bed when Richard arrived. Richard was carrying a bouquet of flowers as he walked in.

"I am so sorry you got messed up in this," Richard said as he set the flowers down and reached across the bed to give her an awkward hug. The guilt was written on his face in the form of palpable grief. "How are you doing?"

"I'm okay," Asha replied, "I didn't get close enough to the building to be seriously injured."

Richard stepped back to survey Asha's overall condition. She had some bandages applied to the arm and leg where the blast blew her backwards on the pavement, causing friction burns and abrasions. There weren't any burn injuries from the flames that he could see and she was probably transported to the Burn Center along with other patients that weren't as fortunate.

"Listen, Asha," Richard started out, not certain how he would finish.

"Richard, it's okay," Asha interrupted. Richard was grateful for that.

"Well, when do you get out?" he asked.

"They haven't told me anything," she replied. "But really, I'm not in bad shape in spite of appearances."

Richard understood that, out of an abundance of caution, the hospital might want to keep Asha for observation. He also realized she was a sitting duck for any further investigation into the conditions that brought her to the Court in the first place.

"How is the investigation going?" Asha asked, effectively changing the subject. "Richard, I think Sisky is responsible for this," she added before he could answer, pointing with her head toward the bandages on her arm. It was a carefully crafted statement to see what he knew.

"No," Richard replied. "We are tracking how this wine is dumped and recovered. We think it's the basis of a money laundering scheme. Sisky may be involved but he's not calling the shots."

Richard never considered Asha's statement to be a reach.

"We think he's a pawn in this operation," he added. "We've tracked huge sums of money traveling through his bank accounts. But he's not driving the scheme. He's merely a customer."

Asha sat motionless in her bed, staring away from Richard.

"Asha…" he started out once more.

"Richard, look," she interrupted again. "I have a confession to make."

For the first time, Richard felt an ounce of pressure relieved from his shoulders, which allowed him to relax them an iota. He stood up straight and waited for the punchline. Asha looked straight into his eyes as she delivered it.

"I'm gay."

"You're….okay," Richard replied, his lips pursed upwards along with his right eyebrow, as if he questioned the voracity of the statement, even though it perfectly completed the narrative he was building up to that point.

"But then…how…" he added.

"Honestly," she said, "I've been in therapy because I was raped as a teen, and I've tried to have relationships with men, but it's just not working."

Richard felt he was just handed a "get out of jail free card." While he was attracted to Asha, he was very much committed to making things work between him and Sarah. Asha was making everything easy for him.

"Oh," was all Richard could offer, followed by, "I'm so sorry."

"So, I don't want you to feel badly about any of this," she added. "I'll be fine. I'll probably be discharged tomorrow."

Richard had no doubts about Asha's assurances. She exuded the kind of understated confidence you might only find in an undercover agent working for a legendary agency.

The two former lovers continued small talk a few more minutes before Richard felt he had satisfied his obligation, and that Asha had no further expectation.

"What are you going to do next, with the investigation?" Asha asked, ever the agent in search of clues.

"I'm not sure," Richard replied. "I've been suspended pending an investigation into the blast, but that won't stop me from poking around."

"Well good luck, Richard," Asha replied, nodding slightly as if to signal the end of the meeting.

"Just let me know if you need anything, anything at all," Richard replied as he leaned over again to awkwardly hug her shoulders. Then he walked out, leaving the flowers where he set them.

Asha waited until Richard was no longer visible in the corridor. Then she reached for her cell phone to message Delaroche:

The Americans are clueless

Richard was about to walk out the glass doors of the hospital when he stopped as if he ran right into them. He looked back at the elevators that had just delivered him from Asha's floor.

Did I just get played? he thought to himself. He stood a few feet from the entrance doors and as people filed past him in both directions, he replayed in his mind the prior fifteen minutes. He was trained at the Academy in the classic technique to gather intelligence from an unsuspecting individual; it was called "Elicitation." And he may have fallen for it.

In the technique, the agent makes a bold statement, the elicitation, to coax the subject into a topic. By making a statement rather than asking a question, the target lets down his or her guard and is more likely to offer information of value. When followed by an expression of disbelief, the target goes even deeper into sharing intelligence they would otherwise protect. Asha had just masterfully played the role of a veteran agent.

Was Asha, in fact, CIA? Richard thought to himself. *Did I divulge too much to her in the course of their relationship?*

He scratched the hair on the back of his neck as he considered the preposterous notion, then walked briskly out of the hospital. He had enough on his mind already.

19

Lt John Underwood was reviewing his "assigned to duty" crew for the coming week, sitting at the bridge of the USCGC *Arowana*. He recognized most of the names and considered these men to be some of the best he's ever had the privilege to serve and lead. Underwood was a third generation Coast Guard officer. His father served previously and his grandfather before that. Underwood stood tall and firm in his uniform, with short, cropped black hair and deep blue eyes. He was handsome enough to earn a role in any Hollywood film that demanded a commanding presence.

Underwood's orders weren't different from any of the other cutters monitoring the marine environment off the coast of Southern California. At that time, the priorities of the Coast Guard shifted from "search and rescue" operations to "migrant interdiction." An increase in migrants attempting to reach the United States from Central America resulted in the Coast Guard detaining and seizing two to three boats every single day. Boats successful in avoiding detection often capsized off the US coast, leading many missions to result in search and rescue operations anyway.

Among the active-duty personnel on Underwood's roster was Jack Tanaka, an Auxiliarist. Underwood recognized Tanaka as a fairly new Culinary Associate that had joined him on the *Arowana* two weeks prior. The rotation of Culinary Associates often depended on the availability of Auxiliarists that had completed the rigorous training in the galley. It was one of the ongoing challenges of the Coast Guard to supply these personnel to dockside ships and those going underway.

He also saw an email coming across from Angelo Spinola expressing concern about Tanaka's background. One email addressed the theory that Tanaka might have been involved in a gang, which wouldn't outright make him ineligible to serve in the Auxiliary so long as he had no prior criminal record. Underwood wasn't inclined to ask questions when he had capable resources to accomplish his missions.

"Good afternoon, Sir," came a voice from just outside the glass enclosure for the bridge. It was Tanaka.

"Mr. Tanaka," Underwood replied, applying his signature stoneface to dispel any theories about what he may have been thinking about at that moment. "What's up."

"Sir, I just wanted to let you know I'm ready to onboard provisions, and we have an extra crate of dry goods to replenish depleted supplies, more than we need for now."

"Do you have space for it in the galley?" Underwood asked while continuing to examine his orders for anything new.

"I'm not sure, Sir, I don't think so," Tanaka replied.

"All right, just put it astern for now," Underwood replied. He made a mental note to have the crate inspected before going underway, thinking that if Tanaka was a member of a gang, it could contain contraband. What he failed to realize was that Tanaka stored the crate of wine *in* the galley, and put an actual crate of dry goods at the stern of the boat.

"Yes, sir, thank you sir," Tanaka replied. And he was gone.

The *Arowana* would be leaving the docks of Sector San Diego later that afternoon, carrying a crate of wine to replace those bottles confiscated off the coast of Alaska.

***

Richard sat in his living room staring at a blank TV screen. A bottle of whisky rested on the coffee table in front of him next to a glass, clouded by fingerprints, containing one remaining sip. His blinds were closed and the room was relatively dark, even though it was midafternoon and the sun was pushing parallel lines of light across the opposite walls of his apartment. He was wearing jogging pants and a faded Michigan sweatshirt. Ironically, the shirt said in bold yellow font, "Whose got it better than us?"

He had been suspended the day prior from his dream job by a man determined to see him fail. He may have unwittingly caused the death of an innocent civilian, while injuring several others.

His perspective since the meeting with Swanson swung 180 degrees from that of a star agent to a careless, self-centered amateur. He tried to push thoughts of despair from his mind but they kept creeping their way back in. Finally, he leaned forward, shook his head, and got up to pee.

His phone, also on the table, recorded missed calls from McAuley, Sarah Goodman, his mother, and his brother Myles. It started to vibrate yet again, and Richard persuaded himself to answer it as he walked back to the sofa, and plopped down on it with a heavy thud.

"Myles?" he said after seeing his brother's name appear on the phone.

"Hi bro," Myles replied, "How are you doing?"

"I'm okay," he said, not quite ready to discuss his employment situation. "How are you buddy?"

"I'm good," Myles replied, adding, "Happy birthday brother!" while doing his best to convey his enthusiasm over the phone.

"Shit," Richard said, "I forgot." Now all the missed calls on his phone made sense.

"You forgot your birthday? How does somebody do that?"

"It's a long story."

"Well, what are you doing to celebrate?" Myles said.

"Well, I might start by looking for a new job," Richard replied.

There were not many people Richard could confide in, but Myles was one of the few in his orbit that would be sympathetic without judging him. So, Richard gave him the full backstory. As a software engineer working at the UC San Diego Computer Science and Engineering Department, Myles was programmed to look at all challenges objectively, without bias, and to tackle problems as if there was a hidden mathematical basis to them.

"That sucks," he said. "So, all the wine got destroyed?"

"Yeah," Richard replied, recognizing that the evidence needed to prove his case was now being bulldozed into a pile of refuse by the heavy equipment brought in after the structure fire. Then, he remembered.

"Oh wait," he spurted out, "I have a bottle. Hang on." The two continued talking about the case as Richard walked outside to his car to collect the bottle from his trunk.

Richard and Myles didn't share much as siblings, but Richard saw his little brother as the antithesis of himself. While Richard grew up as the charismatic, risk-taking and adventurous member of the family, Myles was secure in his place as the young man who didn't have anything to prove. Richard respected this about his little brother and, now that both were grown men, he felt Myles could be a useful confidant as he worked through the fact that he was in deep trouble with the agency. Also, Myles had some experience in the field of cybersecurity, so he likely had legitimate advice to offer.

"So, I have the bottle in my hand," Richard said, spinning it to the back label, "and the back of the bottle has this QR code," he added.

"You know you can reverse engineer a QR code to find the URL it points to, right?" Myles asked.

Richard was dumbfounded. He wished he had consulted Myles earlier. Perhaps the visit to the Court of Sommeliers was completely unnecessary.

"How do I do that?" he asked. He brought the bottle closer to his face, peering at the back label.

"Send me a picture of it," Myles said. "Make sure you get the QR code as flat as possible. Let me see what I can find out."

Richard fell back into the sofa again after his call with Myles. He had not even considered the fact he was sharing sensitive information with someone not vetted by the agency, and without a security clearance. He could have endangered his brother by getting him involved. But none of that mattered to him in that instant.

Richard stood up abruptly, the wine bottle still in his hands. He moved to the kitchen counter and placed it there, in the corner, where it was relatively safe. He then grabbed his car keys and headed back outside.

The first thing he needed to do was to buy a burner phone.

***

Jeff McAuley met Richard at a Mexican restaurant in downtown LA later that afternoon. Richard had been carrying the bottle of wine around with him all day, and it now stood between them on the table.

"I'm going to find whoever did this," Richard said, looking at the bottle, as if it might reveal its secrets by harsh words. In his left hand he held a letter from the FBI's Human Resources Department.

"So, if it's not precious," McAuley said, "what is it?"

"I think it's all about the label," Richard said. McAuley reached for the bottle and brought it closer to him, at eye level.

"Dude we are in the haystack," he said, examining the front label. "And by the way, do they know you have this?" McAuley asked. Richard ignored the question.

"It was bottled in Malta," McAuley continued as he spun the bottle around to look at the back. "Where the fuck is Malta anyway?"

Richard dismissed McAuley's weak attempt at humor. He re-opened the letter which he had read silently several times ever since it was delivered to him that morning. Now, he read it aloud for McAuley.

"Effective immediately," he said, looking at the letter once again, "you will be suspended pending the outcome of an internal investigation. You will continue to be paid at your current rate and have access to medical and dental benefits. You will not be allowed access to any FBI field offices until subpoenaed by Internal Affairs." He folded the letter again, tightened his grip on it, and let his arm fall to the side.

"That sucks," McAuley said, breaking the silence, "what are you going to do?"

Richard looked down, deep in thought. He didn't have a reasonable explanation for the risks he took, because he was oblivious to them. He had lost credibility in the eyes of Swanson, and probably other people, including Jeff and Sarah. His future with the agency was uncertain. All he could do at this point was to significantly raise the stakes, and hope for a bigger payout.

He lifted his head and began to nod gently.

233

"I'm being offered a paid vacation," he said, finally. "Fuck it, I'm going to Malta."

20

A break in a case - as complex as the one in which multiple agents get unmasked and murdered – could take years. And many times, the clues could be literally screaming for attention but the relevant agencies are either under-resourced, distracted, engaged in political infighting, or they dismiss the intelligence as irrelevant or untrustworthy. So, when Katrina Evtushenko first approached the local police department to share her story, it was sent to U.S. Immigration for further investigation, and added to a pile.

Several weeks later, she confided in a neighbor who encouraged her to approach the FBI. It was a terrifying prospect for her, but the increase in stress combined with loss of sleep drove her to it. Ernest Houseman, the Officer in Charge in FBI's Pittsburgh Office, met with Katrina in the same room in which suspects would be interrogated. She was unflappable in answering questions about her involvement in the scheme. She gambled that cooperation was the best path to remaining in the United States, at least in the near term.

Sicily's underworld viewed Katrina as expendable, and they simply did not have the incentive to pursue and punish any of the people they ensnared in their hacking schemes. The Sicilians were already keenly aware that law enforcement agencies were aware of them, and undeterred by it. For this particular operation, it was much easier to replace Katrina, if necessary, with another desperate individual seeking work.

Houseman was unaware of the potential connection between the Sicilian hacking scheme and the unmasking of federal agents. He instructed Katrina to continue her work, not to speak to anyone about her cooperation with the FBI, and to plan for a visit in the coming days where he would silently observe her work. He also put his report on the Law Enforcement Enterprise Portal and Regional Information Sharing System (RISS) that assists FBI offices nationwide to learn about emerging threats.

It would still take more than 48 hours before all the dots were connected.

***

Houseman was looking over Katrina's shoulder when it happened. He leaned in, continuing to hold his cup of coffee. What he witnessed was frightening.

Shortly after signing in to her laptop and navigating to the portal where help tickets were collected, her screen began to flicker. A small dialogue box appeared in the bottom right corner, the kind used to indicate that another party was online and looking at the same information on the screen. The content of the box was in Italian. Katrina turned to look back at Houseman, who took a picture of the screen with his phone.

Next, as Katrina sat in front of the laptop, screens started to change. A cursor could be seen moving across the screen, tapping different options, adding commands to change the view, and going deeper into areas that would have been considered classified to an employee at Katrina's level. Houseman immediately wondered how this activity could escape the attention of the IRS, then realized they were severely shorthanded when the incoming Presidential administration stripped them of personnel.

Katrina felt a rush of adrenalin that she could finally share the horror of what she saw with someone else.

Houseman whispered to her instinctively, as if someone might be listening, "it's like this every time you log in?"

She nodded in affirmation.

Houseman put down his coffee, and pulled up another chair so that he could sit side-by-side with Katrina and take additional photos of the screens being displayed. Meanwhile, the screens continued to change until the computer was showing sensitive information on federal employees including names, addresses, next of kin, photos and more. The screen remained on each page for only a few seconds before navigating back to the IT ticket portal and returning control back to Katrina. The small dialogue box disappeared, and both Katrina and Houseman leaned back in their chairs as if they were on a roller coaster that slowly delivered them back to a level platform.

"That's it," Katrina said, breathlessly. "It's always like that."

Houseman presumed the quick dip into the IRS payroll data was time limited so as not to arouse suspicion. Separately from that session, the perpetrators would combine the IRS data with data collected from other federal and public databases to create a complete profile – leaving the target fully exposed.

Delmatoff messaged Swanson after receiving the urgent notice sent to all senior IRS officials when a breach is known or suspected, even though Swanson would ultimately read about it the next morning in the Daily Director Briefing. Delmatoff had on his computer the photos taken by Agent Houseman. But what he didn't realize is that he was looking at a listing that included covert intelligence agents operating under a thoroughly watertight alias.

"So, we know where to plug the hole, but how do we find who is pulling the trigger," Swanson said the moment Delmatoff picked up the phone, dispensing with all formalities.

"Well, somebody is paying for all this," Delmatoff replied. "You know the new saying," he continued, "follow the crypto."

"Seriously," Swanson said, incredulously, "you can do that?"

"Of course not," Delmatoff replied dryly, "it's impossible."

***

"I'm getting too old for this shit," Delmatoff said aloud as he leaned into the computer screen on his desk, peering at a spreadsheet of transactions that were flagged by his division as suspicious activity related to various ongoing investigations. It was long past quitting time and the offices on his floor were dark and abandoned. He complained out loud whenever he found himself falling down a rabbit hole trying to track new forms of white-collar criminal activity, and many times those complaints echoed down the empty hallways as they did this particular evening. The sophistication of cybercriminals was advancing faster than American intelligence agents and IRS investigators could keep up.

What Delmatoff did not yet understand, in spite of his efforts, was the complex web of financial transactions that loosely connected the sale of VDM wines to the assassination of covert agents. He split his time between various investigations, including examination of potential damage done by the recent data breach, and monitoring any commercial activity on the VDM website, including wines that were once for sale and later removed. He was still operating under the assumption that the wine business was merely an elegant form of money laundering. Delmatoff was a firm believer in Occam's Razor, that is, that simplest explanation is usually correct.

The wine purchases were only available to buyers that Tanaka and the yakuza had already vetted and directed to their website on the dark web. Once the purchase was made in the cryptocurrency Ethereum, it was batched and queued up for "coin mixing" on whatever exchange had not already been closed down by the Treasury Department's Office of Foreign Assets Control (OFAC). Therein lied the challenge that Delmatoff was facing.

Coin mixing combines a buyer's transaction with that of other buyers who happen to be making separate transactions through the system at the same time. It joins the cryptocurrency of two or more users and mixes them together so as to conceal their origin. The user can instruct the "coin tumbler" application to pay the seller in small chunks of the original price, or at a delayed date, so that they cannot be traced back to the original transaction.

In May of 2019, BestMixer.io became the first coin mixer to be shut down on the charge of money laundering. Since then, several other coin tumblers have been closed by authorities including Bitcoin Fog and Helix in 2020, but OFAC found itself in a game of "whack-a-mole" as for every coin mixing operation it was able to block, another two would emerge. In May of 2022 a Sicilian-linked crypto mixing service was used to launder $20.5

million in illicit proceeds stolen from Axie Infinity, a popular video game with nearly 3 million users. At that point the criminal activity began to catch the attention of law enforcement agencies around the globe, including the CIA and FBI.

The Sicilian hackers were on Davis' mind when another call from Swanson came in. Swanson had cross referenced the screenshots from Katrina's computer with another database that contained privileged information on what these employees actually did for the government, databases not available to Delmatoff.

"We are considering the possibility that a new form of APT has hacked into federal databases with the intent to unmask agents," Swanson said. While most of the Advance Persistent Threat groups were state-sponsored groups, their typical mandate – cyberespionage for political influence or economic gain – would align also with Cosa Nostra, 'Ndrangheta, or any of the other mafia clans based in Italy.

"Interesting," Davis replied. "What does that have to do with my department?" Davis felt the question worth asking even though he was examining Sicily's money laundering activity at the time. Also, he was in a foul mood from having his eyes held hostage by his computer screen.

"Well," Swanson said, "intelligence agencies are responsible to protect the identity of their assets, but those agents still have personnel records and they still receive paychecks, right?"

Davis could already see where this was going, and snapped out of his self-imposed trance.

"And if compromised," Davis replied, "a hacker could potentially marry a personnel record with direct deposit payroll data..." he paused to catch his breath before continuing. What he said out loud was already an operating theory. But then, he took the theory one step further.

"And they could use remote ATM or credit card activity to identify the location of a covert agent. Well, fuck me."

Davis felt a wave of shame flow over him that he didn't see this coming. Swanson similarly recalled that Agent McAuley floated the idea a couple days prior that payroll data could be used to connect a covert agent with his or her true identity. Similar scenarios were even covered in cybersecurity conferences the men attended, but the actual threat was considered several years off. The fact both men arrived at the same conclusion, at that very moment, undoubtedly saved lives in the end.

Neither man spoke for another couple seconds as the implications set in.

"Let me see if our department can identify any unauthorized queries," said Davis.

"Davis," Swanson said, "not a word of this to anyone on your side. In case we have a mole."

21

The yakuza and mafia had little in common other than disdain for government, and disregard for the law. While the mafia was a secretive, hierarchical organization that was concentrated deep in a small number of families, the yakuza was more horizontally organized across various clans, and some members were openly proud of their affiliation. Both syndicates operated independently on opposite sides of the world for most of their existence, until a chance meeting in 1984 brought them together.

That is when the Oyabun of Tokyo's largest yakuza clan, Masahisa Takenaka, visited Palermo to learn more about how the mafia was able to operate with impunity across Sicily and much of Italy. Takenaka became leader of the Yamaguchi-gumi after the death of Kazuo Taoka, also known as the "Godfather of all Godfathers", who was responsible for the syndicate's massive growth and success during the 20th century. The meticulously coordinated meeting took place at the oldest restaurant in Palermo, Casa del Brodo dal Dottore in the center of the old city, an unassuming establishment with only six tables in front and a few more in the back.

Takenaka was under considerable pressure, much of it self-imposed, to continue the growth of the yakuza at a time when the Japanese government was introducing effective measures to restrict their activities in the country. He had observed closely the proceedings of the "Pizza Connection Trial" involving 22 Sicilian-born members of the mafia that had built a $1.6 billion drug trade through pizza parlors across the U.S. Customers would order their pie with a "special sauce" that amounted to several grams of cocaine in a Ziplock bag placed inside the cardboard box directly on top of the pizza. The prosecution became the longest criminal trial in U.S. history.

When Takenaka entered the restaurant in September 1984, he was wearing a gray suit and thin black tie. His short jet-black hair, black sunglasses, and distinctive Asian characteristics, immediately caught the attention of the maître-di. Or maybe it was the fact he was surrounded by five other large men in similar attire, who were there to guarantee his safety. His men had already spread word that he sought a meeting with a local leader of the underworld, and Ceasar Costronovo soon appeared. Costronovo's cousin Gaetano "the Uncle" Badalamenti was convicted the year prior for his role in the cocaine dealing operation, and sentenced to 45 years in prison.

"I have a business proposition for you," said Takenaka, through one of his interpreters.

"We love business propositions," replied Costronovo, flashing a smile that endeared him to many of the Sicilians that lived under his protection, and even others that feared him.

The two men discussed a variety of collaborations. Takenaka was particularly interested in hearing Costronovo speak to the activities of the mafia during the prohibition years, as his business proposition involved using the wine trade as the foundation of a money laundering operation. Costronovo was familiar enough with the folklore around those days since he had heard so many stories from his grandfather, and had in fact inherited the mantle to continue what had become a vast enterprise. By the end of the meeting, Costronovo agreed to advise and consult with the yakuza that they could gain control of a Napa-based winery and establish a money laundering operation based there.

The two men parted company after about an hour and a half. Onlookers wondered what a Sicilian gangster and well-dressed Asian man would have in common. They would never know.

Takenaka was murdered shortly after his trip to Italy by a member of a rival clan. Over 1000 members of the yakuza attended his funeral, including his closest confidants. They were effective in wiping away any evidence of the meeting between the two criminal organizations, but set in motion an unholy alliance that would significantly raise the scope of international crimes, involve more actors across the globe, and make perpetrators much more difficult to catch and convict.

As the agent who helped establish that Sicilian hackers were responsible for the collection of sensitive data on federal employees, Ernest Houseman was sent to Los Angeles to assist with the investigation into the unmasking of agents that was gaining the most momentum in that FBI field office.

This was a big break for Houseman who, at only twenty-eight years old, was now working with the most senior officials in the FBI. He personified the prototypical agent, slim, with short, black hair slicked back from his forehead and a permanent serious look on his face. His only problem was that he looked more like a teenager, the curse of looking too young to be taken seriously. Houseman was to report to Swanson who was now short-handed with the suspension of Richard O'Brien.

"Don't spend all day on this," Swanson said, referring to the write-up he requested on the case of Katrina Evtushenko. "And don't forget the briefing at nine o'clock Pacific time today."

At precisely nine o'clock, the FBI seal flashed on the screen within conference rooms across the agency, above a warning that the videoconference session about to begin was intended to be a secure meeting, and that it was illegal for unauthorized persons to view or participate. Moments later, Davis Delmatoff appeared, and introduced his role in the Internal Revenue Service.

"The third-party, non-governmental services that are supposed to protect our data are the ones getting hacked," Davis said, referring to a recent disclosure to lawmakers about a hack into the U.S. Treasury Department. The revelation explained a lot about how agents were being unmasked and was an important part of the puzzle. Third party services were presumed to be "bullet-proof," that's why they were selected in the first place.

"In 2024," Delmatoff continued, "Chinese state-sponsored hackers breached a cloud-based service offered by a company called BeyondTrust. That company licensed an application to provide technical support for the Treasury Office end users. With stolen passwords they were able to override the service's security, remotely access workstations, and access classified documents that were being stored by various users."

Delmatoff was reading from a brief that was drawn up when BeyondTrust first revealed the breach to the State Department, which referred the matter to the U.S. Cybersecurity and Infrastructure Security Agency (CISA), as well as the FBI, to assess the hack's impact.

"Based on available indicators, the latest breach was not from a currently known APT, but more likely from a criminal syndicate based in Sicily," Delmatoff said, ending with a barely detectable sigh, followed by an equally silent, "here we go again."

Houseman took notes, along with most others sitting in FBI conference rooms across the country in various field offices. Also watching from deep within a well-worn sofa was Richard O'Brien, sitting in McAuley's apartment and watching silently from the laptop on the coffee table in front of the two men.

"Dude," said McAuley while staring forward at the computer screen, "if Sarah finds out…fuck, if Swanson finds out…."

Swanson spoke next and said, in a matter of words, what everyone was thinking.

"Sooner rather than later we are going to look like we're caught with our dicks in our hands," he said, treading dangerously with such a crude comment in mixed company. "The data we are supposed to protect is being cherry picked and sold."

Richard thought the metaphor was crude, but not far off.

"So," McAuley said, "are you now going to Sicily as well as Malta?"

Richard opened the map on his iPhone.

"Asha once told me," he said, still looking at the proximity between Malta and Sicily, "there is no such thing as a coincidence. So, yeah, I guess so."

***

If the wine bottle could speak, it would have shed all its secrets, and saved everybody a lot of time. Instead, it stood silently between Richard and Sarah as the two dined on poke bowls in her hotel room. Richard would be leaving for Malta the following evening, and Sarah agreed to drop him at the airport. After all, the Hyatt Regency where she was staying made it convenient to hop over to LAX.

He had been spending more time in Sarah's room lately, as she agreed that the two could remain "fuck buddies" for as long as she was needed in Los Angeles by the agency. At Richard's urging, he and Sarah agreed not to discuss his suspension, but other topics were considered fair game. He poured himself some of the VDM wine he had brought from his apartment, dumped the remaining amount in Sarah's glass, and returned the empty bottle to the center of the small dining table.

"So do you think it's a case of digital delivery, or dead drops?" she said as she balanced a chunk of rice and tuna on her chopsticks, then guided it carefully into her mouth. Richard didn't hear the question. He just stared at Sarah, totally smitten by how beautiful she was, even when she was eating. He reached for his wine glass, and swirled the contents between two fingers as he had learned to do in class. Then, he emptied it.

"I mean," she continued while chewing the remaining food in her mouth, "if it was digital delivery, we would have found the breadcrumbs by now." She pursed her lips in contemplation, then grabbed another chunk of poke, and quickly swallowed it.

"But dead drops are old school," she added, laying the chopsticks back in the bowl. "Nobody invests in labor-intensive efforts like that anymore, you know, actually sitting on park benches." She leaned back in her chair and folded her arms.

What Sarah was referring to was the manner in which the recent assassinations were funded and carried out. The agents working the case had been unsuccessful, to this point, in finding any "breadcrumbs" that might reveal the release of data that resulted in the unmasking of agents, exposing their true identity and location. They also couldn't find any movement of funds that would correspond with the exchange of this data.

There were not many people in Sarah's orbit that she could talk to about an ongoing investigation. But Richard was not in the mood to talk about it. He hadn't spent much time thinking about the case, and was fixated on the fact that this would be the last night he would sleep with Sarah. And anyway, he didn't have an answer for the "digital versus dead drop" question.

The wine knew the answer. And the answer was neither.

22

As soon as Virgin Atlantic flight VS7 touched down at LAX, Nick Sabian turned his cell phone off airplane mode. It was long flight where he endured everything from a colic-prone screaming infant to an argument between passengers over the degree to which a seat could be reclined. Getting off the plane would be as close to an orgasmic experience as he could imagine at that moment.

As he waited for his turn to stand, he passed the time by pulling up the messages queued during his time in flight. He naturally prioritized the message received from Delaroche.

The Americans are clueless

He nodded his head from left to right as he contemplated the implications of the text. While he intended to respect Delaroche's directive, he regretted the eroding relationship between the American and British intelligence services. The two agencies had a long history of cooperation; however, the turmoil created in the United States by the Trump administration's war on its own intelligence community created an air of suspicion and caution on Downing Street that would go on to last for years.

It would take some time to repair the damage done to the relationship, and Sabian for one would have welcomed an improvement. He enjoyed the camaraderie with his American counterparts. Indeed, it would be Delaroche's call, not his and not Chandra's, when and if the Americans would be privy to all that they had learned about the connection between rare wines and even rarer assassinations.

As Sabian processed these thoughts, his opportunity to enter the aisle and exit the airplane had arrived, and his thoughts turned to the meet up with Asha Chandra where he would be debriefed by her, whereupon she would be sent home. He gathered his bag from the overhead compartment, and entered the Tom Bradley Terminal.

***

Asha wasn't proud of how she led Richard on, and, like Sabian, would have preferred to be working with the Americans rather than using them as a source of intelligence. But orders being what they are left no room for complaint or compromise. Richard certainly gave her the opportunity to practice the art of deception, all the way to making a convincing case that she was not a candidate for a romantic relationship.

Sabian and Asha sat in a dark corner of Virgin Atlantic's "LA Clubhouse" at the international terminal, far from the peering eyes of inebriated passengers at the bar. The lounge was relatively quiet given the time of day, and smiles on the faces of passengers pulling rolling bags past the glass doors were in stark contrast to the intense look on Asha's face. She still had bandages on her arm and shoulder, but effectively concealed them under a blazer.

Asha's treatment at the Burn Center, and the fact multiple law enforcement agencies wanted to interview her, made it too dangerous for her to remain in the United States. She would be boarding a red-eye flight back to Heathrow followed by an early morning debriefing with Delaroche. She would go on to receive special commendation on her record as an agent of MI6.

Asha cradled a cup of tea while Sabian perused the file she had handed him moments before. Sabian was hunched over the file on his lap, slowly turning one page at a time as he skimmed the content. The file contained documents tracking the movements of Alexander Sisky, Jack Tanaka, Richard O'Brien, and Sarah Goodman, along with photos she snapped of them and other people ensnared in the investigation. There was also a photo of the VDM wine bottle. Asha was anything if not organized; what she had collected was evidence of just how valued she was to MI6 as a covert agent.

"So, you believe there is a connection between the money laundering scheme and the assassinations?"

"It's the only thing that makes sense," she replied. "The wine isn't re-entering the economy. There isn't a market for it."

"Go on," Sabian said, expecting quite a bit more to effectively connect the dots.

"According to American officials, the labels aren't compliant with FDA regulations, and the wines aren't sold in stores," she said, "they came into the US with an alcohol content low enough to evade labeling requirements. I now believe they are coded with the identities of agents that are operating undercover. That would explain everything."

Sabian was impressed. If Asha was correct, it would explain *nearly* everything. Everything except how the closely protected identities of agents were being discovered in the first place. But that didn't matter as much as stopping the wine from reaching its intended destination. Because if Asha was correct, bottles of this wine out there represented a death warrant for certain agents. Those agents may already be at the other end of a sniper's scope, about to take their last breath. Or as in the case of Gregory Zukov, poked with a lethal drug.

The adrenaline that went missing from Sabian's circulatory system during the twelve-hour flight from London came rushing back into his veins.

"What's my first move," he asked. He respected Asha enough to know she would have the answer.

"I tracked O'Brien's phone last night to a hotel near LAX," Asha replied. "I know he has at least one bottle with him. Or break into Tanaka's storage locker."

"And then..?"

"We need a physical specimen we can examine to reverse engineer the code. I was hoping to steal the bottle delivered to Alexander Sisky. But the police and FBI got in before I had a chance."

"But you have a picture of the bottle here," Sabian said, confused.

"I was too distracted to realize that what I needed was a picture of the back label," Asha replied. "Please," she added, "don't hassle me about it."

Sabian couldn't imagine why that would be necessary; Asha was hard enough on herself. Any agent in Asha's circumstance would have been disappointed to be abandoning a case that consumed so much of her life to that point. Sabian understood; he had nearly two decades more experience than Asha. He would have been a great mentor for her had the two ever operated in the same time zone.

"Don't be ridiculous," he said. As he did so, he reached across to gently lay his hand on her forearm. "You've done an admirable job here, really."

The two sat in silence for a moment, and Sabian spoke again.

"So," he said, removing his hand as he did not want to send the wrong message, "what's next?"

The question laid open the opportunity for Asha to answer for herself, or somebody else.

"Get the bottle from O'Brien. That's your most straightforward first move."

And that is exactly what Sabian set out to do.

***

Sabian knew where Sarah's hotel was located. He proceeded there directly from the airport and waited in the lobby. He was hoping to spot Richard, but Sarah arrived alone, and he recognized her from the photo supplied by Asha. He followed Sarah into the elevator with his own rolling suitcase and held the door open for her when she reached her floor. He followed her down the hall, and exited from the stairwell around the corner.

The following morning, he waited patiently inside his rental car until he saw her drive off the lot. It was time to go back inside, and time was of the essence before housekeeping would arrive to clean her room. Sabian was operating on little sleep and had not yet showered nor shaved since leaving London. All this was fine and proper given the demands of the task before him.

He had performed the stunt so many times before that it no longer made him nervous. The only difference was that it was raining. The drizzle falling in Los Angeles that day was as rare as a cloudless day anywhere else. It combined with a marine layer of fog and shrouded the City of Angels in a funky, wet blanket. He hustled toward the hotel, holding his London Fog trench coat over his head with his right hand, and a large poly bag with his left hand.

Sabian walked into the hotel lobby and then went directly into the men's restroom off to the side of the restaurant. Inside, he locked himself into a stall, and took off his shirt, pants and shoes, leaving him in his boxer shorts and undershirt. Into the lining of his boxers, he put the white side of an expired hotel card key, held in place by the elastic band. He fiddled with the card's location so that it could be easily seen under his underwear. Then, he put back on the trench coat.

From the poly bag he took out two paper cups and lids. He didn't even bother to buy the coffee anymore. Then he left the restroom, both cups in his hands, and took the elevator to her floor. His clothes were left in the poly bag, which he hung from the back of the door of the restroom stall. He wouldn't be long, and would return for them later. He slowly whispered *"Showtime"* to himself as the doors to the elevator opened. He stepped into the hallway, and looked in both directions.

"Oh madam," Sabian said in a loud whisper, "can you please help, she will be furious if I wake her." As he spoke, he walked slowly toward the door to Sarah's room, looking anxiously at the woman from housekeeping that was servicing a room down the hall. At the same time, he looked repeatedly at the cups, pretending to be careful that the invisible coffee wouldn't spill. It was an impressive performance.

"But sir, I cannot open the door for you."

"No, it's fine, I have the key here, in my shorts." He pointed to the hotel card key with one cup in hand as he pushed the trench coat to one side.

She stared at the man's waist. Then pulled the master key out of her pocket.

"It's okay, sir, here you go."

"Oh, bless you," he whispered, "I appreciate it. She'll appreciate it."

The woman smiled and opened the door just enough that he could push it with his shoulders the rest of the way. He did, and slithered himself inside.

"Thanks again, have a good day," he said, smiling back at the woman. As he spoke, the door automatically closed between them. He immediately dropped the cups and got to work.

Sabian noticed that Sarah had placed a "Do Not Disturb" sign on her door, and he hoped that she was a competent agent that did so in order that housekeeping would not snoop nor take anything from the room that could be of value to a counterintelligence agent. He was right.

His first instinct was to inspect the trash cans, believing that it could contain what he was looking for. It did. The empty wine bottle was there, along with a bag containing empty disposable food bowls. He dumped the contents of the bag, placed the wine bottle inside, and pushed this under his armpit.

He quickly looked from left to right for the suitcases, finding one at the foot of the bed, and the other in the closet. He removed two, small GPS trackers from his pants pockets and removed the adhesive from each one. He next opened each suitcase, unzipped the liner slightly, and attached each tracker to the inside of the frame. He did not believe he had any reason to track O'Brien's movements, but decided it best to take advantage of the opportunity as it may not have presented itself again.

Sabian made one final look across the room for anything important that he might have missed, but with the wine bottle in hand he had already found what he came to collect. He stepped outside the room and, rather than risk being seen by the housekeeping staff, he took the stairs back down to the lobby, returned to the restroom, dressed, and left the hotel in the same manner as he had arrived.

***

Delaroche had a huge problem, largely of her own making.

In her role leading the covert agent program at MI6 the past twelve years, she had never witnessed such an existential crisis within the agency. The methodical dismantling of her department by an outside, invisible force was causing anguish and fear among her staff, a staff she devoted her career to protect. Whatever was murdering her agents had clearly penetrated the most carefully safeguarded personal information within the walls of the British government.

And so, against her better judgment, and because nobody could be dismissed as a possible double agent, she authorized sending agents to the United States to investigate why British agents were being compromised, unmasked, and assassinated. But it was illegal to send an agent to operate in a sovereign nation without the express consent of the nation's government, which Delaroche failed to obtain. She was potentially in too deep now that she had sent Nick Sabian in to relieve Asha Chandra, and she stared at the phone wondering if it was time to come clean and ask for forgiveness.

On top of the close diplomatic relationship between the U.S. and U.K., as far as intelligence gathering goes, the two nations were quite literally joined at the hip as founding members of the "Five Eyes Alliance" formed after WWII and including Canada, Australia and New Zealand. It had been hailed in academic circles as the world's most successful intelligence-sharing alliance. Delaroche essentially ignored it because her first priority was to prevent another assassination of one of her own, one of her "children."

She looked at her computer monitor which, now sleeping, reflected back the image of a tired woman that aged more rapidly in the months since agents began to fall. She twisted her wheelchair around to the window behind her desk offering a view of the London Eye that she wouldn't have to look at herself. She sarcastically called it the "London Eyesore" because she found its pandering to tourism offensive when London had so much to offer already in terms of culture, history and the arts.

First and foremost, Delaroche didn't want to initiate a process that might stifle Sabian's progress and ability to move freely in the country. But it was time for her to implement a CYA strategy, so she twisted the chair back and tapped her keyboard to wake her computer. She composed a secure message for the British Ambassador, suggesting he deliver the official request to his counterpart in Washington. Knowing the wheels of motion in the political world would move at the speed of a glacier, she estimated that Sabian had, at most, three more days of free movement.

***

Sarah was not quite ready to put all her casino chips on the square that said "Richard O'Brien," but she was feeling closer to him again since arriving in LA, and wanted to give him something to think about while he was traveling in Europe. They had a few more hours before she had to drop him at LAX for a midnight flight to Catania, followed by a short ferry ride to Malta.

During her time as a divorcee, she joined the growing number of women that visited porn sites, and decided to put some of what she had learned into practice. She was always a confident and secure woman, but never demonstrated this in the bedroom.

So, once they entered her hotel room where his luggage was waiting for him, she started the performance, first putting on a fresh coat of lipstick while sitting at the vanity table holding the cosmetics mirror.

"Richard," she said, as she was applying a wet-look red shade, "did you pack your cuffs?"

"No," he replied, sitting on the edge of the bed and fiddling with the TV remote, "they are in my backpack."

Sarah went to the backpack, dug inside the outer pocket, and pulled them out.

"Nice," she said with a wry smile that Richard failed to notice, "I think they are a different model than mine."

She then went to the hotel bureau where her clothes were stored, and pulled out a second pair.

"No," she said, holding one pair in each hand, "I guess they are the same."

Richard was still not following.

She moved toward Richard and stood between his legs, looking down on him. She unbuttoned the first few buttons on her blouse, revealing a black bra underneath. He leaned back on his arms and looked up at her, not knowing what to expect. Most women would have suggested getting to the airport early, but then, Sarah was not like most women.

"Lie down, officer," she said, pointing up to the pillows and the bedframe against the hotel wall.

Richard was not sure he was comfortable with what Sarah had in mind, but thought it best to play along. He scooted his behind back toward the pillows.

Sarah climbed on the bed next to Richard, took his left wrist and secured it with the handcuffs to the bedframe. She quickly moved to the other side of the bed and secured the other wrist. Richard watched her movements silently, and began to feel vulnerable.

Those emotions went away as Sarah pulled down his pants and underwear, then disappeared below his legs.

23

Sarah appeared at Swanson's office early the next day. After the perfunctory blessing for a "good morning," she got right down to it.

"Look John," Sarah pleaded, "Richard connected the VDM wines to a person of interest right here in your AOR. You have a responsibility to investigate." Sarah was referring to Swanson's "Area of Responsibility," a common acronym to indicate the area over which an agent had jurisdiction.

"It's not illegal to import wine to the U.S., so what's your point," he replied stoically. "And what is O'Brien doing over there anyway. He had better not be impersonating an agent," he said, pausing intentionally before adding, "again."

Not much would get past Swanson and he was already aware that Richard was on his way to Europe. Sarah ignored his response, referring to the time Richard swiped her credentials in order to pursue a suspect at JFK airport in New York. That time, Richard aided in preventing a nuclear bomb from detonating in a populous region of Israel. In reality, he was the hero in that case even after that lapse in judgment.

"The person that rents this storage unit is collecting wines and selling them. That in itself is suspicious because as you know, John, it's illegal to run a business from a storage unit," she said. "I've gotten a look at this guy," she continued, "he's missing a finger on his right hand, so he may very well be a gang member. And he is working with the Coast Guard, but we don't know in what capacity, which is a HUGE concern if he has access to military hardware based on a forged identity."

Sarah's blood pressure was rising as her own prosecution of the case made her realize how all the pieces foretold a potentially serious threat.

"What more do you need, John?"

Swanson rose from his desk and walked around it, leaning on the edge and crossing his legs. The foot that balanced on his knee was just inches from Sarah's lap. He looked down at her, smiling.
"What I need is for you to give us another chance," he said, slowly. "Why are you wasting your time with O'Brien? He's a loser."

Sarah was not particularly surprised by Swanson's advance. The two had dated years prior, when they were both working in the New York office of the agency. It didn't end well and she had sworn off intra-office relationships until Richard came into the picture. She was well prepared to handle Swanson's proposition.

"John," she said, standing up to demonstrate she wasn't afraid of him, intentionally closing the space between them. "As they say, you were merely a short chapter in my life. He's more like a book. Please don't make the mistake of ignoring this case. It could truly be a career-limiting blunder."

With that, she turned around and left Swanson, who was left to process both the insult and the threat.

***

John Swanson despised Richard O'Brien. Richard was more handsome, likable, and charismatic than Swanson. He resented the fact O'Brien was dating Sarah Goodman. But more than he despised Richard, he despised himself. He couldn't help himself from being petty and vindictive toward one of his own.

The reality of the situation gave Swanson little room to maneuver. While he was able to suspend Richard on his own authority, he knew he couldn't make it stick. It was inevitable that Internal Affairs would find that, while Richard exercised poor judgment for visiting the Court without a partner, this in itself wasn't grounds for termination. Also, there was no formal operation named at that point that would have dictated under protocol that he was required to partner with another agent. Richard would be slapped with a warning in the coming days, and an innocuous entry into his personnel file.

In addition to all this, Swanson recognized any intra-agency drama could threaten his goal to ascend higher in the ranks of management, potentially to the role of Director. He was generally recognized as a rising star in the agency for hardnosed tactics that produced results. And then there was the real threat laid down by Sarah earlier in the day. Realizing this, Swanson decided to jump start the investigation into the money laundering case in order to soak up as much credit for himself as possible.

He was given the perfect opportunity when it was reported by the LA police that Alexander Sisky turned up dead. As expected, the Russian consulate did everything they could to deflect attention to the fact Sisky was murdered, suggesting it was probable that Sisky suffered a heart attack earlier in the day. As before, they tried to prevent American interference, but when his wife called 911 after returning from grocery shopping to find him face down in a pool of blood, there was little the Russian government could do to prevent the police from investigating. "There was no time for cardiac arrest once a blunt instrument pierced the coronal suture of the deceased's skull," quipped the pathologist that examined the body in a cloaked rebuttal of the consulate's argument.

There may have been a larger appetite within the FBI to investigate Sisky's murder if not for indifference to the man himself. Sisky had made himself so loathed within the intelligence community that he was like kryptonite, nobody wanted to go anywhere near him. So, when it became known that he was found dead in his home, Swanson merely acknowledged the news without pushing for more details. The LA police could have him; Swanson was more interested in what Sarah had to say about Tanaka.

***

For Tanaka, eliminating Sisky was a major achievement, as it would now force the Russians to accept deliveries in the same manner as all other customers. This time, he didn't even have to get his hands dirty. He hired a contract killer from among the many that were already in use by his clients. He had hired "the Ghost."

It became clear to Tanaka that Sisky had to be eliminated. He had grown increasingly paranoid as he grew older, and was convinced that he was not only under constant surveillance, but that his mail and packages were being inspected before delivery. His insistence that deliveries be made inside his house put Tanaka in increasing danger. And every time Tanaka tried to persuade Sisky to compromise in any way, such as using a neutral dead drop location like an airport locker, Sisky would threaten to expose Tanaka to local law enforcement.

But murder was a bridge too far for Tanaka. The stress and burden he had accepted until now was wearing him down. It started out as an endeavor to prove himself worthy of the yakuza, and offered him acceptance into Japanese culture, however fringe that acceptance turned out. But he paid a heavier price than he ever imagined. He could not discuss his vocation with anyone that he cared about, and his insular life denied him anyone that he *could* care about.

Tanaka decided shortly after contracting out the murder of Alexander Sisky that his next wine drop would be his last. The yakuza would probably be happy to be rid of him, he mused, unless they would offer him something more mundane.

Swanson viewed Sisky's murder as the consequence of a money laundering business that had turned vindictive, and used that theory as an excuse to pick up Tanaka.

"The bad guys are eating their own," he declared. "We need to pick this one up before he ends up the same as Sisky."

***

The *Arowana* lay silently a half mile off the coast in relatively shallow waters. It was a busy day for the crew, with drills for training purposes interrupted by various demands of the Joint Harbor Operations Center (JHOC), including a search and rescue operation for an overturned migrant vessel, and a separate interdiction of drugs from a yacht that carelessly ran into a boater near the entrance to the bay. The owner of the yacht, an American, was transporting drugs he purchased at wholesale prices near the maritime border. He tested positively for cocaine on the scene.

Tanaka was busy cleaning the galley for most of the afternoon as the pursuit maneuvers of the ship caused it to heel from side to side, causing a mess. Fortunately, most of the meals he had to prepare for the crew were already assembled dockside and his role was merely to warm them up. His mind was on the most important task he came to perform, but he would need to wait until sundown.

As day gave way to night, the Pacific Ocean underwent a transformation. Activity from recreational vessels disappeared, and the oceans seem to settle down, even though there was much more activity below the waterline due to creatures that migrated to the surface to feed. The glow of cities was intense as seen from a distance without the impact of light pollution. Stars seemed to multiply well beyond what could be observed on land. Temperatures dropped quickly as there is no microclimate at sea – just space. It was natural and surreal at the same time. And it signaled that it was time for Tanaka to get to work again.

A "Marine Protector Class" cutter is not as large a vessel as some other military ships, but it was still relatively easy to place a crate off the stern of the boat, especially at night when most men are down below, playing cards or streaming movies in their berth. And the stern was where Tanaka stood, silently lowering another crate of wine into the ocean. A water activated strobe light would make it relatively easy to find by a diver with the right coordinates. On locating the crate, the diver would attach lift bags that, once filled with air from his regulator, would glide the crate back to the surface for easy collection.

"Here you go, Captain," Tanaka said as he stepped over the doorjamb and into the bridge.

"Thank you," Underwood replied as he reached toward Tanaka to grab the cup. He looked into Tanaka's eyes with an air of suspicion that Tanaka failed to notice. Instead, Tanaka moved closer to the GPS monitor that he could make note of the crate's location.

"Where are we now?" he asked, as he had done before.

Nothing about the situation would have been cause for alarm had Underwood not received the request from Swanson's office earlier in the day, conveyed via secure message through the JHOC, to observe Tanaka's behavior. It was not the Coast Guard's duty to detain or arrest Tanaka. The extent of their obligation was to deliver him to the appropriate law enforcement agency once they returned to the base.

"Roughly thirty-two point seven degrees north, and one hundred seventeen west. Just off the coast of Point Loma," the captain replied.

"Oh, interesting, how deep is the water here?" Tanaka asked.

"We are in relatively shallow waters," he said, "maximum depth about one hundred twenty."
Underwood silently postulated theories of what was going on.

"Mind if I take a pic again?" Tanaka asked.

"Be my guest," the captain replied, who took note of the coordinates as well.

As Tanaka left the bridge his concern turned to the depth of the water in which the crate was now resting. He knew that the divers he hired to recover it were comfortable to depths of one hundred feet, but uncertainty around the actual depth was cause for concern. However, there was nothing he could do about it once the crate was submerged. He returned to the galley to check on its condition before retiring to his berth. In a little under 48 hours, the cutter would return to base and he would be done with deployments, done with the Coast Guard, and in all likelihood done with the yakuza.

***

Richard was not quite prepared for Malta. For one thing, it was hot, humid, and crowded. The sun blasted the island unforgivably, and the monochrome, light tan buildings in the capital of Valletta made it difficult to tell where one building ended, and another began. And when it came to beginning an investigation, Richard wasn't sure about that either. He decided to start by asking around the various restaurants about VDM wines, and whether they carried them.

Predictably, this approach didn't yield good results. Restaurants were busy, and if Richard was not a customer, he didn't merit their attention. He decided to stop at the Caffe Cordina, one of the oldest coffee shops in all of Europe, to get some respite from the sun and to consider his next move. Here he would find ample shade on their expansive patio which had grown exponentially along with the growth in tourists flocking to the island.

One of the advantages that Richard had not expected was that the Maltese language was a combination of Arabic and various romance languages. Richard studied Arabic at the University of Michigan and it served as his path to join the FBI in the first place, as a linguist and translator. He overheard a couple older men speaking the language, and moved closer to their table. He judged the men to be in their seventies. A small dog slept below them at their table. If they were locals, he thought, they might know something. Malta was a tiny island. Valletta had less than five thousand permanent residents. It was like a big family.

He started with his back to the men, and ordered a cappuccino. He established by eavesdropping that they were talking about what older men generally talk about: their disdain for corrupt government, the price of things, the unbearable weather and even more unbearable tourists. He waited for a comment that he could react to that would appear natural. When the topic turned to women, one of his favorite subjects, he had his opening.

"Your women are beautiful," he said in Arabic, turning himself half way around to look at the men. His Arabic wasn't a perfect match for the Maltese language, but close enough to verify he wasn't an ambitious tourist trying to fit in. The men were startled but not the least bit offended at the interruption. To be acknowledged by a younger man in a respectful manner would typically result in an equally respectful response.

"Indeed," said one of the men in response, "if you can pluck them out from a gaggle of Sicilians."

The three men shook their heads in synchronous agreement. Richard wasn't sure where to go next, but hoped the men would lead the way. They obliged.

"Where are you from, young man?" the other man said.

Richard didn't have the patience to develop the men as sources, and with his limited language skills he didn't necessarily feel qualified for the task anyway. Better, he thought, to test the waters immediately to see if his trip to Malta was a total waste of time and energy.

"I am researching the wines of Sicily and Malta," he said, not feeling he needed to craft a story with any more depth than that.

The two men looked at each other and nodded again. One of them reached for his espresso while the other wiped his forehead with a napkin. It was time to press further.

"I'm looking for VDM wines," he said, "do you know where I can find them?"

At that moment the men realized that Richard was not a tourist, not on holiday, and not in Malta for any good reason. The men looked at each other, and then looked around to see if anyone was listening in on their conversation.

"Son," one of the men whispered, "there are things you should not speak of here, if you wish to live to make poor choices on another day."

Richard now knew he was onto something, but his next question might be his last if he didn't handle it well. The disposition of the men suggested that the VDM enterprise was involved in illegal activity, and the fact this was well known could only mean it had ties to the mafia. He decided quickly to play the role of antagonist, rather than protagonist. It was a gamble.

"Look," he said, "I have information for the caporegime," referring to the local mafia boss. "It will save lives – his -- and potentially yours." Richard stared at the men with as intimidating a look as he could muster.

The men continued to look at each other for silent guidance. Richard's threat appeared legitimate enough. He had the look of a foreigner, his Arabic was passable, and the way he found his way into the conversation had all indications that he knew what he was doing, and was potentially dangerous himself.

One of the men stood, and pointed in the direction of the marina.

"Triq Il-Gdida," he said. "By the water." He then sat back down and stared silently at his coffee.

Richard stood, dropped a ten-euro bill for his coffee, and headed in the direction of the marina, leaving the men to watch him as he turned the corner.

***

Richard didn't realize that "Triq Il-Gdida," translated from Maltese to English, meant "The New Road," however there was nothing new about what he found when he reached it. The road, starting just outside the Victoria Gate near the Grand Harbour, dipped down below the main thoroughfare around the perimeter of Valletta. It was such a narrow road, more like an alley, and could easily be missed. But on either side of Triq Il-Gdida were large wooden doors, curved at the top in a medieval style. The units appeared to be the Maltese version of public storage, close enough to the water that if anybody wanted to transport stolen cash, drugs, or other contraband without detection, this would be a good place to have them ready for export.

Richard walked down the road looking left and right at any signs indicating ownership of the unit. Some were claimed, while others clearly abandoned. There was no question he found the right spot when, at the end, he came upon a small, shiny bronze plaque next to a wooden door that read "CVC Group of Companies" in large letters, and "Vino del Mar" added just beneath it. Looking around the corner, he noticed that the building had another set of doors on the back side of it, facing the water.

Weeds and vegetation were hugging the side of the building and climbing up its walls to claim it. Richard walked around to the other side where there was a small walkway between the building and a concrete ledge, below which was the water. The vertical wood planks that made up the back door had so much decay that if you were standing in just the right spot, you could easily see inside. Richard did, and saw crates stacked high in the back, multiple racks of individual wine bottles, and pallets with even more crates on them.

He found that with minimal effort, he could pry open the back door. The afternoon sun immediately lit up the area, exposing more wine bottles than Richard had ever seen in one place. He stepped inside and walked toward the racks of individual bottles. Most of the bottles did not have any labels on them at this point, but Richard found a cardboard box on the floor and pulled a bottle from it. These bottles did have a VDM label, but what Richard noticed was that the label didn't look anything like the bottles he saw in the U.S. That's when the security guard started to yell.

The guard looked to Richard as if he was no higher than five foot five inches, and probably in his mid-fifties. He wore an authentic looking uniform, but he was too overweight for his shirt, which had missing buttons that revealed his white undershirt underneath.

"Non sei permesso," he yelled angrily.

Richard's prior experience as a translator could have come in handy at that moment, but his Italian was *non bene*. While he wasn't comfortable communicating in Italian, the Spanish he studied in high school would be close enough.

"¿Dónde están los libros?" he said, asking where the books would be that he could study the shipping logs and find where the wine was going.

The security guard, presuming Richard was with a rival mafia gang, was not intending to answer. Instead, he continued moving quickly toward Richard with his baton, holding it behind him so that he could swing at Richard with as much force as possible. Richard was ready.

Unfortunately for the guard, he was not trained for combat, and was hired simply for his ability to intimidate trespassing teens or alert the caporegime of any threats to the business or property. He was no match for Richard.

As the baton swung across the guard's chest, Richard leaned far back and to the left. Instead of hitting him, the edge of the guard's baton struck a stack of wine bottles, causing two bottles to shatter and fall to the ground. A shard of glass bounced off the back of Richard's neck, but he was otherwise unharmed. A pool of wine was now on the floor, along with the shattered glass. Richard jumped back to increase the distance between him and the guard.

"¿CUÁL ES EL PROBLEMA?" Richard shouted, as the guard turned toward him and went back in pursuit.

It would be impossible to exaggerate the amount of adrenaline coursing through Richard's veins at that moment. He was without a weapon to defend himself against a man that was attacking him, his Italian wasn't good enough to communicate effectively, and conversation wasn't on the menu at that moment anyway.

278

The guard once again lunged toward Richard, who fell backward clumsily against another stack of wine, this time toppling dozens of bottles in a colossal crash. Richard rolled to his left, doing his best to avoid the broken glass all around him. Now the guard was nearly on top of him, ready to strike him in the head.

Instinctively, Richard grabbed a broken bottle by the glass throat, and swung it at the guard, slicing a nearly 4-inch gash across his left forearm. The guard looked down at his arm, grabbed it, and fell to the floor, effectively surrendering. He wasn't being paid enough to risk his life by continuing the pursuit. He muttered in Italian to himself, shaking his head.

Richard's pulse was racing from the confrontation, but he quickly gathered his senses and stood above the guard, who continued to hold his arm. Richard was panting with rapid shallow breaths.

"¿Dónde están los libros?" he repeated, this time with enough anger in his voice to ensure the guard understood the risks of ignoring the question again. The guard arched his head back and toward the right side of the room, revealing for Richard a small clerk's desk.

Richard walked over the desk without concern for what the guard might do next. As he walked past, the guard slowly stood and limped out of the warehouse. He would head home and speak nothing about what happened that day.

At the table, Richard turned on a desk lamp that revealed a large, oversized ledger. It had a leather cover and its beige pages were thick paper stock, constructed to tolerate rough handling. It had lines and columns filled with data. Richard leaned over the book, took out his phone, and proceeded to snap photos of the first few pages. Then he flipped toward the most recent entries, and took more pictures.

He looked at the final page with data on it, and noticed a rough pattern. The entries under "Cliente" were limited to a handful of customers, and the shipping locations were either to Los Angeles, or locales near Rome, Palermo, Naples, or Catania. There were a couple entries to other countries. The address in Los Angeles looked very familiar to him, so he punched it into his phone. It was in Temecula California, not far from the wine festival he attended with Asha.

Richard looked up from the book at the bulletin board behind the desk. On it were a few ads for local restaurants, emergency phone numbers, and required city bulletins regarding workplace safety. There was also one business card pinned to the wall, that of Vincenzu di Salvo, a "Dottore Commercialista." This was equivalent to a Chartered Accountant or CPA. His address was in Palermo.

Richard expected to be traveling to Palermo. Now, he had his first appointment.

24

Swanson held the hefty folder on his lap as he leaned back in his executive chair. The report from Internal Affairs was comprehensive including pictures of the blast scene, a timetable of events, witness statements and excerpts from training manuals and various SOPs. The file also included the results of an interview with Richard himself. But it was the cover letter's summation at the bottom of the page that he read with raised eyebrows:

> "While Special Agent O'Brien exercised questionable judgment to have undertaken a field visit without a partner, he could not have known the risk of a later event involving civilian deaths and destruction of property at the same location. The facts indicate this was a preliminary investigation of an unnamed operation; therefore, no partner had yet been assigned to Agent O'Brien. Mr. Rosen (the deceased) was

neither a suspect nor person of interest. Under these circumstances, an attending agent was advised, but not required. We recommend reinstating Agent O'Brien.

This matter is closed."

Swanson was backed into a corner. He knew Sarah had enough dirt on him, including a potential sexual harassment charge, to make good on her claim that his next move could be career limiting. He couldn't continue to isolate O'Brien without risk to his own reputation, especially since rumors that O'Brien had established a definitive link between the assassinations and the wines, fueled by McAuley, had made their way to Swanson's office.

He let out an oversized sigh, then leaned forward and reached for his phone and punched the speaker to hail his admin.

"Get me O'Brien."

***

Richard's sense of urgency began to kick in as he landed in Palermo, a short 250-mile flight from Malta. He had not spoken to Sarah since leaving a few days prior, and worried others working the investigation would announce progress doing web searches, rather than pounding the pavement through good old-fashioned detective work. It would be near impossible for him to fight against conventional wisdom born out of incomplete or hastily done digital research, especially given the fact he was under investigation himself.

The weather in Palermo was not different from Malta: hot and humid, thanks in part to a microclimate created by masses of humanity in close quarters. Richard wore pressed slacks to help distinguish himself from throngs of tourists, a decision he came to question after having walked nearly a mile from where he spent the night.

He made his way behind a group from Germany visiting the Teatro Massimo, and walked onto Via Della Liberta, past high-end shops like Boss, Prada and Rolex. He finally reached a baroque 17th century building matching the address on the business card, once private residences, and later converted to office space. The large, rectangular bronze plaque outside the building indicated the occupants. On the third floor was the office of Vincenzu di Salvo.

The building's elevator was out of order, so Richard climbed the shiny, rounded, marble steps up to the third floor, and found the door to di Salvo's office. It was one of the few remaining original doors in the building, glossy brown walnut with an embedded glass window. In a semi-circle script it read "Vincenzu di Salvo, Dottore Commercialista." Miniblinds behind the glass made it impossible to see what was on the other side.

Richard put his hand on the doorknob and took a deep breath, recognizing anything was possible. As the door opened, a tiny bell tinkled to alert di Salvo, who was in his office beyond a small lobby. Richard could see him there, behind a massive oak desk. There was no receptionist, just a few upholstered chairs along the walls, a coffee table, and some magazines. The walls were adorned with pictures of Sicilian landscapes. Di Salvo looked up when he heard the bell.

"Buongiorno giovane!" di Salvo said, standing from behind his desk to greet Richard. "Vieni qui!"

Di Salvo was a diminutive gentleman of short stature. Richard put his age around sixty. He wore a three-piece brown pinstriped suit, white shirt and mustard colored tie. He had brown eyes behind round spectacles. In every respect, he looked the part of an accountant, apart from the short pony tail resting just above his collar. It compensated for the fact that most of the hair on his head was gone.

"I'm sorry to bother you," Richard started out, still standing in the outer room on the other side of the office entrance.

'il Americano?" di Salvo said as he heard Richard's accent. His accent was distinctly Sicilian.

Di Salvo came around the desk and out of his office so quickly that Richard had the instinct to put his left hand back on the door, in case he needed a quick exit. Then di Salvo reached over with both hands to grab Richard's right hand.

"I love the Americans!" he said with so much joy it could not have been anything but genuine. He vigorously shook Richard's hand before letting go to make a point.

"Look," he said excitedly, pointing to a diploma on his wall Richard couldn't quite make out. "I studied in America!"

"Please," he added, "please come into my office. Tell me your name."

Di Salvo retreated back to his office while looking back to ensure Richard was following. The reception Richard received reduced the amount of adrenaline in his system and allowed him to relax an iota. Di Salvo did not appear threatened, or threatening.

"Thank you for seeing me," Richard said, "My name is Richard O'Brien. I am on holiday here in Sicily, but wanted to ask you about some research I am doing into the activities of the mafia."

This was the opening line that Richard had decided to use as a litmus test for the meeting. The expression on di Salvo's face would speak volumes about whether he was involved in criminal activities, trying to protect sources, or merely afraid to discuss the matter.

"Yes of course," di Salvo replied, "the mafia is one of our most famous exports!"

Richard smiled.

"So," he said, "can you tell me what you know about Vino del Mar?"

Di Salvo didn't hesitate.

"Ah yes, 'VDM' as we call it here. They are one of my clients, but I suppose you know that already, and why you are here. What do you want to know about them?"

"Can you tell me about the company? Where is their wine sold?"

"Oh absolutely! The company is, let's see, about twenty-two years old. It's a small winery, based in Malta. Nearly all their product is sold in Italy. They do send some wines to the United States and other countries, which is probably how you heard of them, is that right?"

Richard was not expecting to hear the company had been operating for over two decades.

"Yes, that's right," he replied. "But I did not know that wines aged in the ocean have been around for so long."

Di Salvo looked confused at Richard's comment, then laughed.

"Oh, I see! You think Vino del Mar means it is aged in the ocean? Young man, 'del mar' doesn't necessarily mean 'in mar.' It's simply a brand for a company that operates near the ocean. There are, in fact, many cities also called 'del mar.' You have one in California, I believe."

Richard had to process that response for a moment. It was clear, however, that di Salvo was very relaxed and prepared to fill in many of the blanks in Richard's understanding of VDM.

"I see," he said, "so VDM has been selling its wine for some time, but recently have they started to join in on this 'ocean fermenting' trend?"

Di Salvo could see that Richard was peeling back layers of story that, at least outside Sicily, was poorly understood.

"Actually," di Salvo replied, "VDM has *not* yet joined this movement, but it's interesting, no, that it seems to have taken off in other parts of the world? I believe there are now four wineries in Italy that offer it. Have you tried it?"

Richard could hardly believe how easily information was flowing from his meeting with di Salvo. He wanted to take notes but didn't want to make di Salvo nervous, if that were even possible. The man was effusive and defied conventional views toward accountants.

"Actually," Richard replied, "I did try a bottle of VDM wines dropped off the coast of Alaska."

As the words left his mouth, Richard recognized it was another litmus test to see how di Salvo would react. Di Salvo pursed his lips, tilted his head, and looked to the ceiling before responding.

"Ah yes!" he said finally. "I know the company sends unlabeled wines to the United States. But they should not be using the VDM brand or label without the company's permission. But please tell me, how was the wine?"

Richard wasn't sure if he was directing an elicitation, casual conversation, or something else. He decided to put his cards on the table.

"Mr. di Salvo," he said, "I am confused. Do you know who controls this company and its global distribution? You work for them, correct?"

At this point, di Salvo's disposition changed visibly. He pursed his lips again and began nodding. But importantly, he never looked at Richard with any outward anger.

"All right, Signor O'Brien," he said, "you are obviously doing important research. Perhaps you are in law enforcement. If this is the case, I would advise you to be very careful. These people don't like to be bothered."

Finally, Richard felt a door opening. But before di Salvo continued, he got up and closed his, then returned to his desk and sat down.

"You know, we have two main branches of the mafia in Italy, the original Cosa Nostra, and the more recent 'Ndrangheta, out of Calabria. The 'Ndrangheta has emerged as the more powerful and brazen criminal enterprise. They control VDM wines. It's well known here."

Di Salvo paused to allow Richard to take the information in.

"VDM is indeed entering the market for ocean-aged wines in Malta. They intend to be the *only* distributor offering wines from Malta and are pressuring the government to give them an exclusive license."

Richard's brain was about to explode. So much of the information coming across was useful, but he wasn't sure where to connect the dots.

"What do you know about their activities in the U.S?" he asked.

"Look, Signor O'Brien, I am just a poorly paid accountant. I keep the books. I look at receipts. I don't ask too many questions."

Di Salvo knew that answer wouldn't satisfy Richard, so he continued.

"As I said, I love the Americans," he said, "and if 'Ndrangheta is sending wines to the United States, you can bet that the customer is not using the products to stand up a legitimate business. There are easier ways to do that without dancing with the devil, if you catch my drift. I do so love American expressions!"

Richard was not sure how much more he could extract from di Salvo, or if any more validation was necessary. He learned from his training that goodwill can evaporate quickly if you attempt to gain too much information in one sitting.

"Thank you, Mr. di Salvo," he said, "this has all been very helpful."

"Oh, you are more than welcome, giovanotto," di Salvo said, standing. "But you should know," he said, smiling, "most of what I told you can be found on Wikipedia."

Richard nodded. The amount of information available digitally was infinite, but much of it was unreliable and, more importantly, didn't make connecting the dots any easier.

"I'll look into it," he said, standing.

"Well, it's been a pleasure speaking with you," di Salvo said, extending his hand to Richard, "but I do have to get to an appointment. I have a nice little old lady, a widow, who needs help with her taxes. And I might ask her to marry me, depending on her assets of course, if you catch my drift."

Di Salvo finished the statement with a playful wink.

The two men walked out of the office together, and di Salvo locked the door. As they walked down the steps, he had many questions about the United States, its politics and people, but interestingly never asked Richard about his line of work. It was very likely he knew already.

When they reached the street, di Salvo asked, "can I drop you somewhere?" He pointed to a fire engine Ferrari parked in a private spot just outside the building.

Richard wasn't sure where he was going next, but he did have an epiphany on seeing the Ferrari, and thought of Delmatoff.

Perhaps it wasn't wise to generalize about accountants.

**

Richard stopped at the first café he found, a few hundred yards from the entrance to di Salvo's office. The mid-day sun was unforgiving and what he really wanted was a beer, but everybody in Palermo would be drinking cappuccino no matter the time of day, so that is what he ordered. Meanwhile the traffic running constantly past the café contributed to the warming of the city, and Richard wasn't sure how long he could last outside. At least he was in the shade.

He tried to make sense of the prior twenty minutes that he spent in di Salvo's office, and had the urge to return to the U.S. as soon as possible to present the evidence he gathered to Swanson, even if it meant passing intelligence through McAuley or Sarah. He opened his phone to type in what he learned that seemed relevant.

- *The VDM company in Malta is sending unlabeled wine to the U.S.*
- *Whoever is collecting this wine is leveraging the VDM brand, potentially in violation of the law*
- *The labels are being created in the US but don't comply with FDA regulations*
- *VDM is operated by the 'Ndrangheta mafia family, raising suspicions about their motives*

291

Was this enough? Richard thought to himself. He wondered if di Salvo would remain as friendly as he was that day if the U.S. Department of Justice were to seek the cooperation of the Italian authorities to subpoena his files. He resolved to simply get on a flight home and to compose a field report on the plane at which time he would hopefully be more articulate.

He switched from the Notes app to the Delta app on his phone to look at flights, but as he was doing so, a message flashed that he had an incoming text. It was from his brother, Myles.

"Do you know Bryan Mazzelli?"

"No," Richard replied. "Should I?"

"How about Nick Sabian?"

"No," Richard pecked into the phone's keyboard his response. "What's this about?" He was mildly irritated that the mysterious interrogation from his brother interrupted his session on the airlines app. Getting a decent seat on the flight required him to concentrate.

"He's an agent in MI6," Myles texted back. "Thought you might be colleagues."

"We're not," Richard replied, anxious to get back to booking his flight, and not the least bit interested in playing "do you know him" with Myles.

"All his details were under the QR code," Myles replied via text. "Like, everything, even pictures of the guy from his driver's license and passport."

"Seriously?"

"He lives on Elm Row in London. He has a daughter; she lives with her mom in Milton Keynes. His favored alias is Mazelli, but he has several others. His given name is Sabian, born 6/22/71. In 2023, he identified a Chinese spy that was using LinkedIn to trick British government employees into handing over state secrets. The same year he led the team that broke up a Bulgarian spy ring operating in the UK and passing intelligence to the KGB. Pretty cool stuff...."

Richard was stunned at the level of detail Myles uncovered, and texted "STOP" to his brother; iMessage was not secure enough for all the detail being shared in that moment. Myles could be forgiven for being absent minded about such things in the heat of the moment. So, Richard called him.

"How did you get all this info?" Richard asked immediately upon hearing Myles' voice.

"Well, it wasn't all that difficult, really," Myles replied, adding, "so, a QR code can store up to four thousand characters. I only texted you five hundred. There's more."

"And that's it?" Richard said incredulously, "you just pointed your phone to it?"

"No, it was password protected," Myles said. "But since it didn't require a username, I used hash cat to authenticate against the resource that holds the data."

Richard wasn't fully clear on what Myles meant, and his younger brother sensed it.

"So, there are, like, a dozen different hacking techniques out there based on different situations," Myles said. "When you don't have anything to go on, you turn to brute force hacking."

"What's that," Richard asked, no longer concerned that he timed out of the Delta app.

"Really you are just pushing forward as many possible combinations as a system can accommodate within any time constraint," Myles replied. "It helps to know the character limit of the password that is required, which I inferred from the size of the field provided once I activated the QR code. To speed things up, I ran simultaneously queries, one assuming it was a five-character field and another assuming a six-character field. It was just a guess, but we got lucky. It was a 6-character field requiring upper- and lower-case characters, and numbers. No symbols."

"How were you lucky?" Richard sought to understand the level of sophistication he was up against. The password requirements themselves sounded sophisticated enough.

"So, you would typically get locked out of a system after repeated attempts within a tight window," Myles explained. "This wasn't an issue, so hash cat – that's the hacking software - was free to push password combinations in 24/7 until it got the right one. It was running for almost ninety hours before it found the password that revealed all that stuff about Sabian."

"Ninety hours?" Richard was impressed.

"Yeah, like I said, we got lucky," Myles clapped back, excited that he prevailed in the task, but determined not to show it.

"A combination like that could take up to 6 days. We'd have found it eventually. My guess is whoever designed this never expected anyone to actually open the QR code, other than the specific person it was intended for."

Richard's heart began to beat so fast and hard that he could feel it pumping, as if he just ran the fifty-yard dash.

"Brother," he said, "this is amazing. YOU are amazing. Who else knows about this?"

"No one," Myles replied, "I worked on it during my lunch hour."

"Great," Richard said. "Let's keep it between us. I am on my way back to the States. I'll see you when I get in."

"Wait," Myles said, "where are you?"

It was too late. Richard hung up and ordered a ride to the airport.

25

By the time the USCGC *Arowana* sailed passed Zuniga Point, representing the entrance to San Diego Bay, the sun was beginning to set below light and scattered clouds, flushing hues of orange, red and maroon above the calm seas and skies. The 12-person crew had completed their three-day surveillance of the maritime border, having achieved an impressive "hat trick," in other words, a successful and significant operation for each of the three days at sea.

On Thursday, as they were making their way into deep waters, they were alerted to a search and rescue operation when a surfer was carried out to sea by a rip tide, and temporarily lost. The young man was found and brought safely on board. The following day, the crew assisted a vessel in distress, boarding it to find the captain was suffering from cardiac arrest. They coordinated with a Coast Guard Jayhawk helicopter to medevac the man to UCSD Medical Center. And on Saturday, as they were making their way back to port, they interdicted a 16-foot panga carrying twelve migrants, desperate to land on American soil. At this point, the crew of the *Arowana* would be grateful to find a hot meal somewhere near the base, and to return to their families.

The FBI's Special Weapons and Tactical (SWAT) Team arrived about ninety minutes before the *Arowana* was expected, joined by the Harbor Police and Sector San Diego's Maritime Safety and Security Teams who were advised and invited to participate in the operation as a matter of professional courtesy. They stood up floodlights from one end of the dock to the other. The agents were not about to take any chances that their suspect might try to jump in the water and swim to an embankment outside the fence line of the base.

The Joint Harbor Operations Command that coordinates activity across multiple maritime agencies was also made aware of the FBI's intent to take a member of the USCG Auxiliary into custody, and advised Lieutenant Underwood that all personnel were to remain on board the *Arowana* pending further instructions. Underwood advised the crew that "due to an impromptu inspection, all hands apart from those assigned to docking maneuvers are to stay in their berths."

The *Arowana* eased its way toward the dock as floodlights illuminated the area, eliminating all darkness and most shadows on its surface. Flying beetles made lazy circles around the lights. The rest of the night sky was black and unseasonably cold. Two "coasties" in their dark blue on-duty uniform grabbed the lines tossed to them and pulled the *Arowana* against the dock.

Six officers dressed entirely in black, wearing bullet proof vests and carrying compact SR-25 sniper rifles stood ready to climb on board. Tanaka was resting in his bunk when they came upon him. He was taken into custody, read his Miranda rights, and zip-tied behind his back without incident. His next stop was a holding cell at FBI Headquarters in Los Angeles. His career as an Auxiliarist was over.

***

Richard stepped into the late afternoon sun at LAX and was relieved to see Sarah's rented Ford Fusion about 25 yards away. She edged the car closer, threw it in park, and jumped outside to give Richard a hug.

"Missed you," she whispered into his ear as the two embraced.

"Me too," Richard replied, too tired to come up with anything more profound.

"Swanson is expecting you," she said, pulling away from his chest, "we have to go straight to the office."

Richard predicted that the case in Internal Affairs would be closed without any recommended disciplinary action, so he wondered whether Swanson came up with yet another excuse to keep him on the margins of the agency. Perhaps he would be given a perfunctory desk job, or something equally humiliating. He was too tired to care, and resigned to whatever fate was waiting to meet him.

During the short drive to the Federal Building, Sarah and Richard updated each other on the events of the past twenty-four hours.

"An MI6 agent?! Operating on American soil!?" Sarah exclaimed as she focused on the chaotic traffic of LA in front of her.

"They took him in? The comic?" Richard countered shortly later. "I hope he'll come up with better material for his act."

"The mafia is involved?" Sarah added, "working with the yakuza??"

This rapid exchange continued for so long that Richard didn't have an opportunity to share how beautiful it was in Malta, and eventually Sarah pulled in front of the Federal Building.

"Richard," Sarah said, stating the obvious, "whatever he throws at you, don't throw back any punches."

"You're not coming in?" Richard asked as he opened the car door.

"I've got some shopping to do," she replied, smiling, "you've been a good boy, and I have a surprise for you."

***

"O'Brien, get in here!" Swanson barked as he saw Richard approach his office. However, the tone of his voice was noticeably different from their prior encounters. In the greatest test of self-awareness he had ever faced, Swanson was determined to see Richard in a new light.

"Get in here, O'Brien," Swanson repeated as he came from behind his desk to greet his new bromance. "Nice work out there."

Richard was not sure whether Swanson was referring to his work on the ground in Malta and Palermo, or the identification of an MI6 agent operating in their midst. He was operating on such little sleep that he wasn't entirely sure he heard Swanson correctly. He had a massive headache from ten hours on a Delta Airbus to JFK, followed by six more hours to LAX.

Swanson grabbed Richard's hand and led him to the seat opposite his desk. At that point, he was sitting on the edge of his desk, just as he did when he propositioned Sarah Goodman.

"Look O'Brien," he said, "I'll get right to the point." Until that point, Richard hadn't even said "hello."

"I'd like to put you in charge of the wine-money laundering-covert assassination thing we've been working on here," he said. "We are not entirely sure of a connection, but you have busted the door open for us on relevant intelligence." Swanson wanted to vomit in his mouth, but he succeeded in getting the offer out of it first.

Richard thought it interesting that Swanson did not even bother to address the results of the investigation recently concluded by Internal Affairs, or the fact he had banished him from the agency prior to that.

"Yes, sir," he replied, thinking that at any moment he might pass out. The pounding inside his brain was relentlessly demanding his attention.

"We've got a search warrant for Jack Tanaka's storage unit, and he's in custody on the eighteenth floor."

"Sir?"

"Form a team, interrogate Tanaka, and get out to that storage unit to collect evidence," Swanson said.

"Yes, sir," Richard repeated, hardly believing what was happening, and wondering if he was in a dream. He wished he had recorded the conversation, just in case.

The two men sat there, staring at each other. Richard thought there may be more.

"Oh, and another thing," Swanson said. So, there was more.

"You get to name the operation," he added. "But don't spend all day on it."

26

Tanaka would be the first to admit his process for distribution of classified information was far too complicated. But in fact, that was his intended design: a scheme so unbelievable that it remained so while performing in plain sight. This would become an operation discussed, dissected and debated for years within the intelligence community, at West Point, and within the FBI Academy.

He often engaged in a silent debate with himself about how best to undertake the challenge given him by the yakuza, playing out various options before dispensing with them as impractical or too dangerous. At least in the case of wine, the yakuza had existing experience and established operations.

Apart from Sisky, all customers were overseas, so there was exposure in nearly every scenario. A single interdiction by customs would shut down his operation while exposing both buyer and seller. The fact was,

Tanaka concluded, every other form of delivery introduced its own challenges and risks. And once he established the infrastructure to conceal sensitive information on wine labels, it was too late to consider an alternative approach. The infrastructure costs had become too high, and he was in too deep with yakuza's mafia partners.

Given the sophistication of Interpol, the FBI and other law enforcement agencies, it was critical to minimize the digital signature of the transactions, so the use of a physical conduit - wine bottles, to the "product" - classified information, was essential. Business could not be conducted in any way that would connect the activity to the parties, and it obviously couldn't look like what it really was. Dumping the wine in the ocean provided the perfect cover, while keeping the valuable intelligence at way more than arm's length – essentially inaccessible – until he was certain that the funding for the purchase went through.

Tanaka considered the use of wine as a decoy to be the most creative part of his plan. He aimed for it to look like a legitimate business, but even if it drew suspicion as a money laundering operation, it would throw off the scent that it was actually far more nefarious. Indeed, Tanaka was proud of how he constructed the whole thing.

He wasn't, on the other hand, proud of his situation, held in a detention room at FBI headquarters, still zip tied with his hands behind his back. That was intentional as Richard entered the room with his cell phone. On the suggestion of another agent, he put a small yellow smiley sticker at the top of the phone to catch Tanaka's attention.

"Do you recognize this?" Richard said immediately on entering the room, and pushing it into Tanaka's face.

"No," Tanaka said firmly, staring at the sticker and believing for the moment that he could legitimately evade an implication of some sort.

Richard turned the phone back to view it, confirming that Tanaka's face had unlocked it.

"Thank you," Richard said, passing the phone behind him to McAuley who walked with it out of the room.

"Is this even legal?" said McAuley to the agent that extended his hand to take the phone. The two started walking down the hall to an adjoining room where they could observe the interrogation.

"We've been doing it since 2018," said the agent, sitting down in the dark room, the one-way mirror providing the only ambient light. He held the phone a few inches from his face.

"He's using Protonmail," he added, staring at the emails he unlocked.

"Shit, that's bad right?" said McAuley.

"No," the agent replied, "actually, it's great."

"Why is that?" McAuley replied.

"We have this guy's phone and he's using the most encrypted email program on the planet," the agent explained. "It means whoever he communicates with assumes their communications are secure and protected. We can exploit that."

McAuley now understood.

"So, we can communicate with his associates and they will think it's him," McAuley stated with confidence, not bothering to frame the comment as a question.

"That's right," replied the agent, plugging the phone into a charger.

The FBI was now in a perfect position to expose the perpetrators and unravel the whole thing.

**

Nick Sabian was deep in concentration, hunched over one of the files on Tanaka's desk, when the garage door flew up and banged loudly against its backstop, fully retracted, and blasting the afternoon sun across the room. At Sabian's feet was his backpack, and inside was the bottle that he took from Sarah's hotel room, which he brought to compare directly to whatever he could find in the storage unit.

"FBI! Don't you fucking move!" came a voice from the cavernous entrance. "Down on your knees! NOW!"

Before Sabian could explain himself, his right cheek was being pressed hard against the cement floor, an agent's hand holding down his head while pulling his arms behind his back and applying zip ties to his wrists.

"Easy mates," he shouted back as he rolled from side to side. "You've got the wrong guy!"

Within seconds from opening the unit, a squad of eight armed FBI police in bulletproof vests were standing around Sabian, who was still face down on the floor. One of the agents helped him to his knees and then to his feet. Richard O'Brien walked through the crowd of agents to get a better look at Sabian. He carried himself with a renewed sense of confidence as the lead investigator on the case, but deferred for the moment to the FBI Police Senior Agent, Donald Berlin, leading the squad.

"What's your name, son?" said Berlin, standing so close to Sabian that little daylight came between them. Standing at six foot three and over two hundred pounds, Berlin made for an intimidating sight, even if not in a bulletproof vest and police uniform.

"Bryan Mazzelli," Sabian replied breathlessly as he tried to stand as upright as possible, a task that would have been easier had he free movement of his arms, and if there wasn't an agent still holding them.

"Bryan Mazzelli, you are in some seriously deep shit," replied Berlin. "We have a search warrant for these premises."

"You don't understand…" Sabian replied, wondering if now was the right time to confess he was a British agent.

Richard heard that name before and it triggered him, especially as Sabian spoke with a thick British accent.

"Wait," he said loudly, opening his phone and looking at it. "I may know this guy….."

He opened the chat from Myles that he received two days before. Looking up, he moved closer to Sabian, as Berlin backed away. Richard was about to take a gamble, but he was pretty confident in the outcome.

"Hello, Mr. Sabian," Richard said, looking him straight in the eye, and extending his hand.

"Pleased to meet you, Mr. O'Brien," he replied. Sabian slowly accepted Richard's offer of a handshake.

The two stared at each other briefly in a form of unspoken respect and admiration.

"It's okay," Richard said, turning to the many agents now standing behind him. "He's one of us. At least I think so."

"We're going to have to see some ID," said the senior agent.

"In my backpack," Sabian replied, "over there."

Richard walked over and picked up the backpack. The first thing he pulled out was an empty bottle of VDM wine. He had seen this bottle before. He looked back at Sabian, holding it out toward him.

"Mate," Sabian said, looking back at Richard, "that bottle has my name on it, quite literally."

"Why do you think it belongs to you?" Richard asked, continuing to examine the bottle.

"Look at the file on the desk," Sabian said. "There is a document with all my personals, and there is a serial number on that document matching the serial number on the bottle. I have to thank you, Mr. O'Brien, unless you were the assassin intending to take me out in the first place."

Sabian was playing with fire, and knew it. But it seemed the quickest way to convince Richard and the other agents that he was, in fact, not the perpetrator of the crimes, but someone investigating them.

Richard spun the bottle around in his right hand. The label was peeling in the same spot as the bottle he shared with Sarah in her hotel. And all of the sudden, Sabian accusing him of being an assassin instantly made sense.

"Did you swipe this from me?" Richard asked, moving toward Sabian with the bottle.

"I plead the fifth," Sabian said stoically, "or is it the sixth? Honestly mate, I'm not sure. I know my country gave you our laws, but then your 'founding fathers' screwed them all up."

27

The night lights of London were in full view on a rare, cloudless night. With her corner office and northern view, Delaroche could barely make out the glow of Westminster Abbey and below, the inky black water of the River Thames that split the city in two. But she wasn't admiring the view. She was on hold waiting for the operator to connect her with John Swanson on a secure line.

"Swanson," the voice said on the other line, as if much closer than it was in reality.

"Mr. Swanson," Delaroche said in the most respectful tone possible, "thank you for taking my call. I know you are a busy man."

Swanson was not impressed by the formality intended to endear or flatter him. And he knew exactly what the call was about.

"Hello Audrey," Swanson replied, dispensing with protocol. He had interacted with Delaroche in the past and it was obvious the level of distrust between the two was quite firmly in place, and content to stay there.

"John, I must apologize for the pedestrian speed at which diplomacy works," she said, "our office directed our inquiry as required but it appears it did not reach you." Delaroche intentionally didn't acknowledge that Sabian was in FBI custody, something she already knew. Instead, she pretended that, as far as she knew, her agent had just arrived and she was calling to alert Swanson's office.

Swanson didn't take the bait, but chose not to escalate matters at that moment. There would be time for that later.

"What can I do for you Audrey?" Swanson replied.

"Oh, John, I merely wanted to call and suggest that you feel free to engage with our agent, Nick Sabian, and to utilize his expertise in any way that it might be useful," she said. "I think you will find that he has a great deal to offer."

"I see," Swanson said, continuing with the charade. He hadn't considered that Sabian could serve as an added resource and wasn't inclined to give him that latitude.

"Yes, John, but do return him in one piece, if you wouldn't mind."

"There will be repercussions, Audrey," Swanson said, finally. He wasn't going to let her go without puncturing a hole in the charade.

"I understand where you are coming from, John," she replied gently, "but at the end of the day, we all want the same thing."

The patronizing comment made Swanson want to reach through the phone lines to strangle Delaroche. On paper, she was correct. On the ground, however, the situation could not be more ambiguous and hopelessly nuanced.

***

The Federal building, outfitted to the specifications of the FBI, had two small interrogation rooms that were a perfect square, with an observation booth in between containing video-cameras, audio-recording equipment, and one-way mirrors looking into each room. There were no furnishings apart from a table and four chairs, and cheap abstract art hanging on the walls to prevent an unpleasant echo on the recorded conversations. It was a matter of protocol that Sabian would be retained in one of the rooms while his credentials were verified. He wasn't surprised, didn't object to his treatment, and didn't expect anything less.

Sabian and McAuley sat hunched over reams of paperwork, looking over the trove of documents taken from Tanaka's storage unit. Sabian's shirt sleeves were rolled up. McAuley leaned back every so often to battle his chronic back pain. Richard walked in with a can of Coca-Cola for each of the men, then sat down.

"Let the record show the interview began at thirteen hundred hours on August 14," he said, directing his voice toward the microphone built into the center of the table. He then looked at Sabien to initiate his line of questioning.

"All right, Mr. Sabian, how did you come to find out about Jack Tanaka," he said.

"We had an agent operating in the wine industry here, investigating the assassination of covert British agents," Sabian replied. "We established a connection between the sale of rare wines and the funding of assassination plots."

O'Brien and McAuley made eye contact at this point, as if to say *our theory as well.*

But a split second later the words "an agent operating here" resonated with O'Brien and images of Asha came flooding back.

"Who is the agent operating here?" he asked. Because Sabian's statement evoked such strong images of Asha Chandra, Richard failed to ask how it came to be that a foreign agent was operating on U.S. soil without the agency being informed.

"You know I can't talk about that, mate," Sabian replied. "It's not relevant, and I'm not at liberty to say."

Nick Sabian had just repurposed Richard's favorite comeback line, and he could barely blame him for it. He continued to stare at him with a menacing look, hoping it might unlock further details, but Sabian just stared right back.

Although it was treated as a coincidence that the bottle containing Sabian's personal details ended up in his hands, in reality there were multiple bottles in distribution to governments and organized criminal syndicates that would like to have seen him eliminated, which explained why Richard also had a bottle with Sabian's details behind the label. Tanaka naturally took advantage of selling multiple "Sabian bottles" assuming correctly that no matter how he was eliminated, none of his Chinese, Russian or Iranian customers would complain.

"So," Richard said, deciding to pivot the conversation, "is it your theory that this is operating as a commercial enterprise, selling off the protected information on agents to various buyers?"

"That's right," Sabian replied. He was relieved that his American counterparts could reach the same conclusion as his government without him having to reveal intelligence he gathered on his own.

"And the buyers have their own mercenaries that can do the dirty work that they keep their hands clean?" It was McAuley this time, adding yet one more piece of the puzzle.

"The buyers have no particular need to touch the bottles," Sabian offered. "Once the purchase has been made, the bottles can be delivered directly to whomever they contracted out to perform the service."

The three men continued to exchange information but it was clear that they were already on the same page. Before they met for a full hour, Sabian's credentials had been verified and he was cleared to leave the building. He opted to remain the rest of the day, with Richard's permission, and simply asked if he could use the restroom to relieve himself and wash his face.

"So," McAuley said, once the two were alone in the room, "have you come up with a name for the operation?"

Richard hadn't actually, but thinking back on the murder of his mentor and others within the intelligence community, he didn't need more than a moment to float a perfect option.

"Yeah," he said, "Operation Fatal Ledger."

***

Richard left the room with McAuley and Sabian and paid a visit to the agent recording the meeting.

"I guess it's time for round two," Richard said as he watched Tanaka sitting in the other room on the other side of the mirror, his hands still zip tied behind his back. "Where is the blade?"

The agent operating the camera equipment opened a desk drawer to his right, and without turning his gaze from Tanaka's interrogation room, held up a box cutter blade above his shoulder, which Richard took from him. Richard then walked out of the surveillance booth and into the adjoining room where Tanaka was beginning to doze off.

He had been detained for over 24 hours and allowed to leave the room only for purposes of using the restroom. Richard understood that he would need to disposition Tanaka within forty-eight hours by either formalizing a charge against him, or releasing him.

Tanaka's eyes opened wide as Richard walked in and placed a bottle of water and bag of potato chips in front of him on the small, square table. Then he walked behind Tanaka and cut the zip ties. Tanaka immediately reached for the water. Richard started to record the session.

"Okay," he said, dropping into the chair opposite Tanaka, "let's talk about what you do for a living, and why you have so many bottles of wine in public storage."

"I'm a wine broker," Tanaka replied as he leveled his head, swallowing a load of water.

"A wine broker?" Richard said, nodding slightly as if he believed it. "And why would a wine broker be dropping wines from a Coast Guard cutter?"

Richard realized that Tanaka could deny the fact he was observed dropping the crate, as there was no eye witness to the act. Fortunately, he got the implied confession anyway.

"I also do some contract work for a wine distributor, VDM, maybe you've heard of them."

"No," Richard said, "why don't you tell me about them."

"The company sells wine that is aged in the ocean; you can look it up."

"We did," Richard replied. "The company is prohibited from operating here because it's illegal to ferment wine off the coast of the U.S."

"Really," Tanaka replied, doing his best to feign ignorance. "I didn't know that. It's legal everywhere else."

"Ignorance of the law is not a defense," Richard shot back. "Why did you have to join the Coast Guard Auxiliary in order to drop the wine?"

"I didn't have to join the Auxiliary," Tanaka replied calmly, "I wanted to serve my country."

"You haven't answered my question," Richard said, as if he was setting a carefully conceived trap.

"I needed a new way to drop the wine as the guy who did this for me was no longer available," he replied. "I was already in the Auxiliary so this seemed a sensible option."

Tanaka delivered the exact lines he had practiced in anticipation of getting caught. Richard stared at him, not bothering to call out the preposterous explanation. Certainly, any member of the Coast Guard would understand the activity to be forbidden, if they even bothered to ask.

"Mr. Tanaka," Richard said, standing up, his arms on his waist, "there are two ways this is going to go down."

Tanaka looked up at Richard, bracing for the worst.

"You will be heading for the federal detention center in LA shortly, to await trial on charges of espionage. That will be in addition to engaging in a forbidden retail business, for illegally dumping potentially toxic materials into the ocean, and for trafficking in protected information."

Richard paused to let the threat sink in.

"Espionage alone is a Class A felony, and you would be looking at twenty to ninety-nine years. Time that you will spend in one of our most uncomfortable federal prisons."

Tanaka hung his head. He had not calculated that so many legal consequences could rain down on him at the same time.

"That's the current trajectory you're on," Richard continued, "but there is another potential path for you."

"Damn, he's good," said Sabian, who had joined a small crowd in the surveillance room, looking in with Swanson and McAuley from the other side of the one-way mirror.

"Yeah," replied Swanson, reluctantly.

"If you elect to cooperate with us," Richard said, "the court will look very favorably on your decision. This approach would go quickly and be over before you know it."

"Think about it," Richard concluded, as he headed for the door to leave the room. As he held the door handle, he turned back to Tanaka.

"Oh, and one more thing," he said, "you can plan on spending a few months in the detention center before your trial even begins."

Richard brought his hand to his chin, pretending to remember an important caveat.

"On the other hand, some detainees – like Jeffrey Epstein – never even get to trial. Suspects that have harmed government officials or intelligence officers are particularly at risk in that environment. They have a tendency to get their asses kicked."

Richard nodded slightly to himself signifying he put it all out there, then left the room.

It took less than 20 minutes for Tanaka to decide to cooperate and turn "state's evidence." On top of the shame it would bring his family, he knew he wouldn't survive incarceration. He'd plead guilty to the lesser charge of contaminating the marine environment, and hope to simply be put on probation. And if Nakajima is somehow killed it would likely ensure that he was not.

Until Tanaka was taken into custody, the investigation into how the distribution of wine bottles led to covert agent assassinations played out like a book with a missing chapter. Now, all the pieces fell into place.

28

By 3:30 in the afternoon, Richard couldn't keep his eyes open any longer. He tasked Agent Houseman to continue the interrogation of Tanaka while he went back to his apartment to crash. Houseman assembled a thorough report to support Operation Fatal Ledger that included the details of how two vastly different criminal syndicates came to be partners.

In the interrogation, Tanaka explained how the yakuza purchased unlabeled bottles from a wine importer in Temecula, how the mafia supplied all the intel for the targets from their Sicilian hacking operation, and various in-kind arrangements between the organizations. He described how they cooperated to launder proceeds through wine sales and vineyard operations, and how this loose fabric of familial clans that thrived on crime and deception had somehow come to be bedfellows, starting with a meeting in 1986 between two aging icons.

To confuse law enforcement, the yakuza taught the mafia how to conduct cybercrime and then outsourced that work to them. Meanwhile, the mafia consulted with the yakuza on how to leverage a wine business to support the art of money laundering. The mafia supplied the wine to the yakuza, and the yakuza gave the mafia a cut of its robust dark web business. It was a marriage of convenience and form of synergy in criminal behavior never seen before or since.

Tanaka was able to identify documents gathered from the storage unit that would reveal bottles in circulation threatening the lives of targeted individuals; however, in that he shredded most evidence, only a handful of vulnerable agents and diplomats could be confirmed. Swanson initiated a series of alerts to government agencies to protect those at risk. But there was unfinished business, and that was to topple the whole enterprise.

***

Richard opened his eyes after his second night back from Europe. His circadian rhythm was seriously out of whack and woke at 4:45 a.m. He stared at Sarah's face for about 10 minutes before finally getting up, getting dressed, and heading to the office. Before leaving, he looked back at Sarah's body still sleeping under the sheets and reflected on how lucky he was.

He walked into the FBI Situation Room on the ninth floor of the Federal Building at 6:50 a.m. This conference room was used primarily for dynamic investigations that had accumulated so much evidence that it would be difficult to summarize in a paper brief. One wall of the room, opposite a row of windows, was converted to a huge bulletin board, and a fair amount of this was covered with newspaper clippings, maps with coordinates, file photos of various "persons of interest," and unclassified reports that pertained to the operation.

Richard set down his coffee and gazed at the impressive amount of information on the wall. This was the first time he realized the significance of the operation he was tasked to lead. He hoped he was prepared.

People began filing into the room, including Swanson, McAuley, Houseman, Sabian, other local agents and analysts, and of course, Sarah, who winked at Richard as she walked near him. Many walked slowly past the evidence wall as if browsing a museum exhibit. Sabian was impressed by the capacity of the agency, as evidenced by an expression of disbelief as he perused the wall. Soon afterward, the staff began to take seats around a massive conference table.

Richard made a few opening remarks and asked each participant to introduce themselves to the others, making a special point of welcoming Sabian as a guest. He thanked the agents for their time and energy in gathering so much valuable intelligence. Then, he flipped open his binder with the bullet points he composed in advance.

"We have a working theory confirmed through interrogation of the suspect," Richard said, "that the yakuza and mafia have partnered in a scheme to sell information on foreign agents of various nationalities, including our own covert agents and 'nocks,' and that the information is being distributed through encryption placed on wine bottles."

"Once the bottles have been purchased on the dark web," Richard continued, "they are automatically paired with a contract killer who receives the bottle and carries out the assassination. The buyers of this information are spending millions of dollars to acquire this information and to fund the murders."

An agent in the room asked the question on the minds of many others.

"Sir, are we able to unequivocally tie the sale of information to an actual murder?"

"Yes," Richard replied, "based on documents we've recovered, we can verify the link between the sale of the bottles and fallen agents, including the most recent assassination of a CIA operative in Havana."

At that point, Sabian raised his hand, and Richard nodded at him. He didn't want his countrymen to be ignored.

"Our government lost an MI6 agent in the UK two weeks ago," he said, "we believe it may have been a revenge killing for his exemplary work in Iran. I believe your former director may have been a revenge killing as well."

"But sir," said an agent standing along the side of the room, "would a foreign government really hire the yakuza for revenge?"

"If it satisfies a strategic goal, absolutely," Swanson said before Richard could respond. Swanson was determined to remain relevant. "And don't forget the fact that the yakuza is a criminal syndicate. Any country's money, rubles, or yen is acceptable to them."

Swanson was correct in that, while the intelligence was scarce, the belief in the agency was that the yakuza would work with anyone and wouldn't regard any political or cultural differences as relevant. It was acknowledged, for example, that the yakuza collaborated with the Chinese government to exploit the market and maximize trade in opium. The relationship between China and Japan was rarely such a productive one.

It was also well known that nation-states were very comfortable outsourcing their assassination attempts; it wasn't limited to China dismantling the U.S. intelligence presence within its borders. The United States had done it to murder members of Al-Qaida. Iran and Russia routinely hired contract killers to eliminate dissidents and defectors.

So, what started as an experiment turned into brisk business for the yakuza and mafia for no other reason than "revenge killings" expanded the potential market for assassinations. It was no longer limited to covert agents but included government officials, opposition leaders, and FBI agents. Conventional wisdom might suggest that governments would not stoop to the level of revenge killings, but for the simple matter that eliminating an agent interfering with a government's activities obviously meant that they couldn't do it again.

***

Richard cleared the conference room in order to retain only those agents assigned to Operation Fatal Ledger, a team Richard handpicked along with an occasional suggestion from McAuley. By this time, he was sufficiently caffeinated to be visibly confident and in charge.

"Okay," he said in a slightly elevated voice, "what have we got since the suspect's detention?"

"We have been reviewing all prior email correspondence between Tanaka and his yakuza handlers and creating a handwriting profile," said Agent Houseman. "We have a pretty good idea on how to mimic his style of communication, and since Tanaka has turned state's evidence, we are using him to refine the messaging."

The rumor about Tanaka's turnaround had generated significant buzz in the building.

"Great," he said, adding, "what's the plan?"

"Tanaka's contact is one of the yakuza clan's highest-ranking officers, probably because he is one of the few assets operating in the U.S.," said Houseman. "We are planning to suggest the yakuza boss meet with a Mexican cartel chief in Honolulu as a convenient neutral ground from which to discuss a deal."

"What kind of deal, and why would we expect him to take the bait?"

"The narrative we are creating is this: the cartel wants help with eliminating law enforcement on the border, allowing them to smuggle drugs and migrants with fewer complications. We are making clear the yakuza's reputation for coordinating clean kills through a network of contract killers. We are suggesting that the cartel chief expects a face-to-face meeting on neutral ground as a minimum expression of respect."

Richard was processing the plan when Houseman offered the catnip.

"This young man, the second in command, is anxious to prove his worth to his father."

"All right," Richard said approvingly, "tell me more about the planned outreach."

"Tanaka has helped us to fine-tune the messages and add details only he and the yakuza would know, you know, for credibility," said Houseman. "We are using the name of Jose Pardillo Guitarrez, a well-known cartel leader, in case they should do a background check of their own."

Richard was impressed by the team he inherited.

"What else?"

McAuley proudly held up a small disc, the size of a thick coat button or coin.

"Check this out," he said. "It's a redesigned Apple Tag the guys in the lab made for us. Small enough in diameter to fit snugly into the cap of a twist-off wine bottle."

"That's cool," said Richard, "what are we planning to do with it?"

"We thought you might like to dive down and replace it with one of the bottles in the crate just dropped. We don't have much time."

"Come again?" Richard asked. He thought maybe McAuley was joking.

"We have the coordinates of the crate Tanaka dropped from the *Arowana*'s GPS. He said the crate would be lifted the day after tomorrow."

Richard was, at that point, just outside the recommended 24-hour window advised before diving after a transatlantic flight. But more importantly, given McAuley's sense of humor, he still wasn't entirely sure what was being suggested was serious. It sounded like a plot from a Bond movie.

"What specifically are you proposing, Jeff?" he asked, squinting and tipping his head as if he was quite confused by McAuley's pitch.

"So, we can produce a bottle for you with the personals of the yakuza boss and put this in the crate, replacing one that is already there," he said. "Instead of nipping at the tail of the dragon, we'd be cutting it off at its head, presuming the bottle reaches a competent contract killer."

"So, we'd have a two-barreled approach," Richard surmised. "Redundancy."

Sabian loved the plan and said so.

"Yakuza members are not likely yakuza customers," he said. "Whoever ultimately receives the bottle won't ever consider the reason why he's being paid to assassinate a yakuza boss, or he may just assume it's being ordered by a rival gang."

Richard stood in silence, processing the proposal, so McAuley repeated the most important point if the mission was to succeed.

"Richard," he said, looking at him with as serious a face as he could muster, "we don't have much time."

29

As might be expected, Richard and Nick Sabian quickly developed a form of mutual respect that would last well beyond their current operation. And as Nick did not have any particular place to go, he was invited to participate in all meetings related to Operation Fatal Ledger. After checking into a local boutique hotel in LA, not far from the Federal Building, he returned to find Richard sitting at his desk, typing up one of many reports needed to account for his activity and expenses. He would be heading down to San Diego within the hour to carry out his team's ambitious plan.

"Mind if I come in?" Sabian said, poking his head in the door.

"Oh hey," Richard replied, "I see they got you temporary credentials. You are legit now."

"Yeah, well," Nick said, "if MI6 won't take me back, I may be applying for something permanent."

Richard smiled. He definitely appreciated having someone like Nick around.

"Say mate," Nick said, "could I interest you in a tiny bit of scope creep?"

The concept of "scope creep," commonly experienced in the consulting world, is not a term heard often within the walls of the FBI. This is because an operation would typically expand not just to the extent necessary, but if it involved saving lives or capturing bad guys, to its full potential.

"What did you have in mind?" Richard asked, checking his watch.

"Look, those other bottles, the ones already down there, they may have details on people we would like to keep alive. I mean, how would you like it if one of them had *your* name on it?"

Richard was embarrassed. Nick had a point. The constant drumbeat of "we don't have much time" led Richard to neglect an important part of any law enforcement mission: to protect and defend.

"That's a fair point," he said. "What do you suggest?"

"Let's see if we can identify more of the bottles and who they are meant to target. Let's go wine shopping."

***

In a hastily assembled meeting, Richard brought together Sabian, McAuley, Houseman, and a few other agents working the case. In addition, he brought in Jack Tanaka from his detention cell, where he remained until a plea deal could be presented to the federal judge. As much as he wanted to maximize time with Sarah, he decided that being seen together in the office might become problematic if their romantic involvement became known. She agreed.

Box lunches were stacked on a table at one end of the room. Members of the meeting filed past that table, grabbed a box and bottle of water, and then started toward the conference table in the center of the room.

"First of all," Richard said while the team was still taking their seats, "I want to thank you all for being part of this team. You guys are great."

The agents acknowledged the protocol displayed in that moment with a slight head nod, and continued unpacking their meal. Richard grabbed an extra box lunch for Tanaka and laid it in front of him.

"So," Richard continued, "where is the new bottle?"

"They're still working on it," said Houseman as he lifted a sandwich from the box.

"Still working on it?" Richard said, a bit alarmed and checking his watch again. "Do they realize I am expected at the base in San Diego this afternoon? Who are 'they,' anyway?"

"Yes, don't worry," Houseman said. "The bottle is essentially done; they are just adding a silicone coat to protect the label. It's being done in the forensics lab, not really their bread-and-butter, but it's the best option on short notice."

Short notice. Those words would haunt Richard if the operation failed to produce results.

As the group ate lunch, Richard drew on the conference room's whiteboard a grid containing a dozen squares. They were organized in three rows of four cells each, just as they would appear in a case of wine. Within each cell he wrote the identity of those individuals known to be included in the shipment sitting off the coast of Point Loma. Only about half the cells were filled in because Tanaka struggled to recall details of the shipment after having shredded most evidence of it. The lives of three American agents and two British agents would be saved by the removal of those bottles from the crate, a direct consequence of the scope creep that Sabian recommended.

"I suggest we replace this bottle," Richard said, pointing to a bottle in the second row from the top. "This man was recently incarcerated in China for murdering a business rival, so this bottle is probably to exact revenge. But it's more likely the contract killer collecting the bottle would take down another man of Asian heritage without asking too many questions about it. Mr. Tanaka, do I have that right?"

Tanaka nodded in agreement.

"Some contract killers will only assassinate Asians, and some will only kill the British and the Americans," he said.

"Okay," Richard said, determined to keep things moving quickly, "what identities of other American agents, British agents, or diplomats are in that crate that we want to protect?"

He looked at Tanaka, whose expression was blank. He looked at Houseman, who, in the slightest manner possible, shrugged his shoulders. He looked at Sabian, whose face reflected the ambiguity of the moment. Richard was under the mistaken assumption that most of the identities were known.

"So, half the bottles could be anyone," Richard said, hoping the group wouldn't settle for such uncertainty.

There was a brief moment of silence as the team had nothing to offer.

"This is bullocks, mates," Sabian said out of frustration. "We can't let those bottles reach their destination. We should just destroy the whole lot."

What Sabian didn't realize is that the United States would not back down from a big investment in a bad idea. Richard needed to make a decision, but he didn't see an obvious path. A chimera of potential failure hung over the meeting as the group felt there was a higher probability that a proven contract killer would succeed than any effort to capture Nakajima alive.

Richard proceeded to free associate, not entirely sure where it would lead.

"All right," he said, "this whole plan was predicated on taking out a highly ranked member of the yakuza in the event we miss the opportunity to take him into custody. This was to be our backup plan, our failsafe."

"Let me remind everyone," he continued, "about the yakuza's scope of crimes: drug trafficking, human trafficking, sex trafficking, cybercrime, extortion. That's just a partial list, guys, to which we can now add the assassination of our own people." Richard was demonstrating the leadership he always knew was within him.

"So, let me ask by show of hands, how many of you feel we should just destroy the crate completely and potentially forgo the opportunity to eliminate this bad actor? Would you be able to sleep with the knowledge you let him get away?"

Richard looked directly at Sabian as he finished the thought. No hands were raised. If Richard wanted to talk his way out of a dangerous scuba diving mission, his free association exercise was not the best approach.

"Okay then," Richard said, "if we removed all bottles but one, that will look suspicious to whomever collects the crate," he said. "And if I pull half of them, that would look suspicious as well. I can't imagine the bad guys collecting the crate are going to call customer service, but something about this plan doesn't feel right, like we would tip someone off."

Heads nodded gently across the room. Then, predictably, Sabian floated the obvious.

"We have to replace all of them."

***

The Jayhawk helicopter gently set down on the tarmac at the U.S. Coast Guard base in San Diego. It was five o'clock in the afternoon. Richard hopped out, ducked as much as he could under the still rotating blades, and jogged over to meet a small team of men waiting for him outside the aircraft hangar where additional helicopters were maintained.

"We appreciate the assistance, Sir," Richard said as he extended his hand to Lieutenant Underwood. "As you know, we don't have much time."

"Happy to help," replied Underwood. Although Underwood wasn't able to take Richard to the drop site on the *Arowana*, he was able to arrange for the USCG Marine Security Response Team to take him out on one of their rigid hull inflatable boats. These boats were commonly used for search and rescue operations when rescue divers needed quick access to the water.

Richard himself was growing weary of the "haven't much time" declarations as it only served to amp up his own nerves at a time when it was important to have his wits about him. While the first bottle was produced in the lab shortly after the close of the noon meeting, he waited another two and a half hours for the lab to replicate eleven more. By the time the task was nearly complete, he had to arrange to be transported by helicopter in order that the mission could be carried out in time.

Richard was experienced in diving to sixty feet in daylight, but this particular dive would be closer to ninety feet, and the ambient light would be limited. He understood it would take too long to find and brief a diver working in any agency that could accomplish the mission in time. In another 18 hours the crate would be lifted by Gabriel Rios. Swanson, doing his best to turn over a new leaf, didn't hesitate to approve the operation.

The mission was to dive at the GPS coordinates provided by Underwood, where Tanaka dropped the crate of wine. They would proceed to lift the crate with air bags, and replace it with a new crate containing bottles with identical labels and QR codes, revealing Nakajima's identity as the target. Each bottle would be equipped with a modified air tag fitted inside the bottlecap.

A petty officer brought a wheelbarrow to the side of the helicopter as the blades slowly rotated to a stop. These were used on base to transport materials to the marine dock. Richard jogged back to the aircraft to assist the young man. He pulled out his gear bag and heaved it into the wheelbarrow. The petty officer reached inside the cabin and pulled a small wooden crate with the word

"PERISHABLE" stenciled in paint on the side, and followed Richard with it. Once everything for the mission was removed from the helicopter, Richard rejoined the men waiting outside the hangar.

"Lieutenant Holmes is expecting you, and we found another diver to assist you," said Underwood, adding "good luck" before walking away. He had more confidence that Richard knew what he was doing than Richard himself.

Another petty officer approached him from the other direction.

"Good afternoon, sir," he announced, with a broad smile. "I'm Petty Officer Third Class Scott Van Dusen, but my shipmates call me 'Scooby.'"

"Is that because…?"

"Yes, sir, I am a diving fanatic. Happy to accompany you on this dive," he replied. "We are, what sir, looking for something on the reef? Here, let me help you with that."

Scooby lifted a small crate containing a dozen wine bottles, and laid it gently on top of Richard's equipment. Richard explained the goal of the dive as Scooby pushed the wheelbarrow toward the dock. It was now a bit more complicated than originally planned, but Scooby never heard the original plan and was up for anything underwater; the more challenging, the better.

"Sir," Scooby said, "do you understand how to ideally search for something underwater?"

"I assume you take coordinates from the anchor?"

"No, sir," Scooby replied as they reached the dock, "you swim in broad circles around the anchor so you are never too far from it. That's more efficient than swimming in the completely wrong direction."

Scooby hopped onto the boat, and Richard passed the gear down to him, then climbed onto the boat himself. Lieutenant Holmes was standing in the middle where the controls and wheel were located. The small inflatable boat tipped from side to side as another man boarded. Richard nearly fell over the port side as he was unprepared for the movement.

"Ready?" Holmes barked. Richard grabbed the side to steady himself, then nodded. He was grateful he remembered to take Bonine an hour prior.

Scooby looked relaxed. Richard was nervous but refused to show it. Within a few minutes, they were racing out of the bay and toward the coordinates provided. It took about forty minutes to reach the site. The crewman positioned in front of the boat threw the anchor and line over the side.

For the following twenty minutes, Richard and Scooby suited up in silence. Scooby kept his eye on Richard for any assistance he might have needed, the sign of a competent and conscientious diver. Eventually, he helped Richard get his arms through the buoyancy compensator vest as Richard couldn't quite move his left arm back far enough to loop it through.

"Okay, sir," Scooby said, "we want to move with purpose but not risk overexertion."

"Got it," Richard replied as he looked over the gear now surrounding him. He grabbed the regulator in his hand and took a few breaths from it, one of the most important pre-dive exercises.

"And we want to be returning to the boat with no less than one thousand psi," Scooby added, "so please let me know when you reach that point. I may also point to your gauge to ask that you show it to me."

Scooby then reviewed a few common hand signals with Richard to ensure they could communicate effectively underwater.

"Any questions, sir? Are we ready to go?"

Richard wasn't sure he was ready. But he nodded his head in agreement.

"You go off that side first," Scooby said, sparing Richard the inevitable moment when the boat would rise off one side from the changing weight distribution.

Richard did a backroll off the port side of the boat, and Scooby followed quickly afterward. The two sank toward the bottom, gently holding the anchor line and allowing it to run through their gloves.

Richard looked for any sign of the ocean floor. All he could see was a green haze as he descended down the line ahead of Scooby. The cold temperatures began seeping into his wetsuit, running down his back and giving him the chills. At twenty-five feet, he paused to equalize the pressure in his ears, then continued downward. At forty feet, there was still no sign of the bottom. According to the GPS, the depth was approximately ninety feet, thirty feet deeper than he had ever been. Then, suddenly the ocean floor appeared and rushed so fast toward him that he nearly hit his head on a coral head that held the anchor in place.

He grabbed the massive boulder to avoid drifting in the current and pulled the depth gauge to look. He was ninety-four feet down, and the temperature was fifty-five degrees. He thought he was shivering because he was nervous, but then he realized it was extremely cold. Seconds later, Scooby floated by his side, not bothering to hold the anchor line, in perfect control of his buoyancy. Richard could not help but be impressed.

The two men kneeled on the ocean floor, facing each other next to the anchor. Scooby attached a strobe light to the anchor, which illuminated the area for one split second every five seconds. He then gave Richard the "OK" sign, which he reciprocated. Scooby then made the 360-degree motion with his hand by drawing an imaginary circle. Richard nodded in agreement. Scooby started out first, with Richard close behind.

Within a few minutes, a second strobe light was seen, and the fact its pattern was different gave immediate indication they had found the crate of wine. Scooby took a compass reading so that he would not make the mistake of reaching the wine crate, but be unable to see the strobe light on the anchor. Richard watched in admiration of how easily Scooby maneuvered underwater. The two began to approach the crate.

As Richard came within fifteen feet of the crate, a random assortment of wildlife came into view around it, picking at the wood as if it were a source of food. The crate definitely aroused the curiosity of wildlife, and the dive lights flashing around the scene attracted even more small fish, darting in all directions, in what became a carnival-like atmosphere some ninety feet below the surface. A large California Sheepshead was hovering over the crate, as if to protect it from intruders. The Sheepshead was only about three feet long, but its vibrant red and black stripes, combined with four protruding teeth, made it look more intimidating than it was in reality. Richard used his right arm to push the Sheepshead back, and it obliged but merely floated backward a few feet to observe the two men.

Richard and Scooby kneeled again, this time at the side of the crate. Scooby checked his dive computer to determine how much time they would have before requiring an additional decompression stop on the way to the surface. He held up his palms with all ten digits visible and flashed them once to Richard, signaling ten minutes of bottom time available. Scooby realized the two had more time than this but wanted Richard to focus on finishing the task as quickly as possible. They still had to allow time to return to the boat before starting up the line, as well as to provide for any other unforeseen complications.

Richard grabbed the crate from both sides to stabilize himself against the current, which was pushing him in opposite directions about every seven seconds. He watched as Scooby pulled from inside his vest a yellow rubber bag about the size of a large balloon. The bag had a line that could be attached to one end of the crate with a carabiner. Richard proceeded to mimic Scooby's movement, pulling a second bag from his own vest, and threading the line through one of the wooden slats on the crate, pulling it from the other side, and securing it. The men looked at each other to verify the task was complete once each bag was attached.

Scooby gave an exaggerated nod to Richard that they were ready for the next step in the process. Both men inhaled deeply, then each took the regulator from their mouth, guided it into the underside of the bag, and pushed the regulator's' purge button to release air into the water. As they did so, the bag inflated quickly and began to lift the crate. The men guided the crate upward in order that none of the bottles would break or fall out, and then returned to breathing on the regulator. It was important to leave no trace the crate was ever there.

Richard held the crate, suspended a few feet off the ocean floor. Then, another light from above revealed itself. It was the replacement crate being lowered by the boat. Lieutenant Holmes had followed the men's bubbles as they broke the surface of the water, a twist in the mission that had not been discussed, but that ultimately saved time and the need to return to the boat's anchor. Scooby grabbed the replacement crate and guided it to the floor, then releasing the line that had lowered it down. He fidgeted a bit with the crate and its strobe light to ensure it was stable on the ocean floor, and not likely to be overturned by the current.

Scooby pointed to Richard's air gauge to see how much he had left. The gauge read 900 psi, which was just enough for a safe ascent. Richard did not realize he had been hyperventilating due to the stress and anxiety of the dive. Scooby placed his palms together to form a "V" shape, then flashed the "thumbs up," indicating it was necessary to return immediately to the boat; no time for sightseeing. They each held one side of the crate, which provided some ballast in absence of an anchor line, and helped to prevent an uncontrolled ascent to the surface.

Between the periodic ocean surge, cold and dark conditions, breathing from a bottle of gas, and operating under a time limit, Richard could barely produce enough adrenaline to stay on task, but still, the operation was a success. And they had ample wine for a post-dive celebration.

30

"The yakuza will figure out very soon that we have their man in custody," Houseman said as he stood outside the analyst's office cubicle. "What have you got?"

Richard put Agent Houseman in charge of drawing Nakajima out of the shadows in rural Japan and into a space where he could either be apprehended by U.S. Marshals or eliminated by an assassin's bullet. In the first case, the Bureau would be publicly celebrating a massive win, which was preferred; in the latter case, they would be practicing deniability and celebrating in private.

"Here is what we came up with," the analyst said, handing a piece of paper to Houseman. "Take a look." Houseman read the draft email to himself.

Honorable Wakagashira,

I've been approached by a spokesman for the leader of the Sinaloa cartel operating out of Tijuana. The leader's name is Jose Pardillo Guitarrez. He requests a meeting with you to discuss a cooperation to eliminate law enforcement personnel at the U.S./Mexico border so that they may operate more freely. He proposes a meeting in Honolulu as neutral ground and is prepared to wire an advance immediately after the meeting.

Wakagashira, this is a matter of showing respect to the cartel, which is part of their culture. I understand if you do not wish to travel, but Guitarrez will see this as a sign of weakness and indicated he would reach out to another oyabun.

Please advise if I might assist in setting up the meeting.

Houseman looked up at the analyst. "And Tanaka has seen this?"

"Yes," the analyst replied. "He helped us set the tone. He explained that Nakajima is desperately seeking the approval of his father so that he may take his place someday, and that with proper security measures, he would likely make the trip."

There was a brief discussion earlier in the day with Swanson about sending a parallel series of messages to the cartel leader, but this was quickly abandoned when it was agreed the benefits outweighed the risks.

Nothing Houseman could see might represent a cloaked warning to Nakajima in the proposed email. "All right," he said after pondering the matter. "Let's go with it."

***

"Dude, this is like jumping from a moving train on a bridge into a fast boat," McAuley said. "The timing has to be perfect."

"I've seen Tom Cruise do it," Richard replied, without looking up from his laptop while recognizing Tom Cruise had never done anything remotely similar. He was busy looking at the layout of hotels in Honolulu to find the best one for the meeting where they planned to apprehend Nakajima. He preferred an airy, outdoor setting where his agents could be watching the action without the risk of being detected. What he didn't realize was that Nakajima would be dictating the venue.

"Okay, Batman, riddle me this," McAuley quipped, "how do you expect to sync the meeting in Honolulu with the contract killer's receipt of the bottle, that he gets it before Nakajima leaves the island?"

Eliminating Nakajima in Hawaii would be infinitely easier than trying to penetrate the tight security he enjoyed in his native Japan. But in order for it to work, the assassin would have to arrive in Hawaii before Nakajima left it. And Nakajima would be leaving quickly if not apprehended first.

"Hey," Richard complained, "may I remind you, Joker, this was *your* idea. Where is the bottle now?" Richard asked.

"We are tracking its movement across Mexico," McAuley said, referring to the GPS transmitter in the wine's bottle cap. "If it has to get farther than Cuba," he added, "not even Robin can help you."

***

The yakuza are capable of generating fear and respect. The Mexican cartels, on the other hand, are capable of generating only fear. So, nobody was surprised when Nakajima initially scoffed at the idea of traveling to the United States to meet the man known as 'Guitarrez.' Nakajima's initial response was to not respond at all.

"We need to give him something else," Houseman said to Richard. "Maybe he is also skeptical that the message is from Tanaka; maybe he senses a trap."

"Work with Tanaka to share something that legitimizes the message and creates urgency," Richard replied, gently grabbing Houseman's shoulder, "emphasis on urgency."

Houseman prodded Tanaka to compose something only the yakuza's inner circle would know about with respect to their business activities. The second message had the urgency of an existential threat to Nakajima's influence.

Honorable Wakagashira,

Mr. Guitarrez is aware of our operation to unmask American and British agents and offers to pay over $1M for the identification of any American agents in Tijuana shadowing the Sinaloa cartel. Moreover, he said he will take his offer to the 'Ndrangheta family if you do not meet with him. Please advise.

It was well known in the criminal underworld that the 'Ndrangheta was already operating in Latin America, directing cocaine shipments from there to Europe. One of their leaders was captured on the streets of Bogotá in 2025, but it was understood that many more "capos" were moving freely in the region and expanding their footprint. This was exactly the threat needed to seduce Nakajima to attend the meeting.

Within twenty-four hours of sending the message, Nakajima consented to the meeting.

"We're on," said Houseman, "it's showtime."

***

Steven Daniels lived in Miami, a short flight from Havana. He resided in a predominantly gay neighborhood, close enough to South Beach that he could spend evenings there and meet up with prospective clients when needed.

Daniels would have no need for the bottle once he took the information from it. Like other contract killers involved with Tanaka's program, he actually appreciated the ruse. It kept him safe from the risk of having any obvious incriminating evidence in his apartment. He could land in Havana, take a taxi 20 km to the cruise ship terminal, and claim the bottle assigned to him as the crate was being delivered and unloaded from the Cuban tanker *Vilma*. He could be back in the U.S. later that afternoon while the remaining bottles were transferred under heavy guard to the *Neustrashimy,* a Russian patrol ship.

Daniels could hardly believe his luck once he downloaded the details from the bottle at a restaurant near the cruise terminal. He had an existing assignment on the West Coast already, offered by the CIA Special Activities Group. What he didn't realize was that, thanks to the GPS tracker in the bottle cap alerting the FBI to its arrival in Cuba, he was under immediate surveillance by agents dispatched out of the U.S. Embassy nearby.

From face recognition technology, Richard's team quickly identified Daniels as a former Navy SEAL.

***

A line of five black Mercedes sedans traveled in single file through the Tamagawa Tunnel en route to Haneda Airport in Tokyo, one of two large airports serving the city, but with fewer tourists and a diminished presence by law enforcement. Inside the third vehicle from the front, in the front passenger seat, was Hiroshi Nakajima.

This would be Nakajima's first visit overseas in service to his father, and he was not about to take any chances with his security. Nakajima was superstitious and would never travel in the fourth vehicle nor sit in the fourth row of an airplane for the simple reason that four is pronounced "shi," which also means "death" in Japanese. He would routinely switch his seat in any of the other vehicles, in either the front or back, just in case a rival gang might try to prematurely end his career.

If Guitarrez was going to dictate the general meeting location, Nakajima was going to dictate the venue. He chose a resort he knew to be sufficiently crowded with tourists that, with minimal security, he would not stand out among them. Also, he wanted to meet as close as possible to the private landing strip at Kalaeloa Airport on the west side of the island, where he would arrange to land.

Houseman quickly messaged the location to Richard, who was having a beer with McAuley when the notification of a secure message popped up on his phone.

"Mina's Fish House at The Four Seasons Resort Oahu Ko Olina, at 7:00 p.m. Monday," Richard said aloud, looking at the text. He looked at his calendar. It was Thursday.

"Dude, you are going to Hawaii!" McAuley said aloud. "Man, can I carry your bags?"

Richard's first thought was to bring Sarah.

"So, we need to get our men, and our man, over there as soon as possible," he said. "You know what they say…"

"We haven't got much time?"

McAuley chuckled at the overuse of the phrase. Then, he recognized a potential glitch.

"Can we assume Daniels knows he needs to be in Hawaii on Monday?"

Richard wasn't sure but had an idea.

"He's former military, right? Let's give him a hint."

***

Febri stepped out of the shower at the Hampton Inn, a few miles east of the Four Seasons, and considerably cheaper. He was delighted to be back in the Pacific region and considered the Hampton a vast improvement over the hotel he had in Cuba. After drying off, he swept the complimentary shampoo, conditioner, and other amenities into a polybag with his arm and threw it in his luggage. From his luggage, he put on an oversized Hawaiian-themed shirt that he bought in the airport and blue jeans.

He pushed a Beretta 92 pistol inside his pants and pulled the shirt over it. Looking in the bathroom mirror, he was satisfied the gun was concealed. Then, he put a folding knife with a three-and-a-half-inch blade in his front pocket, and this was similarly concealed under the flowing fabric of the shirt.

He looked at his watch; it was five-thirty. He checked the app built by Giuseppe to confirm his target hadn't moved since he checked in; he would probably be having dinner at the hotel. Febri might not have a better opportunity to catch him alone and off guard. It was time to go.

***

Richard and Sarah were lying on the king-size bed at the Four Seasons, propped up by pillows and facing a large balcony that afforded a view of the ocean. Richard was trying to find the motivation to leave her side and take a shower. He wore only a pair of black underwear.

"Tell me honestly," he said, "would I be Jerry or George?"

Richard was referring to the long-since canceled *Seinfeld* series that lived on in the form of short reels on social media.

"Well," Sarah said, grabbing Richard's hand and squeezing it gently, "let's see. Jeff is definitely Kramer. SWANSON is George."

She paused to consider the rest of the cast, then continued.

"I think I'd make a decent Elaine. How do you feel about Newmannnnn?"

"Not funny!" Richard replied, jumping off the bed. "I need to shower and shave."

Sarah admired Richard's body as he walked past her to the bathroom, then looked at the time on her phone.

"Yeah, you better get going," she said aloud. "Do you want me to go with you?"

"We've talked about this," Richard said in a serious tone, popping his head out of the bathroom to emphasize the point. "You are officially off-duty. It's not worth the risk. Please, trust me. I can manage this."

Sarah expected Richard's response but felt obliged to offer one last time.

"All right," she said, "I'll behave. But no celebrations without me, okay?"

"I promise," he said.

***

Steven Daniels's flight was delayed, and by the time he checked into the Residence Inn on the west side of the island, it was nearly four-thirty. He would not have time for a shower.

He didn't understand exactly how he was included in a Signal chat among intelligence agents that revealed when and where Nakajima would be on the island. Perhaps it was a mistake; it certainly wouldn't be the first time a chat message that was intended to be secure ended up including the wrong people. Or perhaps the contractor for the job was actually his own government.

He threw open the door to the hotel and tossed his bag on the bed. With any luck, he would be able to finish the job that evening and perhaps spend a couple of days in Oahu diving the reefs. Then he remembered he had *two* jobs on the island; no doubt he imagined two targets that had a history with each other. It would be nice if they simply killed each other, Daniels thought, sparing him the effort. Whatever the two men had in common, Daniels understood it was best not to ask questions when it came to accepting these assignments.

He laid out on the hotel bed all the weapons he felt were necessary for the operation.

He looked at his laptop to reconfirm the meeting location on the secure chat — the Four Seasons Hotel, about three miles away.

***

Nakajima stepped out of the shower and immediately felt he needed another one. He was not accustomed to the high humidity of the islands. He would be pleased if the meeting went quickly so he could return either that evening or, worst case, first thing in the morning.

A call came in on his cell phone from one of his security guards, staying in the adjoining room.

"Wakagashira, it's almost time," said the man.

"I understand," Nakajima replied. "Have you been to the restaurant?"

"Yes," the man replied, "we have good options to see everything."

"Very well," said Nakajima. "I'll be ready in fifteen minutes."

Out of an abundance of caution, Nakajima wore the same suit as his bodyguard, though it was also abundantly clear which man was more intimidating.

As he held the hotel door handle, he looked back at his room and wondered if it would have been wiser to have the meeting with Guitarrez there, then recognized that if the meeting was a ruse, he'd be trapped in the room with no way to escape.

As he left the room, he whispered "ganbatte" to himself, the equivalent of "wish me luck."

31

Richard arranged with the hotel management that the restaurant would be officially "fully booked up" in order to protect hotel guests from any danger. He enlisted the help of local agents to sit at tables so that the restaurant would appear to be busy. There would also be agents wandering around the area, monitoring the situation but instructed not to interfere. Richard would be seated at a table in close proximity to where the host intended to sit Nakajima. The situation was as controlled as it could be under the circumstances.

A local FBI agent of mixed heritage, Jared Leota, was selected to play the role of Guitarrez. He had more Polynesian blood than anything else, but Richard was confident he could play the part long enough for

Nakajima to be isolated from his security and captured. Leota's picture was sent to Nakajima by Tanaka's proton account in advance, along with a fake profile detailing his role in the cartel.

At precisely 7:00 p.m., Nakajima arrived at the podium in front of the restaurant. He was flanked by two of his security guards.

"Good evening, Mister...," said the host as he looked down at his ledger showing reservations for the evening.

"Nakajima," replied the yakuza boss, airing the slightest annoyance that he would have to speak to anyone other than one of his subjects.

"Oh yes, Mr. Nakajima," replied the host, "right this way."

The host led Nakajima to the middle of the restaurant, which had been determined in advance to be ideal, as any escape would require navigating past half the other tables. The security guards did not follow but instead positioned themselves at the edge of the patio representing the restaurant's seating area. Richard pretended to be eating a meal at the nearby table and kept his head down most of the time. But his heart started pounding as the shadow of Nakajima passed him.

"I believe there are two in your party, correct?"

Nakajima nodded, then added, "yes."

"Very well, we will bring your guest to the table when he arrives. Enjoy your evening with us."

It didn't register with Nakajima that the host knew his guest was another man.

It was decided that Leota would not appear until 7:08 p.m., allowing Richard's team the time to fully observe the environment. Between FBI agents at tables and on the perimeter of the patio, combined with Nakajima's guards, the area was already a combustible situation. Then Steven Daniels arrived, followed by the Ghost. There were more concealed weapons in the restaurant than in a bar full of thugs with serious insecurities and unfaithful wives.

At 7:08 p.m., the host brought Leota to the table. According to plan, the two men would talk briefly while the agent hoped to record Nakajima admitting that he was responsible for the operations that led to the assassinations of covert agents.

"Where is your security?" Nakajima asked as Leota took a seat opposite him.

"See the two men over my shoulder?" Leota said. "And over by the bar, they're mine."

Nakajima looked at the men in the distance. They did not look Mexican to him. In fact, they had a remarkably light complexion. One man looking back, apparently Febri, did a very poor job of concealing his interest in the meeting.

"So," Leota continued, fully embracing his role, "can we talk business?"

Nakajima's superstition began to kick in. There seemed to be a lot of men wandering around with no particular place to go. That is when he noticed one of the men in the distance bring his hand to his ear. That was all Nakajima needed to see to get spooked.

"Would you please excuse me a moment?" Nakajima said, standing. "I'll be right back."

Leota didn't flinch but looked around for feedback. He was under instructions to detain Nakajima only when Richard gave the word from the nearby table. Richard was too focused on obtaining a recorded confession to realize that Nakajima was abandoning the meeting.

Within seconds, agents began to move in the direction of Nakajima, who ducked into the kitchen and began to run through it. One of his bodyguards followed, while the other guard left the scene to bring a car around to the back of the hotel. The operation was quickly falling apart.

Richard followed the men into the kitchen, which was organized as a long row of metal counters with cooking surfaces every few feet and pots and pans hanging above. Immediately he heard the screams of employees being shoved hard to the side, followed by the sound of huge steel bowls, pans, and pots being smashed against each other or falling and rolling on the floor. Steam was filling up the area with ingredients landing where they didn't belong. At one point, Nakajima pushed aside an employee carrying a pot of soup, which ended up sloshing on the floor, causing Richard to slip and fall when he reached the same spot. By the time he got himself to his feet, Nakajima had exited the back of the restaurant where he had a car waiting.

Steven Daniels left the scene at the first sign of trouble and headed directly to the airport. Febri was stationed at the nearby bar, observing the chaos in relative obscurity. It was impossible to interpret what caused the ruckus, but Febri correctly concluded that there were too many plainclothes law enforcement officers for him to safely stick around. He decided that this was not the night he would succeed in fulfilling the demands of his current contract.

The men rushing through the kitchen left a mess in their wake and were shortly thereafter out the back door and into vehicles that headed to the airport. Nakajima was screaming at his bodyguards for failing to detect the ruse while simultaneously thinking of how best to punish or eliminate Tanaka. Richard was on the car's police radio requesting support. Daniels was already at the airport, getting into position.

The main road into Kalaeloa Airport was via Midway Street. However, to save time and avoid any police they may have encountered at the main entrance, Nakajima's driver took Saratoga Avenue, jumped the curb, and drove over the grass toward the private plane that was preparing to taxi to the runway. The car busted through the fence, bounced into and out of a trench, flew almost a foot in the air, and landed hard on the grass again. Birds that were resting on the fence or feeding on the grass flew off in all directions.

The car was only a hundred yards from the plane as the pilot slowly rolled the jet in their direction on the tarmac, aiming to close the gap so that the plane could take off quickly. He ignored commands from the air traffic control tower, which was only beginning to understand the situation on the ground.

By the time Nakajima and his bodyguards had abandoned the car and scaled the stairway for the plane, Daniels had positioned himself in the grass near the other end of the runway. What he had not expected was that Richard's team would be crashing the scene and risking the success of his operation. As the jet began to turn toward the runway, three police cars entered from the other side of it, lights flashing and sirens blasting. Unfortunately for Richard, his team was woefully unprepared for what happened next.

The plane's engines began to roar loudly as it moved in the direction of the oncoming vehicles. The pilot would attempt to lift off without the length of runway for which he was trained in order to rise above the oncoming cars. For a larger commercial aircraft, this would have been suicide. But this plane was a Learjet 75, capable of getting airborne with a velocity as little as seventy-eight knots.

As the front wheels began to lift off the runway, Daniels fixed his gun on the wings. Daniels understood that many planes carried fuel in bladders fixed in positions on the wings between the flaps. In a WWII study of planes that were successfully shot down but recovered, planes were able to continue operating after taking gunfire so long as enemy fire did not penetrate the fuel bladders. As part of his training, Daniels learned of this vulnerability but never practiced taking a plane down.

As the plane lifted off completely, the altimeter immediately began broadcasting the warning when insufficient altitude is detected:

"Pull up!"

But the pilot couldn't pull the plane up. It was constrained by "ground effect," the condition when a plane hasn't gained sufficient altitude and is being pulled back to the earth while it attempts to gain enough velocity to overcome the effects of gravity.

"Pull up!"

The oncoming police vehicles might have presumed the pilot was playing a game of "chicken" until it finally began to rise high enough to avoid a crash. The landing gear of the plane snapped off one of the flashing lights as a police car passed under it. It was that close.

Daniels discharged his weapon six times before the plane flew over his head at the end of the runway, doing his best to hit the spot between the flaps, a space no more than 2 feet wide. Four of the shots were a direct hit to the left wing, causing fuel to immediately shoot out of it. Police lights continued flashing across the scene as Richard, Daniels, and others on the scene watched the plane fade away in the distance. Daniels then disappeared himself.

The Learjet was destined to crash into the Pacific Ocean, but the pilot had a choice. He could travel west against the headwinds toward Japan or east, where he would benefit from the wind pushing the plane and not risk being upended by strong oncoming winds as the plane lost power. He chose probable death over certain death. Nakajima was not happy about it.

"We must return to Tokyo!" he yelled at the pilot. The pilot was the one person that Nakajima could not will into compliance.

"We would not make it," the pilot replied, continuing to look forward as the instruments showed the fuel gauge needle inching its way toward zero.

"But we would be in international waters!" Nakajima replied, determined to find a solution where he walks free.

"It would make no difference," the pilot replied. He was right.

As the pilot carefully navigated the Learjet 75 toward the sea several miles from the mainland, he raised the cockpit so that the water would glide under the belly of the fuselage. But as contact was made, the plane created a wave of water that shot in front of it and, once the velocity of the plane began to slow, the wave caved on the cockpit, forcing it down. Even though the pilot was strapped in, his head lunged forward and smashed against the roof of the cockpit, rendering him unconscious.

The smell of jet fuel penetrated the air from a pool forming around the fuselage as the plane bobbed up and down on the waves. Nakajima and his team struggled to get up.

***

Bill Whitmarsh was in third place when it happened. At first, he thought perhaps it was an apparition, brought on by nearly two weeks at sea and the fact he was severely sleep-deprived from the journey. His shipmates were equally spent from the voyage, which originated in San Pedro, California.

The *Makani* was on the final leg of the race, the TransPacific Yacht Race, more commonly known as "TransPac." The skies were partly cloudy, the weather was humid, and winds were steady. The sun had just disappeared below the horizon, leaving hues of orange and purple across the skies. The Catalina 38's spinnaker was full, and the sailboat was slicing through the water at a speed of twelve knots. They were about fifteen hours from the finish line, which was at the lighthouse near Oahu's Diamond Head.

Bill and his crew were on track to improve their performance from the year prior when he saw a small plane crash into the water off the starboard side, about a quarter mile away. The rest of the crew was looking in the wrong direction, toward the islands, when it happened. But they could definitely see the splash, which would have been mistaken for a whale breach had Bill not seen the fuselage on approach.

Bill immediately took to the marine radio, verified it was on Channel 16, grabbed the handheld transmitter, and began speaking slowly and deliberately.

"Mayday, mayday, mayday," he called out, "this is the sailing vessel *Makani*, this is the sailing vessel *Makani*, this is the sailing vessel *Makani*." He took a deep breath before continuing, determined to follow the proper protocol while remaining calm.

"Our call letters are: Delta, Oscar, Seven, Zero, Echo, Foxtrot. I repeat: Delta, Oscar, Seven, Zero, Echo, Foxtrot. Our location is approximately 21.58 degrees North and 156.95 degrees West, just off the island of Oahu," he said.

"There is a plane down, I repeat, a small private plane down. Survivors may be in the water. We are proceeding in that direction to render assistance. Over."

Bill's crew looked on in disbelief.

"Bill, we will lose the race," said his first mate. Bill ignored the comment.

Shortly after competitors in the race heard the mayday announcement from the *Makani* on their radios, they saw it peel off from the procession of boats heading for the islands. Within a minute, three more boats diverted to join in the rescue effort.

The control tower at Kalaeloa Airport had already reported to the Coast Guard base on Oahu that gunshots were fired on the runway at John Rodgers Field, expecting the plane would not get far once the fuel tanks were hit. They lost visual confirmation of the plane's location shortly after it fell below 200 feet, but the *Makani*'s mayday call enabled the Coast Guard to quickly mobilize its Maritime Safety and Response Team and fast boats in the direction of the crash.

The first Coast Guard asset to reach the site was a Jayhawk MH-60, which buzzed low and directly above the *Makani* in order to get a visual of the boat in case it represented a threat. Bill cranked his head behind him as he heard it approach, then up, and then in front to watch the helicopter racing toward the scene.

In spite of his superstitions, Nakajima did not purchase a jet with an automatically deployed life raft as would be found on most commercial airliners. However, he and his three bodyguards were able to exit the craft and held onto seat cushions for flotation. The waves pitched the men up and down, but they were otherwise safe so long as resources reached them in time.

As the Coast Guard helicopter hovered over the scene, one bodyguard panicked, pulled his Glock revolver, and took a shot at the helicopter, aiming for the pilot. Nakajima was too overwhelmed to yell at the man who made a perilous situation even worse.

A nimbler helicopter than the Jayhawk, a Dolphin HH-65, arrived with Richard on board. Richard was kneeling directly behind the pilot so that he could view the scene, his hands on the back of the pilot's seat. Like the others on board, he wore a helmet with an integrated microphone to offset the noise from the helicopter's engine and blades. He saw the bodyguard holding the gun and pointing it at the Jayhawk.

"Can we sit on him?" Richard said through the helmet microphone. Richard was not clear if the Coast Guard units had the weapons on board to neutralize the immediate threat, but what he wanted to avoid at all costs was a situation where the bodyguards might climb on board a boat and take the passengers as hostages.

"Yes, sir!" replied the pilot.

The Dolphin maneuvered itself directly above the bodyguard, creating a whirlpool effect known as "rotor wash." From the perspective of the bodyguard, it was like being in a hurricane, with a column of water rising in a circle all around him. Even with the help of the seat cushion, he couldn't avoid ingesting water and becoming overwhelmed by the effect of the helicopter hovering relentlessly just a few yards above his head. He succumbed to the pressure, gagging repeatedly, and passed out. Letting go of the cushion, he disappeared under the water.

After the demonstration provided by the Dolphin, the Jayhawk pilot broadcast a message on loudspeaker to the scene below.

"This is the United States Coast Guard," he said, "if you are carrying a weapon, you must drop it immediately or you will be considered a threat and you will experience the full force of the Coast Guard."

Nakajima and his bodyguards looked up, resigned and exhausted. None of them wanted the same experience as the one that just drowned before their eyes.

"Do not board the civilian vessels," the pilot continued, "we have a rescue boat en route. I repeat, do not board the civilian vessels. We request the boats in this area to keep their distance from the crash survivors."

The pilot was taking orders dispatched by the USCG Hawaii Operations Center, which assumed control for the developing incident. He was advised that only swift action would prevent a hostage situation from developing.

By this time, there were two helicopters and three sailboats in a circle around the plane, which was still floating. The wind and spray bouncing off the ocean as a result of two helicopters overhead played havoc with the sails on the boats, so they lowered them and followed instructions to keep their distance from the crash survivors.

The Coast Guard Sentinel-class "fast response" cutters USCGC *William Hart* and USCGC *Oliver Berry* arrived within minutes and took the three men on board. A Helicopter Rescue Swimmer dropped earlier from the Jayhawk pulled the pilot out of the cockpit and brought him to the *Oliver Berry*.

Nakajima was now in US custody. No extradition was necessary. And a criminal enterprise responsible for the murder of intelligence agents and law enforcement officers was shut down for good.

32

A warm, fragrant breeze floated through the open window in Richard's bungalow. After the successful conclusion of Operation Fatal Ledger, he upgraded his room as a reward to himself, and for the couple of weekend days before he was expected back at work in Los Angeles. Large palm leaves attached to a ceiling fan circled slowly over his head, bringing fresh air to the crisp, white bedsheets that covered him and Sarah. He opened his eyes and replayed the prior twenty-four hours in his head. He was reminded of the cartoon character, Jimmy Neutron, whose favorite expression at the end of every episode often found its way into pop culture: "for once, everything turned out perfect."

Meanwhile, Sabian joined Asha Chandra by returning to work in the United Kingdom. Delaroche debriefed both of them, but there would still be necessary hearings, criticisms, second-guessing, and documentation necessary before closing the files on the case which led to the assassination of several MI6 agents. An unreasonable amount of written testimony conveniently left out the fact that Delaroche broke with protocol by failing to inform the Americans of their intent to deploy agents to the United States.

Steven Daniels remained on the island. He had one more job to do.

Richard and Sarah spent a good part of the morning in their room, musing about how things might change when they returned to work on Monday. Richard hoped he could convince Sarah to move in with him. Sarah was not ready to give up her role in the Detroit bureau. He was at least successful in persuading her to join him that evening on a boat cruising under the stars, and began preparing the dive gear he brought along for it.

"You're wearing a knife on the dive, why?" Sarah asked when Richard pulled the sheath from his luggage and inspected the blade.

"Hey," Richard replied, "you never know." And this was true; he didn't know. But Richard believed that a dive knife attached to the calf was always a good look, whether you were diving or not.

***

The dive boat at Waianae Small Boat Harbor had the capacity for eight divers and four guests. It would still go forward with the excursion with six divers, but any fewer than this and the trip was barely a breakeven proposition for the dive operator. By the time Richard and Sarah showed up at 8:00 p.m., there were only four divers waiting.

Richard had heard about "blackwater dives" during his open water training and was nervous that he might miss the opportunity to experience it unless more people showed up. As Sarah was not a certified diver, she would join the boat to enjoy a moonlight cruise along with three other tourists and not count toward the minimum number of divers.

"Don't worry," said the boat captain, "we almost always get enough divers, especially on a weekend, and tonight the conditions promise to be spectacular."

No sooner had he finished that statement than a man in his forties showed up. They were now at six divers, and the excursion was a go.

"Ladies and gentlemen," said the captain in a bellowing voice, "please follow me down to the boat where we will have the dive briefing."

Nine customers fell in line behind the captain to walk down the thin wooden dock to the boats. The dock creaked under the pressure of so many people at one time. All of the leisure boats they passed were secured to the dock and dark inside. Only the dive boat would be going out this late.

As they approached the dive boat, the scene lit up. The boat's deck lights revealed a group of young men preparing the dive equipment on the boat, securing tanks to the sides and testing them to ensure each had a minimum of 2,750 psi of air. Rinse tubs were being filled with water, and stations were being set up where each diver would sit to gear up. It was an impressive sight to see the level of coordination being conducted on behalf of the group.

"All right everyone, gather around," said the captain. "As you can tell, this is not our first rodeo, and you will be in excellent hands tonight with this crew."

Nobody in the group would have cause to challenge the statement.

"Tonight," the captain continued, "you will witness what has been recognized as 'the greatest migration on earth.' It's truly a mesmerizing experience."

The divers were giddy upon hearing the statement that caused them to pay $235 each for the privilege to be there.

Every night, billions of zooplankton and phytoplankton make the trip from the cold depths of the ocean to warmer, shallow waters. The combination of tiny animal larvae and photosynthetic organisms creates the foundation of the entire oceanic food cycle. Witnessing the migration can overwhelm the senses if topside weather conditions are good and seas are calm.

"So, as you know," the captain said, "we will be heading far enough offshore that there is nothing but ocean below us. In some spots, it may be ten thousand feet of ocean, far too deep for us to anchor."

"We will tether each of you to the boat where you will descend to about twenty feet. From there, you will enjoy the show. Just be sure to be properly weighted that you are suspended below the boat and that you shine your light away from the other divers."

Blackwater dives had grown in popularity, but due to constraints on how many divers could participate and locations to support it, it remained a bucket list item for many. The dive boats would space out six to eight divers on either side of the boat with enough room between them that they wouldn't be shining their lights at each other. The lights were critical to seeing the creatures that would emerge. Outside the laser-like image created by the light as it penetrated the dark water, everything was as black as black can be.

As the boat left the marina, Richard left Sarah to mingle with the other guests who were not diving. He was not concerned with the fact she was talking with a man who came alone and appeared to be in very good shape. Richard was finally secure in his relationship with Sarah, and besides, quite amped up about the dive experience waiting for him. He took the time to familiarize himself with the dive equipment that he was renting for the excursion, sitting at one of the stations where he would be making a backroll into the water.

After about twenty-five minutes underway, the boat began to slow down, and the captain reappeared.

"All right everyone," he yelled, "it's time to suit up."

The young men who were originally preparing the equipment were now assisting each diver to put on their gear, which included a buoyancy compensator, a life vest for divers with a regulator and tank attached, and a weight belt to ensure they would effectively drift down the length of the line which was attached to the boat. Loud hissing noises were heard as they turned on the air in each tank. The divers were chatting away and excited to be there, filled with anticipation of what was about to happen.

The crew instructed the divers to breathe on the regulator to ensure it was delivering air to them and they were comfortable to proceed. Then, they attached the diver to a line that was secured to the boat so they would not drift off once in the water. It was all happening very fast, perhaps too fast for those divers who were not entirely confident in their skills. This realization hit home when the captain spoke again.

"All right everyone," he said, "the pool is open."

A couple of experienced divers on the port side of the boat immediately stood up, backed up to the rail, and flipped backward into the water. This caused the boat to sharply rock back to the starboard side, making it difficult for the other divers to stand up.

Richard prevailed, and, not wanting to be the last one in the ocean, fell backward off the side and into the black water below. Soon after, all divers were in the water, tethered to the boat, and suspended thirty feet below it.

"My goodness," Sarah said to the man who remained on the boat, "it's quite an operation."

"Yeah," he replied, looking out to sea, "I'd love to do this someday."

Sarah found the man to be a bit awkward in his demeanor but didn't let it concern her. Instead, she leaned over the side of the boat to see Richard's light shining in the other direction.

Down below, Richard was wondering when the show would begin. He didn't realize that once divers displace so much water, they displace organisms as well. He lay motionless in hopes that he would see something worthy of his attention.

Then, they arrived. The telescoping image created by his light began to reveal creatures all around him. Most were no larger than a quarter, but they had fantastic shapes and colors and emitted a fluorescent light source of their own. The first creature looked like a tiny shrimp, with hundreds of legs moving feverishly to propel it forward. Then a thick ribbon twisted, curled, and floated in the water column like it was performing ballet. A translucent but chromatic creature burst with color, spinning slowly in circles. It was a never-ending parade of one bizarre creature after another. "Mesmerizing," Richard thought, was an understatement.

As he continued to move the light slowly across his field of vision, he noticed that the light of the diver to one side was moving farther away. Then, he felt intense pressure in his ears, as if he was sinking. Horrified, he realized he was no longer tethered to the boat, and the boat was drifting away. Also, he was no longer in thirty feet of water; he was fifty feet below the surface and descending rapidly.

He quickly grabbed the air inflater hose to his buoyancy device and carefully added a few puffs of air. It was critical that he not overdo it, or he might find himself in an uncontrolled ascent that could cause his lungs to burst. Simultaneously, he tried to swim back toward the boat.

Sarah was watching the scene play out but had a delayed reaction because Richard's light was always moving, and it was not immediately clear that he was in trouble.

"That's odd," she said, loud enough that the man could hear, "it seems he's farther from the boat than he was a minute ago."

With the help of a little extra air and some feverish pumping of his legs and fins, Richard was able to get back next to the boat when the closest diver slid behind him. Richard instantly felt himself being pushed down again, as if a giant hand from below was pulling him into the depths. He started spinning in place to try to understand what was going on as he felt the weight behind his back. He was hyperventilating and using up his air as he continued downward.

In actual fact, it was Febri, the diver next to him, who removed his own thirty-pound weight belt, and looped it over the back of Richard's tank, where he couldn't see or reach it. This time, Sarah sensed something was up, and so did the man observing the water with her, as a torrent of bubbles from Richard's frantic breathing broke the surface. The man jumped into the water after Richard.

By the time Steven Daniels reached Richard, they were in about fifty-five feet of water, close to the maximum depth of a professional free diver. But if anyone was skilled enough to save Richard in that moment, it was a Navy SEAL trained in deep water rescue. Daniels first motioned to Richard to share his regulator, a technique known as "buddy breathing" that all divers learn, but few ever have to rely upon as if their life depended on it. Daniels put his arm around Richard to steady the pair while grabbing the weight belt off the back of the tank and letting it fall.

Within a few seconds, the two men were stable in the water column, rising slowly with Daniels guiding the way and managing the air in Richard's buoyancy device so that they would have a controlled ascent. They continued to share a single source of air, passing the regulator back and forth as they floated up. When they came to within fifteen feet of the surface, Daniels took one last, deep breath from Richard's regulator, then handed it back and displayed a "thumbs up," indicating Richard should proceed to the surface. He then took the knife from the sheath on Richard's leg and swam in the direction of the boat.

Febri was no match for a Navy SEAL, but he wasn't even aware of the situation, confident that he had succeeded in sending Richard to the bottom of the ocean. The killing was clean, and the death would be ruled an accident as a result of a line that somehow detached from the diver. Febri was playing the inevitable news story in his mind when he felt two giant arms collapse around him from behind. Steven Daniels had arrived to work.

Daniels put one hand across Febri's mouth, then drove the knife forcibly through Febri's neck, pushing it hard enough that it nearly exited the other side. Febri struggled briefly, then went limp. Blood started gushing out from his neck and mixing with the saltwater. Then, Daniels pulled out the knife and cut the line holding Febri to the boat. Finally, he punched a hole in the buoyancy device with the sharp point of the blade to release any air holding Febri in the water column and let him go. Febri, the Ghost, disappeared into the inky black water within an instant.

Daniels was successful in murdering one of the two men he came to kill in Hawaii.

***

The moment that Daniels left the boat, the captain and crew initiated the "man overboard" protocol. They brought the tethered divers back on the boat, positioned the floodlights where Sarah pointed to the underwater disturbance, and threw a couple of floating rings in the same direction. A few seconds later, Richard emerged. He got back on the boat before Daniels and explained to the captain, breathlessly, that another diver attacked him underwater and Daniels saved his life. The other divers kept their distance, spooked by what they didn't quite understand, and miffed that their dive was cut short. On Richard's advice and promise of reimbursement, the captain offered everyone a refund and an opportunity to return the following night.

Police and paramedics were on hand when the boat returned to the dock in the dark of night. On medical examination, the paramedics found Daniels had ruptured an eardrum from the rapid descent to reach Richard. Daniels, Richard and the boat captain were subject to questioning by the police, but the fact Richard and Sarah produced their FBI credentials allowed the law enforcement presence to relax somewhat, as the police report could defer to the agency's handling of the incident.

"You're CIA?" Richard said incredulously as he sat next to Daniels on the curb next to the police vehicles, towels draped around their shoulders and still dripping wet from having been in the ocean twenty minutes before.

"Sort of," Daniels offered, mindful of the risks of saying too much.

While the CIA doesn't conduct full-scale military operations, their highly secretive "Special Activities Center" was known to hire mercenaries when diplomatic options were exhausted, not practical, or simply not an option. Daniels explained to Richard he was contracted to kill Febri, "the Ghost," one of the most highly productive assassins in the world. Richard remembered Febri as being a key suspect in the recent murders of covert agents, but would never have guessed that Febri would come after him. The gravity of the matter was not lost on him, and he felt himself shivering even though no longer cold.

"So," Richard said, trying to lighten the mood for his own benefit, "you've been quite busy since arriving in Hawaii?"

"Yeah," Daniels replied, "you could say that."

Only much later, on further examination of Tanaka's records, did the FBI conclude that the Ghost was hired by Dennis Spence, the man Richard pursued in Operation Carbon Paper and who was thought to have committed suicide in Hong Kong. Obviously, portions of that theory would need to be revisited.

Richard and Steven Daniels became fast friends for the limited time they had left on Oahu. Richard was in awe of Daniels and his prior military record. He learned that Daniels was counting on the income from killing the target on the bottle from the crate that was replaced. And yet he had the humanity to save Richard's life. So, Richard promised to arrange for Daniels to meet John Swanson and potentially become a contractor for the FBI, because one never knows when a contract killer can come in handy.

***

Richard looked out the window of the plane as it lifted itself away from the Hawaiian Islands, and they faded in the distance. He was sitting next to Sarah in the first-class cabin on their return flight to LAX, a perk he earned from his loyalty to Delta Airlines and the occasional upgrade certificates they provided him.

He leaned back, closed his eyes, and thought about the intensity of the past couple of days. He successfully dismantled a murder-for-hire operation, dealt serious blows to the capabilities of the yakuza and mafia, and survived an attempt against his life. Then he realized—if he was still alive, Dennis Spence might not be as satisfied with the outcome of the weekend and could come after him again. He chose to set that thought aside.

The dinner service started immediately after the plane reached its cruising altitude, and trays were being laid out in front of them by the flight attendant. Richard and Sarah began reorganizing the food on the various plates, opening napkins, and wiping their hands with sanitizer.

"So, just to let you know," Richard whispered after the flight attendant moved to the row behind them, "I might ask you to join the mile-high club with me tonight." He looked at Sarah with a devilish smile.

"How do you know I'm not already a member of that club?" she replied back, nonchalantly, while poking at the entertainment system on the seat back in front of her. She intentionally chose not to look in Richard's direction.

Once again, Richard thought, Sarah exceeded expectations and knew how to push his buttons. He felt certain that Sarah carried many secrets with her about her past, but he would never jeopardize what they had in that moment to request any details.

"Can I persuade you to spend a few more days with me in LA?" he said hopefully.

"We'll see," she replied, continuing to look at the LCD screen. "If you are a good boy."

Richard blushed like a schoolboy. Images of being handcuffed to the bed frame came flooding back, and he concluded he got the answer he wanted.

A moment later, the flight attendant returned and leaned into their seats, broadcasting a wide smile.

"May I offer you a special treat we have to accompany your dinner?"

She held a bottle in her hand that looked like it had been dragged through a garbage dump.

"It's wine that's been aged in the ocean," she said, pushing the bottle forward so they could clearly see the label. "It's from Malta," she added.

Sarah and Richard shot a stunned look at each other; Richard's mouth hung open.

"It's a new thing," said the flight attendant, "seriously, everyone is talking about it."

ACKNOWLEDGMENTS

My first novel, *Con & Consequence* took exactly one year to write. *Cease to Exist* took a year and a half. *The Wine Broker* took me two years. If writing was getting any easier, those metrics would be different.

Nevertheless, it's a labor of love, and I am gratified that I have the time and the audience to produce literature that informs while it entertains. I've learned a great deal in the course of researching topics from wine to cybercrime. I hope my readers value the opportunity to learn as much as I do.

I am indebted to many people that assisted me in this adventure. My sister Diane Klein was there to guide me when I needed a helping hand. The editor of my earlier work, John Cannon, went above and beyond in his evaluation of my first draft. Whenever I had a question about how to best pair a bottle of wine with either an innocuous or nefarious activity, my good friend Dr. Jerry Kolins was there for advice. My friend Rob Jafek helped me understand the physics of flight that brought down the yakuza's plane. Finally, Professor Wendy Novicoff from the University of Virginia, a recognized expert in quality, reviewed the final draft.

Most importantly, my wife Inna gave me the freedom and space to write, including a sabbatical in Europe to research scenes and to ultimately bring the project over the finish line.

Thank you all for your support and encouragement.

ABOUT THE AUTHOR

Ian Rodney Lazarus has been publishing technical articles and opinion pieces in various magazines since 1989. *Con & Consequence* was his first novel, drawing from his international business travels across five continents, followed by the sequels *Cease to Exist,* and *The Wine Broker.*

A native of Detroit and graduate of the University of Michigan, he now lives in San Diego with his wife and three children. He is a certified sailor, advanced scuba diver, and "Six Sigma" black belt. He also serves as Staff Officer, Publications, for the U.S. Coast Guard Auxiliary.

More from Ian Rodney Lazarus

Con & Consequence

Cease to Exist

Available from most online book retailers.